RUE MARQUIS de SADE

By the same author:

WITCH-QUEEN OF VIXANIA
SLAVE-MISTRESS OF VIXANIA

RUE MARQUIS de SADE

Morgana Baron

This book is a work of fiction.
In real life, make sure you practise safe sex.

First published in 1996 by
Nexus
332 Ladbroke Grove
London W10 5AH

Copyright © Morgana Baron 1996

Typeset by TW Typesetting, Plymouth, Devon

Printed and bound by
BPC Paperbacks Ltd, Aylesbury, Bucks

ISBN 0 352 33093 7

One

The sign came on and told her that she could unfasten her lap strap, but she didn't. She didn't, even though the broad band of woven plastic was making it hard for her to take a deep breath and its edge was biting into the soft swell of her hips. Charlotte had pulled the belt far beyond snug when she'd buckled it. It was tight enough to hurt.

It wasn't that she was nervous of landings, it was just an old habit. She always wore her belts cruelly tight. Charlotte didn't feel comfortable otherwise. Charlotte never let herself think about how that habit had started. There were a lot of things that Charlotte didn't let herself think about.

There were things, physical things, that felt nice in ways that made no natural sense. She was often stirred in un-natural ways by sensations that wouldn't have stimulated any normal woman. Charlotte didn't understand why that should be – or perhaps she dared not understand.

There was the seductive texture of silken cord, for example, like the one that she always tied so tightly around her waist when she wore her short satin robe. Why would running a cord through her fingers make a pulse throb between her legs? Why had the simple act of tightening a leather strap around a travelling case when she'd packed made her so moist that she'd had to change her panties?

Why was it that she sometimes masturbated in a way that she was ashamed of? She'd done it two days before her flight. She'd taken two silk cords from the heavy drapes in her bedroom, tied one around her own slender waist until it creased her skin and distorted the subtle dimple of her navel, stood in front of the tall mirror, and watched herself rubbing the other cord over, and into her sex. Soft friction. So supple, yet so threatening.

She'd saturated the cord. That was another of her shames, the way her sex gushed when she had an orgasm. That too, had to be perverse. Other women didn't do that, surely?

No one who knew her suspected that she was so twisted inside. How could they? Charlotte was the picture of innocence. Her hair was long and blonde, tumbling around her face in natural ringlets. Her eyes were big and blue, though golden flecks showed in her irises in the right light. She had lips like plump pink pillows and a tiny overbite, just enough to let a glisten of pearly white teeth show when her mouth relaxed.

Charlotte's neck was slender, her shoulders snowdrifts that had been carved by the wind, and her breasts were high and plump, but not so large as to appear overtly provocative unless they were bare. Naked, they displayed their unnatural nipples; virginally pink, but too long, and too fat. They were like flat-topped cylinders of flesh, not pointed cones. Charlotte had pinch-me nipples. They begged to be nipped, twisted, tugged. They were the sort of nipples that showed through thick sweaters. Charlotte took great care to always wear thickly lined bras.

The rest of her body was slim, right to her tiny high-arched feet, slim and girlish and innocent. And it was all a shameful lie.

Deep inside her, where she dared not look, she was a slut, a harlot, a whore, a bitch in heat. Beneath the pure and natural exterior, she was utterly debauched and totally depraved.

But it was best not to think about that. The thoughts might lead her back along a long dark tunnel, to a place and a time where guilt lurked. Warm guilt. Warm, wet guilt. Warm and wet, and squirmy. Tempting. Enticing. There was surrender there, waiting in ambush like a cruel lover.

Charlotte's thighs squeezed together. She moved against the sadistic tightness of the seat belt. Her body felt the restraint and enjoyed the pain that her mind carefully ignored.

So she sat there, tightly confined, while most of the other passengers on the AeroSteinreich flight filed past, befurred and bejewelled, or wearing shorts or jeans, and disembarked into the clear Swiss noon. Charlotte allowed herself to feel smug. Three-piece suits! Fur coats! She could always tell the infrequent flyers by the way they dressed. She knew better. Even at only 20 – almost 21 – she'd crossed the Pacific twice and the Atlantic a dozen times already. This trip had been a long one: from Ridge River to New York, then across the Atlantic by Concorde, and then from London Heathrow to Geneva. There'd only been one short stop-over.

She was glad she'd known enough to wear scuffed trainers, baggy rugby pants and a loose sweatshirt. It was far better to be comfortably scruffy on purpose than to dress up in your best and then have grunginess forced on you layer by layer, with each hour of flying time.

And there was no one around to disapprove. It wasn't as if her father, her stepfather, was still alive. It wasn't as if her stepsister was on the plane.

What was their relationship legally? Charlotte's biological father had died before she'd been born. Her mother had remarried when Charlotte had been three. Her husband was the only father she'd known. Then, a year after her mother had died, when Charlotte had been a young teen, father had remarried Veronica's mother. It made for a strange family: a father and two daughters, with no shared blood. Sisters by adoption? But the sisters had become close – too close.

Stepsisters! Stepsisters! Somehow not being related by blood diluted her guilt. No. She didn't think about that. Anyway, she'd been young. She'd been so vulnerable. And it was over. Over. Even when she saw Veronica again, probably at the hotel, it'd be different now. If Veronica tried to be the way she had been back then, Charlotte could deal with it now. For sure. Absolutely. Anyway, Veronica had most likely changed. She had to have changed.

3

At seventeen, the last time Charlotte had seen her step-sister, Veronica had been precociously svelte, dark, elegant, arrogant, and cruel. Especially cruel. But Charlotte didn't think about that.

Of all the things that Charlotte deliberately didn't think about, Veronica's taste for cruelty was the most important.

'There's a complimentary buffet in the airport lounge,' the stewardess said. 'We'll be laying over for about an hour, ma'am.'

'What? Oh! Buffet? No, I'm not hungry.'

'Then may I bring madam a drink? It's gone twelve. The bar is open.'

'A drink? Um, white wine?'

'Certainly, ma'am.'

'And some of those smoked nuts?'

'Right away, ma'am.'

Charlotte watched the stewardess's retreating back sway along the aisle and wondered how she managed in those heels. AeroSteinreich obviously put appearances before comfort or efficiency. The Lear jet only seated sixty, but the service was far above first class. The steward and the stewardess had been kept hopping right from the take-off in London.

Most airlines choose their staff with looks as a factor, but AeroSteinreich outdid any airline Charlotte had ever flown on. The steward was tall, blue-eyed and blond, with a deep dimple at the blunt point of a strong chin. The stewardess looked, and moved, like a prima ballerina. It wasn't just the uniforms, although they were certainly stunning enough. The colours were gold and forest green, just like the duchy of Steinreich's flag. The cut and styling might have been Christian Lacroix. Both of them wore short, flared, green suede boots; his with cuban heels and hers with four-inch spikes. His tight-fitting green serge pants matched her long straight skirt, but the man had the advantage when it came to walking. The woman's skirt was ankle length, and dramatically tapered. The only concession to practicality was a back-slit to just below knee height. His gold shirt matched her gold blouse, and each

4

of them wore a short fitted jacket in the green, plus green hats; his a smart cap and hers a pert pill-box. The only other colour on either of them was a ruby teardrop pin over the right breast.

If Veronica had been on board she'd most likely have seduced one of them between London and Paris, and the other between Paris and Geneva. This stop-over might well have become a three-way orgy.

Charlotte's capricious imagination called up a picture: the stewardess dishevelled and skirtless, bent over the back of one of the seats, her bottom a bright mottled pink from Veronica's spanking, and the steward naked at Veronica's feet worshipping, perhaps sucking on the heel of her boot, his fist a desperate blur as he pumped himself towards an orgasm.

But perhaps Veronica had changed.

Or perhaps she hadn't. That was a frightening – yes frightening – thought. When it feels like the skin of your belly is cringing on the inside that's fear, isn't it? It certainly can't be that other thing. It can't be unbidden, unwanted lust. Not even if Charlotte felt a betraying warm trickle between her thighs.

'Excuse me, ma'am?'

The stewardess leant across and pulled the tray down from the back of the seat in front. Her perfume was strong. It rode upon the waves of damp heat radiating up out of the woman's cleavage. Close up, she didn't look so much like a ballerina. Ballet dancers aren't usually so well developed. Ballerinas' breasts don't sway enticingly when they lean over, dragging the tips of erect nipples across the taut fabric of their blouses.

Charlotte swallowed. 'Thank you.'

There was no denying it. Her body was betraying her. Her crotch was soaking. The cloth of her rugby pants was probably darkening with the moisture. It wasn't fair! Other girls didn't start oozing the moment a sexual thought crossed their minds.

Other girls even had orgasms without gushing their juices. Damn! Why had she been born a freak?

It'd been another of the things that Veronica had teased her about.

'Come for me, Charlotte! Squirt it! Come like a man!'

'Like a man.' That was the shame of it – or part of the shame. Not being able to hide her betraying body's wicked needs – that had been the other part. Thank God for the shielding tray. If it hadn't been for that, the stewardess would probably have seen Charlotte's lust, plainly written in the essence of her body, written in a spreading stain at the juncture of her thighs.

Charlotte drained the wine in her glass and poured herself another from the half-bottle that the stewardess had brought. There were only two ways to deal with her body when it did to her what it was doing now. She could go to the little bathroom, pull her pants to her ankles, straddle the toilet and let her fingers do those shameful things. She would let herself spasm, and spurt out her disgrace, and then she'd have to wash, and hope that the act of wiping her sex didn't start the dreadful process all over again.

Or she could try to blank those seductive thoughts out of her mind, and wait, and wait. Eventually her body's shameful need would fade.

But with Veronica in her mind, and the old memories rising unbidden, it would be hard. She and Veronica used to play, in the copse behind their father's house, with Charlotte tied to a sturdy young oak with a rope, bark rough on her barely-budded breasts and down-shaded pubes, the cord biting into the small of her back, and Veronica's fingers pinching and tweaking, or slithering wickedly into Charlotte's forbidden crevices.

Then there was the hot summer attic, on the day that Veronica had found the old chests that were bound with broad leather straps. Veronica had found uses for those straps. And the nights that Charlotte had lain alone in her bed, fearing and yearning for her door to open, and Veronica to creep in, and do those dreadful things.

Then there had been the wardrobe. That had been the worst torment. Whenever she'd refused to obey Veronica's warped demands, it'd been the old oak wardrobe in the attic that'd persuaded her to obey. Two hours in the cramped dark with her wrists tied behind her back had seemed like an eternity, and then Veronica would come in and join her.

By then Charlotte had always been eager to do whatever was required of her, if it got her out of that awful place. By then she was ready to play 'Mistress and Slave Girl', and the worst of it was, she'd enjoyed doing the depraved things that Veronica had made her do.

It was unnatural! When people made love, it wasn't right that one of them should be a slave to the whims of the other. And women didn't make love to other women. That was even more unnatural. And if they were sisters – even stepsisters – that made it even worse, didn't it?

Then why was it that the two boys she'd allowed to know about her body's shameful reactions had failed to move her? Why had it seemed so insipid, when they'd done their best to please her, and to hide their disgust when she'd soaked their sheets with her belated but copious spending?

Why had she lain beneath Rob's sweaty thrusting body, with thoughts of Veronica's cruelties blindingly bright inside her head? Why was it that she'd watched Gene's gentle fingers brush her nipples, oh so delicately, and found herself craving the vicious tweaking that Veronica had inflicted on them so often?

Was she that depraved? Could there be no love for her that wasn't also debauchery? A man and a woman, moving softly together, with no pain, no bondage, neither dominating the other, united in sweet love?

It was Veronica's fault! When Charlotte's mother had died, and father had brought his new wife home from Spain, along with his new daughter, Veronica, Charlotte had been devastated. She'd withdrawn from the world, from her betraying father, and from her new step-family. Had father comforted her? Of course not! There was no comfort in that iron man. It had been Veronica who had stolen into Charlotte's bedroom that night, and crept into Charlotte's bed. But it hadn't been comfort that Veronica had offered. It hadn't been consolation. Veronica had offered perversion. And Charlotte, to her shame, had accepted the gift with open arms. Even twisted love had seemed better than no love at all.

But that was over now. When father died, piloting his private plane across the Andes, Charlotte had taken the opportunity to escape. She and Veronica had gone their separate ways. Veronica had gone to Madrid, her former home, and then to Paris, and then Charlotte had lost track. She'd immersed herself in her dancing, first, in Winnipeg, Canada, and later in New York.

She'd sworn to herself to forget Veronica, to never see her again. But then the letter had come from the lawyers who administered the trust funds. It had been in father's will. Now that communism had withered, and their father's homeland was free again, she and Veronica had to go there, for a month at least, or else forfeit all claim to the fortune that waited for them on their 21st birthdays. Their birthdays were just days apart.

Charlotte had considered giving up the money, but if she did it would all go to Veronica. That thought was unbearable. Veronica was the enemy.

'Love thine enemy.'

No, there had never been love. It had just been lust – unnatural, twisted lust. And it wouldn't start again, no matter what. Veronica had no control over her now. None at all.

But the thought of being with Veronica again, for a whole month in the same hotel in father's homeland, the tiny duchy of Steinreich, was perversely thrilling.

The whole damned country was only two thousand acres! It wasn't room enough for the two of them!

What would she do if there was a connecting door between their suites, and one night the door opened and Veronica was to come in, the way she had so often done when they'd been in their late teens?

Charlotte would send her away. Of course she would.

But why was there wetness and tingling between her thighs? Why was her throat so dry? Why did her nipples prickle?

Charlotte poured more wine. A half-bottle drunk fast would send her to sleep. She wouldn't think about Veronica again, not until she had to, not until she got to the hotel in Steinreich.

Her thoughts drifted and twitched to a vision of Veronica's gleaming thigh, the smooth swell of her belly, the curve of her hip.

Fight fire with fire! If her body insisted that she think erotic thoughts, there were other people she could fantasise about – natural people! There was that handsome steward, for instance. Any normal lusty woman would be inspired to think about sex with a man like that.

Charlotte let her thoughts drift. She imagined that she was on the plane, but she wasn't wearing her scruffy rugger pants and sweatshirt. For some reason or another she was wearing just a thin oyster-pink slip and a pair of matching silk-finish hose. The blond steward had brought the wine: vintage champagne. After he'd poured, he'd lingered. The poor man was so struck by the vision of her loveliness that he couldn't tear himself away. In her dream Charlotte crossed her legs slowly, very elaborately, knowing that the sight and hiss of silk on silk would torture the poor fellow.

Yes, through her lowered lashes she could see the cylindrical bulge in his green serge pants twitch and throb.

'May I, madam?' he asked, his fingers at his zipper's tab.
'Very well,' she said, graciously.

The zipper hissed. He put his hand into the opening and fumbled out a magnificent length of pale blue-veined penis. Lying in his sweaty palm, it uncurled, and engorged.

Charlotte smiled secretly. It was the sight of her stiff nipples protruding through the silk of her slip, and his view of her slender white thighs, that made his flesh inflate until it ached. It was in her power, and hers alone, to grant or deny him release.

A glistening purple helmet emerged. The steward pulled back on his foreskin and began to stroke himself.

'Did I give you leave to do that?' Charlotte demanded.
'I thought . . .'

Charlotte uncrossed her legs and touched her left knee

with the tip of one almond nail. She noticed that her nails were filed to long points, and painted a deep crimson, although in real life she kept her nails trimmed short and never coloured them.

'Come closer,' she told him, 'and lay it there.'

He hunched into the narrow space and crouched low enough to obey. The head of his sex was already moist. Charlotte's kneecap could feel warm wetness soaking through her stocking.

'The other leg,' she said. 'Roll my stocking down.'

His fingers trembled. His face was flushed. As soon as he had the silky fabric hanging loose from her knee, she said, 'That's enough. Put your thing back in place.'

The steward held his penis pressed to her left knee. Charlotte lifted her right leg and crossed it over her left, trapping the head of his cock in the warm soft pocket behind her knee.

He groaned his lust.

'Put your hands behind your back,' Charlotte ordered.

When he'd done as he'd been told, she said, 'Now you may move it.'

His hips rocked, carefully. A fraction too much movement, and he'd pull himself free. There was no way for him to know whether she'd let him start again if he made an error. The taut silk over the hardness of Charlotte's gleaming kneecap, and the yielding softness of her flesh pressing down, were two contrasting sensations, tantalising him where he was most sensitive.

He gritted his teeth and slid forward and back, butting and dragging, driven mad by an ecstasy that one false move could snatch away, perhaps forever.

'He's going to come soon,' the stewardess gasped.

Somehow or other the woman had sensed what was happening and had crowded in behind the steward.

'Did you want to play with yourself while you watch?' Charlotte asked her.

'Yes please, ma'am.'

'Then you may.'

The woman unbuckled her green suede belt and dug her

thumbs into the waistband of her skirt, forcing it down over her hips as she wriggled and squirmed it over her plumply rounded buttocks, and down the statuesque columns of her thighs. Apart from a frilly moss-green garter-belt and matching stockings, the woman was naked beneath her skirt, just as Charlotte had suspected. The black bush at the juncture of her thighs had been trimmed close and was already dewy. With the skirt still wrapped around her calves, she spread her knees obscenely wide. The fingers of one hand parted the lips of her sex, giving her other hand access to the intimate pinkness. Two fingers, clamped together, hooked into her flesh and withdrew glistening with her juices. She had found her clitoris. With one slippery finger pressing each side of her clit's head, she humped at her hand, jerking the sweet polyp between her fingers' pads.

Neither of Charlotte's eager victims could have been comfortable, crowded into the narrow space, stooped and juddering, but the power of their lust overcame all discomfort.

Charlotte leant back in her seat and sipped her champagne, aloof. Lesser mortals were slaves to their lusts. She was stronger. That was her favourite fantasy: having that strength of will.

Charlotte was just as strong as Veronica was.

No! Veronica wasn't in this dream. Veronica wasn't allowed to be in it.

The steward jerked faster. The stewardess was panting.

'You are so lovely, ma'am,' the steward gasped.

'She's beautiful,' the stewardess agreed. 'Cold and cruel and beautiful.'

That's not me, Charlotte thought. They're describing Veronica. Then she said, 'You are close to your orgasms, aren't you? Both of you?'

The steward nodded, speechless. The stewardess hissed a long, 'Yesss!'

'Then you must both stop.' Charlotte uncrossed her legs, leaving the steward thrusting at the air.

The man choked, 'But ...'

11

The woman spluttered, 'I'm so close . . .'

'Enough!' I said. 'Have you no self-control, either of you? Rearrange your clothing. Make yourselves decent. You may fetch me more champagne, and then we shall see.'

A voice like the crackling of electricity said, 'Still the total slob, I see.'

Charlotte shook herself awake. She blinked her eyes open. Yes, it was the voice and the tone that she knew so well. There, standing in the aisle, frowning down on Charlotte in that incredibly disapproving way that she'd always had, was her stepsister, Veronica.

Two

'You haven't changed one bit,' Veronica continued. 'Have you no pride?'

'I . . .' Charlotte started.

'Don't make excuses! Look at yourself, and look at me. Father must be spinning in his grave to see you looking like that.'

And their father would certainly have approved of Veronica, just as he'd always done. She might have just stepped off the cover of a fashion magazine, except that she wasn't showing any cleavage. She was dressed like a jockey, in parti-colour silks. Her high-necked blouse was divided into four squares, two green and two gold. Her glossy pants had one green leg and one gold one. They were tucked into gleaming black riding boots. To complete the effect, Veronica had her sleek black hair tucked under a gold jockey's cap with a green visor. She was also carrying a riding crop.

On anyone else the outfit would have looked slightly ridiculous, but Veronica wore it like an empress at a costume ball. The greens in her costume put emerald glints into the inky blackness of her eyes. The silk clung to her nipples' points and draped over her breasts' curves. The pants moulded themselves to her strong slender thighs and cupped the prominent mound between them. As always, what Veronica wore simply reminded you that beneath her clothes she was stark naked, and incredibly gorgeous.

Charlotte tore her eyes from her stepsister's braless breasts.

As a teen, Veronica had needed no support for her perfectly shaped bosom. Charlotte had hoped that by now,

now that they were both twenty, there might be some sign of sagging, but no. There was no justice in this world.

'Stop gawking and let me sit down,' Veronica snapped.

Charlotte scooped her newspaper off the aisle seat, spilling inserts to the floor. She kicked them under the seat in front, hoping that Veronica hadn't noticed.

'Don't you give your sister a nice big hello kiss?' Veronica asked as she sat.

Charlotte leant over automatically, and recoiled sharply as she felt the warm wet probing tip of Veronica's tongue slip between her lips.

'Still daydreaming, I see.' Veronica smiled. 'Who were you fantasising about? What's his name? Or was it a "her"?'

Charlotte began to protest, but Veronica had reached under the tray and found the damp cloth at Charlotte's crotch.

Charlotte pushed Veronica's hand away and said, 'I didn't expect to see you until the hotel.'

'How many flights would you expect there to be, into a postage stamp sized country like Steinreich?'

'I hadn't thought.'

'You haven't read up on our father's homeland? You should be ashamed of yourself. Here!' She pulled a green and gold brochure out of the pocket of the seat in front. 'A proud history, wouldn't you say? Never in a war, and always a safe refuge for the oppressed. You really should have read this, sister dear. Knights Templar were first, heavy with the Saracen gold they'd looted during the Crusades. Then it was heretics fleeing the Inquisition, followed later by some of the Inquisitors. Our homeland took in Romanovs, when the Russian revolution came. Mandarins and their concubines fled to Steinreich from imperial China when the emperor discovered an assassination plot. We gave a home to a number of wealthy southern gentlemen after the American Civil War. Then there were assorted kinky friends of King Farouk's, once he was deposed.'

'There was no need for anyone to flee America, surely?' Charlotte interrupted.

'Only those who refused to give up their slaves.'

'Slaves?'

'There were no anti-slavery laws in Steinreich. Still aren't come to that.'

'There are slaves in Steinreich?'

'Did I say that? Do pay attention, dear. I just said that there were no actual laws against slavery, if someone did just happen to have a slave or two.'

'That's barbaric!'

'Is it? Perhaps. Maybe the slaves who came over with their masters enjoyed being slaves. You, of all people, can understand that, surely?'

'What do you mean by that?'

'What do I mean?' Veronica pinched Charlotte's thigh, making her wince.

'Don't do that!' Charlotte said, as sternly as she could.

'It's like that, is it?' Veronica smiled. 'All grown up, are we? No more naughty children's games? You don't obey your big sister any more?'

'You're just one week older than me,' Charlotte protested, 'and things are different now.'

Veronica's nails traced lines up Charlotte's thigh to where she was still damp.

'Then why are you quivering, Charlotte? You were wet when I sat down, but you're wetter now. Why is that, dear sister?'

'I'm not!' Charlotte denied, feeling herself blush.

'And you're pouting! Don't you remember what I do to naughty little girls who pout?'

Charlotte shrugged. 'Don't be ridiculous. As you said, neither of us is a child now.'

'You think age has anything to do with it? Listen to me, Charlotte. Some are born to command, and some to obey. I'm a commander. I've given instruction to men and women twice my age, and been thanked for it. You, on the other hand, Charlotte, were born to serve.'

'Not to serve you, I wasn't.' Even as she said it, she realised that her lower lip was jutting and her cheeks were pouched.

15

Veronica flicked her crop sideways, stinging Charlotte's thigh. 'I told you not to pout, young lady!'

'I'm not pouting,' Charlotte lied.

'Look me in the eyes!'

Charlotte knew from past experience what obeying the command would lead to. Veronica's eyes could drink her soul. Once she allowed herself to be sucked into those hot black pools, her will would drown. She would cease to exist as a rational human being. Some primitive ancestor would take over; an ancestor who knew that the only way to survive was to submit, and that unconditional surrender would be rewarded by total ecstasy.

She'd have to be crazy to let things revert to the old ways. But her body was craving. Her body had been roused and frustrated, and roused again. Charlotte's body told her that it wouldn't hurt to go along with Veronica, just once. It said that it'd be better to start off with Veronica on the right foot, to give in to her just once. It asked her to wallow in the old forbidden joys that only Veronica could bring, just once.

It needn't happen again. Charlotte would sit Veronica down once they got to the hotel and explain to her, sternly, forthrightly, logically, that this would happen just once. Like a kiss hello. A gift on meeting.

'Look at me!' Veronica ordered.

Charlotte twisted her body against the tight cutting edge of her seat belt and obeyed.

Black as Satan's darkest secret, Veronica's eyes claimed their mastery over Charlotte's will. As the other passengers reclaimed their seats ready for take off, she began quizzing Charlotte.

'You were fantasising when I came aboard, weren't you,' she said.

Charlotte cleared her throat and said, 'Yes.'

'About me?'

It took a moment's thought, then Charlotte said, 'No. About the steward.'

Veronica grinned. 'I saw him as I boarded. Quite a hunk. The stewardess is very attractive too, don't you think?'

16

Charlotte's mouth was suddenly very dry. She tried to swallow.

Veronica's gaze hardened. 'Admit it! You were lusting after both of them, weren't you!'

'I – it was – in my dream – it was the other way. It was them who wanted me.'

'Really?' Veronica drawled. 'My my! So the little slut has some spark in her after all! Isn't that interesting. And their wanting you made you hot, did it?'

Charlotte's voice was husky. 'Yes.'

'And wet?'

'Y–yes.'

'You still get soaking wet at the first thought of sex, don't you?'

'Yes.'

'And when you climax, you still come just like a man, don't you.'

Charlotte bit her lip. 'Yes.'

'Because under that sweet and innocent look of yours, you're really a slut, a tramp, a bitch in heat, aren't you?'

'N–yes.'

'What are you? Tell me, bitch!'

'I'm a slut,' Charlotte confessed. 'I'm a tramp. I'm a bitch in heat.'

'And you'd do anything to get off, wouldn't you? Anything at all. With anyone, any time, any place, anyhow.'

'Not with just anyone, Veronica.'

'But for me? Tell me, Charlotte!'

Charlotte felt her face burn from the shame of it. 'For you, Veronica? Yes.'

'Say it!'

'For you, Veronica: anything, any time, anywhere.'

'And you want it right now, don't you, Charlotte? You want one of your sloppy wet orgasms, don't you? You're desperate for it. You crave it, don't you?'

'I – we're on a plane, Veronica. It's public, Veronica. Please?'

'Don't whine! "Anywhere, anyhow," you said.'

'Yes, Veronica.' A tear trembled at the corner of Charlotte's eye.

'Then ask for it, you whore!'

'Ask?'

Veronica's lip curled. 'You say, "Please Veronica, please allow me to have an orgasm".'

'Please Veronica, please let me have an orgasm.'

'We'll see. Put your right hand on your naked belly, inside those disgusting ugly pants. OK – now what do you feel?'

'My tummy, Veronica.'

'And?'

'And the beginning of my mound, and my hair.'

'Your pubic hair,' Veronica corrected.

'My pubic hair.'

'The hair on your sex.'

'The hair on my sex.'

'Is it still the way I remember? Is it still fine and soft, with a slight curl?'

'Y–yes.'

'But it's wet now, isn't it? Soaking wet with the juices that you've been spilling? Plastered to your skin by your own juices?'

'It – it's damp.'

'And does it still smell and taste as sweet?'

'It – I don't know.'

'Then smell it, Charlotte! Get your fingers lower between your thighs. Rub your fingers in it. Get them wet with your juices. Rub the insides of your lips where it's fresh. Are you doing it?'

Charlotte grunted and nodded, her eyes still lost in Veronica's.

'Then take your hand out, bitch!'

Charlotte obeyed.

'So! Smell your fingers! Are they musky? Is it sweet?'

'It – yes. Yes, Veronica. My fingers smell of my juices.'

'And taste? Lick them, slut! You know you love the taste of a woman.'

Charlotte's tongue lapped out. 'Yes, Veronica. I taste good.'

'Then suck them, bitch!'

Charlotte put two fingers into her mouth and sucked.

18

'Now put them back into your pants. I'm going to make you play with yourself, you filthy little whore. You'd like that, wouldn't you.'

'Yes, Veronica. I'd like that a lot.'

'What do you want to do?'

'I want to play with myself, Veronica. I want to masturbate.'

'Because you know that I'm watching you, right?'

'Yes, Veronica. I want to play with my sex, knowing that you're watching me.'

'And what does that make you?'

'A horny little slut, Veronica.'

'Then do it!'

Charlotte shoved her hand back into her pants so eagerly that she rocked the tray and her wine. The lips of her sex were longing to be manipulated. Her clitoris craved her fingers' touch.

'Pull on the right lip first, Charlotte! Get a good grip on it, with your finger and thumb, and tug it!'

Charlotte moaned.

'Now rub! Work that slutty lip. Your thumb is inside, isn't it? Smooth that soft flesh, Charlotte. Rub the ball of your thumb over that slickness.'

'I want to . . .'

'To play with your clit? It doesn't matter what you want, Charlotte. You will do as I instruct, isn't that right?'

'Yes, Veronica.'

'Then pull yourself open. Spread your thighs, and pull.'

The tray rocked again.

'Are you spread wide?'

'Yes, Veronica.'

'Wet and wide, and oozing, isn't that right?'

'Yes, Veronica.'

Veronica licked her lips. Charlotte could see the hunger blazing in her eyes. Strong as Veronica was, Charlotte's lust was getting to her, spreading like a contagious disease.

'Three fingers, Charlotte. I want you to push three fingers up inside yourself. Higher. Push beyond your lips, up into your vagina.'

'Y–yes, Veronica.'

'Keep looking at me. Don't let your eyes roll. Now, is it hot up there? Hot and wet? Can you feel those smooth little bumps?'

'Yes.'

'Stroke them, Charlotte. Rub them with your fingertips. Like little nodules, aren't they? That's where the glands are, Charlotte. That's where your sweet juices come from. Scratch them, Charlotte. Scratch gently with your nails.'

Veronica's name strained between Charlotte's clenched teeth. It might have been an accusation, or it might have been a prayer.

'You're running with it now, aren't you, my little Charlotte? You're flowing. It's trickling out of you.'

'It – it's so wet!'

'And it's going to get wetter. Bunch your fingers, Charlotte. Make a cock out of your fingers. Now do it! Do it to yourself! Up and down, Charlotte. In and out. Screw yourself with your fingers!'

Charlotte's thighs spread even wider. Her legs straightened under the tray, and beneath the seat in front. The tray shook. The wine glass shuddered across to the bottle, and clinked against it. The clink became a rapidly vibrating tinkle.

'Stop,' Veronica told her.

Charlotte froze, her fingers still embedded to her knuckles. Her thighs convulsed and squeezed together, trapping her fingers in their spasming grip.

'You didn't come?' Veronica demanded.

'No, not yet. Please?'

'Take your fingers out.'

Charlotte forced her legs to relax and part. Slowly, reluctantly, her fingers slithered out, leaving her vagina aching with emptiness.

'Please, Veronica? Let me come. I need it.'

Veronica's full red lips twisted. 'You need? What do your needs matter? Don't you understand yet? After all the time and effort I put into your training? You are supposed to please me, not yourself. What you want or need is irrelevant. If it pleases me that you should have an orgasm, then you shall. If I decide that you won't, then you won't. Is that understood?'

'Yes, Veronica; but please?'

'Then don't let me hear another word about what you want. You're wearing a bra, aren't you?'

Charlotte bit her lower lip. 'Yes, Veronica. It's quite pretty.'

'I am displeased. You will be punished later.'

'But . . .'

'But what? You didn't know? You didn't think? That's all irrelevant.'

'It fastens at the front, Veronica. I could take it off, if you wanted me to.'

'I'll tell you what I want. Don't whine at me, and try to get out of your punishment. It never did work and it never will. But your discipline can wait. We always finish what we're doing, don't we, Charlotte? One thing at a time. Where was I?'

'My breasts,' Charlotte whispered. 'My bra?'

'Oh yes! Put your hand up inside that revolting sweatshirt, Charlotte. Put it up to your left breast. Now fold the top half of the cup down and tuck it into the bottom half. Make it like a half-cup, you little bitch. Make sure that your nipple is above the cup, you understand?'

Charlotte fumbled beneath her shirt, her eyes never leaving Veronica's.

'Now the other cup.'

'Yes, Veronica.'

'Are you done?'

'Yes.'

'Now you'd look better if I had you take your shirt off, wouldn't you? You'd look more like the cheap little whore that you really are.'

'Yes, Veronica.' Charlotte started to worm her arm back down.

'No! We aren't done yet. Now you're going to play with your nipples. You'll do it right, or I'll make you pull that shirt up to your chin and show the steward and the stewardess what a slutty little bitch you really are.'

'Please no, Veronica.' Charlotte could feel herself flushing, either from shame or from pleasure, at the thought of making a cheap display of herself.

'You want to!' Veronica accused. 'You'd like to show yourself. You dirty little bitch! I should have you pull your shirt up over your breasts and drag those pants down to your ankles, and call the attendants to watch you while you finger that wet slit of yours into a froth! That's what you want, isn't it?'

Veronica's finger reached out to the 'press for service' button.

'No, Veronica, please no!'

Veronica pressed. 'Keep your hand where it is.'

'We're about to take off,' the steward said. 'Is there something I can bring you ladies once we're in the air? You are the only passengers for Steinreich, so anything at all?'

Surely Veronica was going to look at the man? If her sister released her eyes, just for a moment, she could break the spell. But Veronica didn't. Still gloating into Charlotte's eyes, she said, 'Champagne for both of us, once we're up. Steward, if we're taking off, shouldn't our belts be fastened?'

'Yes, ma'am. I see your friend's already snug.'

Still without turning away from Charlotte's gaze, Veronica gave a little twist to tell the man to take care of her belt for her. Charlotte cringed. He'd have to stretch across Veronica to do it. He'd have to grope between them. Surely he'd notice something strange? Two women, staring into each other's eyes, not even acknowledging his presence with so much as a glance? And she had her arm folded up inside her baggy sweatshirt, with her breast cupped in her palm! He absolutely had to notice that something strange was going on.

But he didn't seem to. 'How's that, ma'am?' he asked Veronica.

'Tighter.'

He pulled. Veronica sucked her stomach in. 'Tighter.'

'Ma'am?'

'Yes. That'll do.'

The plane rolled and howled. Charlotte felt that familiar sinking feeling.

'Your nipple,' Veronica said.

'But we're taking off.'

'Pinch it!'

'He'll be back in a moment.'

'You're arguing with me. That's two black marks. You know what three means? You remember?'

'Yes, Veronica.' And she did remember. There'd been bamboo canes in the garden shed. Bamboo canes to beat her and hooks in the wall, and twine to tie her wrists to them. Three black marks had meant a trip to the shed, back then. Charlotte sucked her lips in and pinched her nipple.

'And roll it.'

'Yes, Veronica.'

'Now pull on it. Pull it hard.'

The plane was still climbing. The warning light was on. The steward wouldn't come back, not just yet.

The light blinked and told them they could unbuckle.

'Veronica!' Charlotte pleaded.

'Now squeeze your whole breast.'

The man might not notice if she squished her hand in close and pressed her breast flat.

'Shall I unbuckle you, ma'am?' he asked Veronica.

'You may,' she said.

'And you, ma'am?'

It took Charlotte a moment to realise that he was talking to her. Her world was bounded by her sister's eyes and the bruising pressure of her own hand at her breast, kneading so hard that she could feel the muscular tissue deep in her flesh.

'No – no thank you,' she croaked.

He poured the champagne into flutes and retreated.

'Shall I call him back?' Veronica grinned. 'Shall I ask him if he'd like to watch you play with yourself?'

'Please no.'

'Then keep working at that nipple, bitch! Get your other hand down between your legs. I feel generous. I'm going to let you have an orgasm.'

'Thank you, Veronica,' Charlotte whispered.

'Is your clit's head exposed?'

'N–no.'

'Then pull back on its hood, you silly little slut! How else are you going to play with it? Now get it between your fingertips, just like you've got your nipple. Now roll them both! That's it! Tweak them. What a nasty little girl you are, Charlotte. Here you are in a public place, with serving-people likely to come along any moment, and what are you doing? Playing with yourself! Masturbating! You stink of sex, you filthy child.' Veronica gripped her riding crop and began to tap a slow rhythm with it on the thickest part of Charlotte's thigh. 'You lewd brat. Do you know what they do to obscene children who can't keep their hands off their own bodies?' The tapping came faster, and harder.

Charlotte shook her head, but her eyes didn't move. She didn't even blink, although her eyes were watering.

'They tie them up, so that they can't play their disgusting games, and then they whip them. What do they do?' The crop's beating was a blur now, as it kept time with Charlotte's fingers as they rolled and strummed with frantic urgency.

'They tie them up,' Charlotte panted. 'Tie them up and whip them. Veronica! Please Veronica! Please let me!'

'So you do remember! Very well. We might as well get this obscene exhibition over with before you cause me any more embarrassment. On three.' The crop lifted, hovered, and slashed down. 'One!' Up with the crop again. 'Two!'

Charlotte arched up, her body straining against the bondage of the strap across her lap.

'Three!' The crop cracked. Charlotte bucked. For the first time her eyes left her sister's, and rolled back into her head. She let out a long shuddering sigh, and sank back into her seat.

Veronica poured two flutes of champagne.

Charlotte rubbed her thigh.

'Two black marks, remember.' Veronica smirked.

'No, Veronica. It's over. It really is over. That was just "for old times sake". I have a perfectly normal sex – love

24

life now, Veronica. I don't need your kinky little games, and I refuse to play them ever again. Do you understand?'

Veronica raised one perfectly shaped eyebrow. 'Why, I do believe that you really have grown up, Charlotte dear. You're right, of course. We'll both be 21 in a matter of weeks. In Steinreich that's the age of majority. We must act like mature young women, not naughty little girls. I agree: we'll put the past behind us. We have equal inheritances, so father must have considered us equals. So be it: from here on, just stepsisters. And, I hope, friends. Agreed?' She reached her hand across Charlotte and took hers.

Charlotte shook Veronica's hand. 'Agreed. Will you excuse me? I have to go to the bathroom.'

'Of course you do.' Veronica laughed. 'And I won't even tease you about why.'

There now. That hadn't been too difficult, thought Charlotte as she wiped herself.

In her seat, Veronica opened a snakeskin-bound note book and took out a gold propelling pencil. She turned to a page that was already headed CHARLOTTE, and underlined her sister's name. Beneath it she wrote, 'Two black marks', and the date.

25

Three

'You get changed in the bathroom. Take a quick shower if you like. I'll unpack my things and change here,' Veronica said.

'What shall . . .?'

'Something suitable for sightseeing. Walking clothes. They eat late here. It's hours before dinner yet. We should take advantage of every opportunity. There's lots to see according to the guidebook.'

Charlotte took her duffle and overnight bag into the bathroom. It was wonderful, the change in her stepsister. Charlotte had been nervous all the way to the hotel, and doubly so when she'd seen that the lawyers had booked them both into the Borgia suite. The bathroom was as big as the living room in her New York apartment, and although the drawing room had three armchairs and two couches, it still looked underfurnished. There was just one gigantic bedroom, with two empress-sized beds.

Veronica, however, had been champagne-giggly all the way, and had offered Charlotte her choice of the rather ugly beds. Charlotte had tensed. She'd been sure that her sister would make some remark about two beds being one too many, but she didn't.

'You pick, my dear,' Veronica had said. 'Which drawers would you like? I'll take this end of the closet, and you take that one, dear.'

Could it really be that easy? Is that all it had needed? Could she have rebelled all those years ago? Just stood up to Veronica once, and ended the domination? And did that mean she'd really been just as guilty as her sister – her stepsister? Had she been a willing victim?

Knowing how Veronica loved to show off her knowledge, Charlotte had asked her sister, 'Are those ugly headboards and footboards antique?'

'Traditional, anyway.' Veronica had shrugged. 'All those round holes bored through the wood are something to do with some weird nuptial customs, or maybe they're religious. The guidebook is a bit vague.'

Washing herself, and deliberately keeping her mind blank as she soaped between her thighs, Charlotte congratulated herself. Perhaps it was going to be a real vacation, not a constant battle. She should relax. She should soak in the sights and sounds of her father's homeland and maybe, just maybe, there'd be romance for both of them. Perhaps they'd meet some nice young men, and flirt their way into one of those innocent holiday affairs that normal young women enjoyed when they were far away from home.

Maybe there'd be more than romance. They were almost 21. This was Europe. There'd be men, not boys. European men were so much more sophisticated than the boys she was used to, back in Ridge River. Perhaps there'd be a man who could rouse the passion in her, and who wouldn't be shocked when she got so damned wet. With a man like that, she could do the sexual things that she'd always wanted to do, and never dared.

The hard bar of soap slid up between the lips of her sex, pressing firmly against her inner lips as she imagined it: an imaginary man kneeling at her feet, with his aristocratic face trapped between her thighs, his thin-lipped mouth on her sex, his strong thick tongue deep inside her.

The soap squirmed in her hand, twisting to present its narrow end to her fleshy channel. Her palm flattened on its base, and pushed. Her inner lips parted against the solid pressure. The soap slid higher, one end slipped into her, forcing the folds to part.

A girl has to be clean, doesn't she?

And the fantasy man's tongue moved higher, to her clit,

27

where its tip vibrated as fast as a humming-bird's wing, but with firm insistence.

The soap was all the way in now. Charlotte squeezed her internal muscles, forcing it down and out, and then pressed it back up with her palm once more.

And she'd warn him, of course. 'I come wet,' she'd say. 'I gush.'

He'd nod his understanding and lap harder, thirsty for her nectar. Then she'd feel herself getting slicker and slicker as her internal muscles tensed she'd just let her climax flow, wet and strong and so, so liquid. He'd press his open mouth over her sex, taking every drop, sucking it out, swallowing and gulping and nuzzling, eager for more.

Charlotte convulsed inside. The soap shot out, followed by a gush of clear essence: essence of Charlotte. Without thinking, she lifted her palm to her lips. It smelt of lemon and salt. Her tongue flickered out, tasting herself.

No! That was perverse. Sex was good, but solitary sex was a perversion. Find a nice man, fall for him, and then enjoy virtuous, normal, loving sex. That was the right way.

With adventure in mind, she towelled herself dry, and sorted out the briefest pair of panties that she owned. They still weren't that sexy. Cotton never is. But there'd be shops, right? Perhaps, like real sisters, they'd go shopping together, and Veronica would help her pick out some sexy underclothes. It might even be fun.

She'd brought two pairs of jeans. One was baggy and comfortable. She struggled into the other pair, and tucked in a white Oxford-cloth shirt. Then she sucked her stomach in, as she tugged the zip up. Drawing her breath in further she pulled the belt a notch tighter than it had ever been fastened before. Then she joined Veronica in the bedroom.

Veronica was wearing trousers as well. Except hers had been tailored from slubbed silk, and fitted her so well that she looked as if she'd been dipped up to the waist in a vat of denim-blue dye. Charlotte blessed the gods that her sister's matching waistcoat was less snug, even if it did leave her slender arms and stark white shoulders bare.

Veronica pulled on her second snakeskin boot, and

picked up a handbag that was covered in the same mottled skin. She let a frown flicker across her face as she saw how Charlotte was dressed, and said, 'Let's go, sis. The duchy of Steinreich, in all its decadent glory, awaits!'

The main street, *Cesare Strasse*, was six lanes wide, but cobbled. *Via Lucrezia* cut across it at almost a right angle, but not quite, and was just two lanes narrower. The rest of the streets were tangled insanity. The broadest were about eight feet across. The narrow ones could barely take two people walking side-by-side.

There were shop signs in English, French, German, Italian, and a few in some even more exotic scripts. Charlotte thought she recognised Cyrillic, and what might have been Hindi, Chinese, and possibly Japanese. Many of the shops had three-dimensional signs hanging outside: brass boots, imitation vials of perfume, a haunch of beef and a wine bottle. You didn't need to know the language to read those.

The people were just as varied. Charlotte had visited London often enough, when she'd been living in England, and knew New York reasonably well. She was used to ethnic neighbourhoods, but Steinreich was even more of a melting pot than New York.

A golden-skinned, cat-eyed Eurasian girl passed by, holding the hand of a handsome coffee-tinted man. A typical Steinreich couple, Charlotte thought. He'd been in a three-piece suit, and she was wearing a short dirndl skirt and a peasant blouse that left her shoulders and half of her breasts bare. That was typical as well. She saw clothes from every famous fashion house and designer. And there were more outfits similar to the one the Eurasian girl had worn. Charlotte guessed it to be the local peasant costume, much like that of Bavaria, but far sexier. There were several variations. Some of the girls wore bare-shoulder blouses, but others showed long expanses of bare midriff from the tops of their skirts to just beneath their breasts. Further still, some wore waistcoats like the one Veronica was wearing, except they laced up over naked cleavages.

It was warm, but Charlotte was still a little shocked to see as much bare skin on display as she'd expect to see on Wreck Beach, Vancouver, or at a Greek island resort. Or perhaps not quite as much. None of the women were actually topless, none of the men were barechested, though some of each came close. One of the couples she'd seen in bib-fronted lederhosen had been wearing nothing else but boots, which isn't the way lederhosen were designed to be worn. Their bibs covered the front but not the sides. On the man, that wasn't so bad. On the woman it had been far too revealing for Charlotte's peace of mind.

She and Veronica paused outside a shop window. The display was of junk jewellery, mainly brightly coloured wooden squares, with circular holes cut in to make bangles. Charlotte had noticed a number of girls and women wearing them on their wrists.

A pair of lovers came out, giggling; he had his arm around her waist. The girl was carrying an oblong parcel.

'They're handsome people, aren't they,' Veronica remarked. 'It's the mixture of races that does it.'

Charlotte remembered what her sister had told her about southerners bringing their slaves, and all the other refugees. 'They seem prosperous,' she said. 'What's the local industry? I thought this had been an austere communist country until recently.'

Veronica laughed. 'They practised their own brand of communism. When Steinreich found itself behind the Iron Curtain after World War Two there was an instant and painless revolution. Some of the nobility simply packed and left, to wait out the new regime in Rio or Monte Carlo. The old duke and his family stayed and were put under house arrest. That was no hardship, I can tell you. As for the rest of the duchy, it was business as usual. The Chamber of Elders became the Chamber of the People, with the same people running things. Instead of tourists from the west it was the Party élite from the USSR, Albania, Rumania, Cuba and China.'

'So the duchy lives on tourism?'

'Some. Mainly it's from overseas investments. I told you

that they welcomed refugees – well they did, and do – but only rich ones. Every time a despotic regime falls, and some dictator who's robbed his country's treasury runs away and disappears, this is usually where he ends up.'

'That's terrible!'

'I guess. It's certainly profitable. And, there being no taxes, a lot of companies are registered here. It's a living. It's also probably why the people are so good looking. When some despot runs, he usually takes his favourite ladies with him. Whether it's wives or concubines or his choice of whores, the ladies are usually very attractive.'

'So that's why there are so many languages?'

'And such a variety of food. Let's go nibble something ethnic.'

Veronica took Charlotte's arm and steered her across the street to a vendor's cart. Four of the local marks, less than a British pound, bought them a hot kebab each, served on a bed of rice in a fold of edible rice-paper. They walked and ate in companionable silence until they came to a wine-vendor.

'That was spicy,' Charlotte said. 'I could use a cold drink, but isn't it a bit early for wine?'

'The sun will set soon, but the people here start drinking early, anyway. Get used to it. American colas cost three marks for a small bottle. The local wine is fifty pfennigs a litre. It isn't very strong. The locals drink it all day. Only tourists buy the soft drinks.'

They took their paper beakers of wine into the park and sat under a brooding elm.

'Are you getting excited?' Veronica asked. 'This time next month we'll both be rich.'

'Rich? I wonder? How rich is "rich" do you think?'

'Our mutual stepdad didn't say much, did he? But reading between the lines, pretty rich I'd guess. When he left here he managed to take enough money out so that he never had to do a day's work, didn't he? And he let slip a couple of times that he'd left more behind than he'd taken. I wouldn't be a bit surprised if there was a title as well. Dad always had an aristocratic way about him.'

31

'But we wouldn't inherit that, would we? Even if he'd been a count or something, we aren't blood, just adopted.'

Veronica shrugged. 'Who knows? Perhaps there's land, and the title goes with it.'

'Land? Land must be very valuable, here.'

'Just like Tokyo. You and I could retire in Sybaritic luxury on what half an acre was worth, dear sister.'

Charlotte thought about that for a while. Before coming to Steinreich, it had all seemed vague, like a dream. Now she was here, her potential inheritance seemed real. She really would have to learn more about her stepfather's country.

'Veronica,' she said, 'our suite is the Borgia suite, and the two major roads are called Cesare and Lucrezia. What's the connection with the Borgias?'

'That goes way back. Cesare and Lucrezia used to visit a lot, when things got hot for them in Italy. The story is that they even had a child here: a daughter. She was left behind in the care of the current duke, and eventually married him.'

'But Cesare Borgia was Pope, and Lucrezia was his sister.'

'Yes.'

'But that's incest!'

Veronica grinned. 'So it is! How shocking!'

Charlotte flushed and changed the subject. 'What's that big building, Veronica?'

'*La Musée de Sainte Clothilde*. She's the patron saint of Steinreich. There's a big festival each year to honour her.'

'I've never heard of her.'

'Nor has the Catholic Church. She's strictly local. It's an interesting story. Legend has it that back in the seventeenth century the duke, Rufus the Third, took a fancy to the daughter of a French count. The Duke tried to get his hands on the girl in a number of ways: offering her father a fortune for her, trying blackmail, and whatever other dirty tricks he could think of. Daddy refused him, and sent the girl to a convent for protection. The count died mysteriously, and the convent suddenly got rich. A month later the girl appeared at the castle – that one up there.'

Charlotte followed Veronica's pointing finger. She hadn't noticed the castle before. It glowered on a high crag on the side of Mount Steinreich, far above the city. 'What happened?' she asked.

'Rufus took her to his bed, of course – his and his wife's, as the story goes. He was a kinky duke, apparently. Clothilde was a dutiful daughter, and determined to honour her father's memory, but the duke saw her potential, as it were, and was sure that with the right persuasion she'd become his willing whore. He devised an elaborate series of disciplines, to teach her a lesson and to convert her to his perverse way of thinking. That's what the festival is all about: the trials of Saint Clothilde. It's like a twisted version of the Stations of the Cross.'

Charlotte crunched her empty cup and dropped it into a bin. 'And what happened to her, in the end?'

'The stories vary. Some say that she proved impossible to corrupt, and ended her days in the dungeons. Others maintain that racked with sudden shame and guilt at her response to the duke's training she found an opportunity to jump to her death. Still others will tell you that he was successful, and she became just as debauched as he and his duchess were, and lived wallowing happily in sin for ever after.'

'But they made her a saint! But if she'd become Rufus's whore?'

'There are different definitions of sainthood, in Steinreich.'

Charlotte thought about that for a moment. 'What did he do to her, Veronica?'

'Curious? There's nothing like the idea of a beautiful young maiden being forced to perform perverse sexual acts to rouse one's prurient curiosity, is there? Come on. There's time. Dinner isn't until nine here. Let's visit the museum and find out.'

The entrance hall was lined with portraits of past dukes and duchesses. Beyond that it was a wax museum. Or more like an X-rated chamber of horrors.

The first alcove contained a tableau in wax, showing a

33

tall imperious man, in plum velvet doublet and breeches, at the centre. A long-haired blonde girl in a flowing white off-the-shoulder dress that was made of some gauzy, semi-transparent fabric knelt at his feet, her face upturned and tear-streaked. There was a wreath of white roses on her head. Her hands were fastened behind her back by some sort of wooden block, with two holes for her wrists.

Behind the duke was a bed, similar to the one in their hotel suite. Lying in the bed, but with the satin covers pushed down to her willowy waist, was a vulpine-faced black-haired woman, beckoning. The upper part of the woman's torso was bare except for the dramatic cascade of midnight hair that curled over and around her proud and naked breasts.

'Those things on the girl's wrists . . .?' Charlotte began.

'You noticed? A bit like the ones in the shops, aren't they? Girls wear them in honour of Saint Clothilde at festival time, which is soon. I understand that this year's festival is an extra special one, for some reason.'

'But in the shops they're just single blocks. The ones on Clothilde are double – more like wooden manacles.'

'Yes they are. That's exactly what they are; wooden manacles. They're lined, so as not to mark the skin. Much kinder than ropes or handcuffs, don't you think? You'll see double ones soon. Some of the more devout women and girls wear them publicly during the actual week of celebrations.'

'I can understand wearing single blocks as jewellery, but to manacle yourself – well, it seems a bit much.'

'There's no women's lib here, Charlotte. When a woman puts those on it's considered a sign of devotion to a husband, or a lover. They even form a part of the wedding ceremony here.'

'Then, when I get married, it'll be somewhere else. I won't be treated like some man's property.'

'Perhaps you just haven't met the right man yet.'

Charlotte hugged herself, although it wasn't cold. 'You surprise me, Veronica. I can't see you letting yourself become some man's slave.'

34

'Perhaps. Perhaps not. The right man? And if I'd had to endure what Clothilde suffered? If I'd learned the lessons that she was taught?'

'You?' Charlotte laughed, nervously. 'Never! You're too independent. If you ever settle down with one man, it'll be him who'll have to beware.'

'You may be right. Just don't warn him, OK?'

'I promise.'

'And I won't warn your man, when there is one, about you and some of your stranger sexual preferences.'

Charlotte let it pass. 'Let's see what comes next.'

It was the same three people, in the same room. Clothilde was bare now, and bent over a chest with her upraised rear to the audience. Her floral wreath lay crushed and trampled on the flagstone floor.

Rufus was standing by, chin in hand. The other female – the duchess, Charlotte guessed – was standing with her legs spread. She wore a black silk gown with a dramatic *décolletage* that left her breasts half naked; her hand was raised and held a willow wand. Clothilde's buttocks were criss-crossed with livid weals.

Charlotte clamped her thighs together. For a moment she'd seen herself in Clothilde's position. The thought had started her sex tingling.

'They started with gentle persuasion, I see,' Veronica remarked.

'If that's gentle, what would be extreme?' Charlotte asked.

Veronica took her sister's arm in steel fingers. 'You've had worse,' she hissed, 'and thoroughly enjoyed every second of it.'

Charlotte wrenched herself free. That part of her life was over. She didn't want to be reminded of it.

Clothilde was still naked in the next tableau. It was a different scene and featured some sort of stocks. It was so low that Clothilde was bent over at the hips, with her upper body parallel to the floor. The duchess, her robe dishevelled and one nipple bared, was standing beside the saint and reaching beneath her to cup one sweet young breast. The duke was holding a jar, perhaps some ointment, and had been frozen in the act of smoothing a palm over one of Clothilde's buttocks.

'Is the duchess caressing Clothilde, do you think?' Veronica whispered into Charlotte's ear. 'Or do you think she's pinching her nipple?'

Charlotte pulled away again. There was a warm slick feeling between her legs.

The next scene was set in another part of the same dungeon. Two great timbers had been fastened together to form a splayed triangle. The double-block at Clothilde's wrists had been chained to the apex, leaving her dangling. Now there were single blocks on each of her ankles. The duke was in the act of fastening an ankle to one of the uprights while his wife was tugging viciously on their victim's other leg, stretching it out to fix to the other timber. There were strange implements hanging between the flaring torches attached to the stone wall, and more were laid out on a bench.

'That poor girl,' Charlotte gasped. 'They're going to split her in two.'

'You're a dancer, aren't you?' Veronica said. 'Didn't you take some yoga as well? You can do the splits.'

'But I've never been forced to do them. I've never been spread and tied that way.'

Veronica stroked her sister's arm. 'There, there. You're young yet. There's no need for you to be jealous of Saint Clothilde. Maybe you'll get lucky, and some nice man will tie you up the way you like. If you can't wait for Mr Right, Charlotte dear, I volunteer.' She leant closer, her lips an inch from Charlotte's ear. 'I'd tie you up, if you asked nicely. We could act it out. You be Clothilde and I'll be the duchess. Haven't you noticed that we look a bit like them – you like Clothilde and me the duchess? I quite fancy the duchess's role. I'm starting to get hot, Charlotte. Looking at these displays is making my nipples prickle.' Her voice dropped to a hoarse whisper. 'I need someone to suck on them, Charlotte.'

Charlotte hurried ahead to the next display. It was similar to the previous one, but with Clothilde reversed. Now she was hanging by her ankles. The duke held a ewer. He was pouring something into Clothilde's sex while the naked duchess stood by with an oversized and intricately carved ivory replica of a penis in her hand.

'Did they have those things in those days?' Charlotte asked.

'Dildos? They're among the oldest tools known to humanity. How do you think prehistoric women amused themselves when their men went off hunting mammoths?'

'I've seen enough,' Charlotte said.

'Squeamish? It gets even more interesting as the display goes on, or so I've been told. There are things that they do to her breasts, and things that they put into her body.'

But it wasn't squeamishness that made Charlotte want to turn back. She was getting that dangerous glowing feeling between her legs. Her juices were starting to flow. Somehow she couldn't stop thinking of herself in Clothilde's place. If it got any more arousing the dampness might soak right through the denim of her jeans. But she wasn't going to tell her stepsister that. Veronica was already getting ideas without any encouragement.

Back in their suite, to Charlotte's surprise, Veronica was still being friendly. In the past, when Veronica had been thwarted, she'd been a bitch until Charlotte had been punished. Perhaps it was another sign of how their relationship had changed.

'Did you get a close look at these holes in the headboards?' Veronica asked. 'They've been cut with a thread, to take a wooden screw. That must have been how the old Steinreichians restrained their brides. Can you imagine it? Some poor virgin, on her wedding night, her arms stretched up over her head? There'd be no "but darling hubby, a nice girl just doesn't do that sort of thing" would there?'

Charlotte shrugged, and looked closer. 'But there are holes in the footboard as well, and the headboard goes so high! There are holes almost to the top; to the ceiling. Why would they? How would they use such things?'

'There's more than one position, you know.' Veronica chuckled. 'A tall girl, literally screwed to the head and the foot, would be suspended in mid-air. Now that could give a man ideas, I bet. It does me, but then I'm still horny from seeing what the duke and duchess were up to with poor Clothilde in the *musée*.'

'Women weren't so tall, back then.'

'Perhaps they had shorter beds. Or they stretched their women to fit.'

'You really don't think that.'

'I'm joking, you silly goose. Nevertheless, what if you had one ankle fixed up there, and the other way down here? Or all four blocks could be fastened to the headboard with the girl spread-eagled, ready for the man who likes to do it standing up. Well, it does make one think, doesn't it? You could even suspend her upside down. That might be difficult, though.' She tapped her lower lip with a fingernail. 'But what if you had two men? One could lift her while the other fastened the blocks, and then, what with there being the two of them . . . Did you ever make it with two men at once, Charlotte? Or a man and another woman? Or with two other women?'

Charlotte squirmed inside her jeans. 'Shouldn't we be getting ready for dinner?'

'Let me have the shower first, then. What are you going to wear?'

'Wear? I hadn't thought. I've got a trouser suit that's quite smart.'

'You aren't in New York now. Civilised people dress for dinner.'

'But I haven't brought anything. Perhaps I should have bought something while we were out.'

'We're close enough in size. I'll lend you something.' Veronica opened the closet. 'Here, try this.'

The dress was red satin. It was short, with a teasingly low *décolletage* and spaghetti-thin straps.

'I don't suppose you brought red stockings, either? Nor shoes?'

Charlotte shook her head.

38

'You'd take an English eight, US six? I thought so. To-morrow we go shopping, but you can use these for now.'

Charlotte picked up a diaphanous crimson stocking. 'How do I keep these up?'

'They're hold-ups. The tops grip your thighs. You don't need garters or a suspender belt.'

'Oh. But those shoes!'

'Heels a little higher than you're used to? You'll get used to them – and we won't be doing much walking.'

'Thank God!'

Charlotte undressed and put a robe on while Veronica showered. When her stepsister emerged in a *crêpe de chine* wrap, that made Charlotte ashamed of her shabby terry cloth towelling robe, she took her turn. When she'd finished, she returned for the clothes that her sister had lent her and went back into the bathroom to change. Maybe they were just stepsisters now, but the thought of undressing in the same room as Veronica still made Charlotte's belly quiver. She'd probably have to eventually, though. That was a bridge she'd cross when she was forced to.

'No, no, no!' her sister snapped when she emerged. 'That'll never do! Come here.'

Charlotte tottered over on heels that made her feel like she was on stilts. Veronica, sitting on the edge of the bed in what looked like oyster-pink silk pyjamas, pushed her hand up under Charlotte's dress and, before she could recoil, snatched Charlotte's cotton panties down to her knees.

'What do you think you're doing?' Charlotte squealed.

'Relax. I'm not attacking you. I never was the attacking kind, remember? The dress is satin, you silly little thing. It clings. It's not made to wear anything beneath it. That ridiculous bra will have to go, too.'

'My bra?' Charlotte gulped.

'I can see the straps. Even a strapless bra wouldn't look right, though. Oh well, it'll just have to go.'

Feeling as scarlet as the fabric of her dress, Charlotte kicked the offending panties off her ankles and fled to the bathroom before Veronica could do anything more to embarrass her.

39

Charlotte walked into the dining room close behind her sister, feeling that every eye was on her. Anyone who so much as glanced her way would be sure to notice that she was almost bare, especially her breasts. Those outsized nipples of hers might as well have been naked for all the silk concealed.

It was some consolation that the way that Veronica's pants clung to her behind showed that she wasn't wearing any underclothes either.

And what if she got aroused, somehow? What if her sex did its dreadful thing, and started to ooze? No! It wouldn't happen. It mustn't happen. She'd just have to discipline her thoughts, that was all. There'd be no thinking about what she'd seen in that awful museum, for instance.

When she sat she tried to blank out the sensuous feel of the satin under her thighs, and on her sex. No!

'I phoned down and ordered for us while you were in the shower,' Veronica said. 'I thought that after all the travelling we'd need an early night, so this'll save time. We're having steak tartar, and lobster bisque, with a Caesar salad on the side – except they call it a Cesare salad, of course. Then fillet mignon, with asparagus. I didn't order us any dessert.'

'If we're going straight up to bed after, we won't want too much on our stomachs.'

To Charlotte, after living for three years with diet-conscious dancers, the meal sounded sinful, and dangerously overloaded with red meat. She didn't dare argue, though. Things were going so well, between her and Veronica, she didn't want to spoil it.

The waiter brought a wine that Charlotte didn't recognise.

'What an attractive salt cellar,' Veronica mused, holding it up and fondling it. 'So heavy – I'm sure it's solid silver. Don't you admire the shape?'

'The shape?'

'Just like a cock.' Veronica rubbed her thumb over the domed top. 'And it must be – what – six or seven inches? Nothing spectacular, but adequate. I've had smaller.'

Charlotte squirmed and mumbled something.

'I really covet this salt cellar,' her sister went on. 'In fact, I want it.'

'Perhaps they'll sell it to you.'

'Sell? You're no fun. Here.' She handed the silver cylinder to Charlotte. 'Steal it for me.'

'What? Steal?'

'You've done it before to please your loving stepsister.'

'That was . . .' She'd been about to say 'different', but it wasn't. She was placating Veronica now, by not complaining about the meal. She'd been placating Veronica then; back when Veronica had forced her to be a petty thief, stealing sweets from the local shops.

'Do it!' Veronica snapped.

'But I've got no purse. I mean – how?'

'I told you it was shaped like a cock, didn't I?'

'You mean?'

'Do it, Charlotte, and perhaps I'll forget the black marks. We can really start fresh as loving stepsisters. Do it to show that you love me as much as you would a real sister.'

'I . . .' But she was already dropping her hand, with the cellar, beneath the table cloth. 'I don't know how I'll . . .'

'You want help? You want me to drop my napkin, and bend under the table, and do it for you?'

'No! No, I'll manage.'

'There's a good girl.'

The silver felt cold through Charlotte's stocking top, chill against the bare skin high inside her thigh, and colder still as it nudged the lips of her sex. They parted easily, as they always did.

Rob, the slightly more experienced of the two lovers she'd had, had once told her that with other women he'd had to part their lips for them. But with her it was easy; shamefully easy. Her sex welcomed invasion whether it be from a finger, or a cock, or even from cold silver, so it seemed.

'Is it all the way in?' Veronica asked, eagerly.

'A – half-way.'

41

'Then push it, my sweet little obedient bitch. Shove it deep. It'll have to go all the way, you know. And then you are going to have to squeeze it, so it doesn't fall out. Can you squeeze it for me, Charlotte? Make believe it belongs to that dishy airline steward you were lusting after.'

Charlotte parted her thighs a little wider, and squirmed. It slid. It went in so easily. Soon the splayed base was against her lips, and then it too slithered into her secret flesh. It felt hard. It felt, to her shame, good. Another wriggle, and a prod with her fingertips, and it was snug, with a spare inch between its base and her opening.

'I can't sit like this for long,' she complained.

'Don't whine. Here comes our soup. Waiter! Why is there no salt at our table?'

Charlotte sat with her knees clamped together and endured the meal. When they were done Veronica led her out of the dining room.

'These heels,' Charlotte whimpered. 'Veronica, with these heels and this thing inside me, I can barely walk.'

'Why don't we take the stairs up?' Veronica said, just as if Charlotte hadn't spoken. 'After all that food it'll be good for us, and it's only two floors.'

Clutching the banister and walking with her thighs pressed together, Charlotte made it up a flight and a half before she felt the metal begin to move. It had been inevitable. The humiliation, the fear of discovery, Veronica's cruelty in making her undergo this degrading experience, had all served to make her sex seep. And there was the effect of the thing itself. Each time she lifted her leg, she could feel the unyielding rigidity of the thing inside her. It pressed against her soft flesh almost painfully. It was no wonder that her juices were slicking her thighs and soaking into the tops of her borrowed stockings. That liquid was meant by nature to serve as lubrication. Her body didn't care that the intruder was an unnatural one.

With her channel so well oiled, no matter how hard she clamped down, the salt cellar began to slither.

Charlotte froze in place, one foot already up on the next step. 'Veronica!' she hissed. 'I'm losing it!'

Veronica, icy calm, simply took one step back and down behind her sister, and reached up under Charlotte's skirt, between her thighs. 'So let it go then,' she said.

Charlotte relaxed, squeezed a little, and felt the cellar plop out into Veronica's waiting hand.

Veronica held the glistening cylinder to her nose. 'Yes, you are still as sweet as when you were younger. Very well, you tried, even though you failed. We'll count that as one black mark paid for. That means you still owe me one.'

Charlotte fled up the stairs. She was in bed with the lights off when Veronica came into their suite.

'You realise that you are a thief now, don't you?' she said as she put the salt cellar on the dresser. 'Do you know what they do to thieves, in Steinreich?'

Charlotte mumbled, 'No,' into her pillow.

'There's no probation here, not even for first-time offenders, and they don't have room for a prison. If they catch you, Charlotte, they'll brand you with a "T" for "Thief", on your right breast. Would you like that, Charlotte? Can you imagine it? Think about being tied by thin cords with your back to a wooden post. Being stripped naked to your waist, and then some masked brute of a man with a white-hot iron, coming closer, and closer, and your poor nipple cringing. You beg for mercy, but he ignores your pleas, and then comes the incredible searing agony as . . .'

Charlotte's sobs drowned out the rest.

43

Four

Charlotte woke stiff from holding herself tense all night. Veronica had her right where she wanted her, didn't she? She had a sword to Charlotte's throat.

Charlotte knew her sister too well to think that she wouldn't take advantage of her power. Sooner or later there'd be a reckoning. Veronica doted on having her step-sister in bondage, whether it was physical or mental.

Sometimes the suspense was the worst.

Veronica had made her wait six weeks for her punishment, once. By the end of the fifth week she'd been ready to beg for it. When it'd come it hadn't been so very bad: no pain, just humiliation. Veronica had brought that cheap village girl, Betty something, home, and made Charlotte pleasure her. Veronica had been in charge of the whole thing, giving them both her instructions, telling them exactly what to do to each other and when.

Perhaps it'd be something like that again. Veronica loved to watch, and she loved to 'direct scenarios', as she called it. There were bound to be whores for hire in Steinreich; better class whores than there had been back in the village.

But no. Veronica was older now, and more sophisticated. Charlotte's punishment would probably be a lot worse now than it had been back then.

Charlotte shivered under the covers. If Veronica became aroused it mightn't be so bad. If she just ordered Charlotte to do intimate things to her body. There'd be the shame of it, of course, but it'd be an old familiar shame, shared just between the two of them. It was the thought of Veronica bringing other people into it that worried Charlotte most. Private shame is more bearable than public humiliation.

Her thighs were squeezing together. She felt damp in the folds of her sex. At the thought of being forced into having sex with strangers? Surely not.

'Come on, sleepy-head! We've shopping to do.' Veronica's voice betrayed no trace of the evil glee that she had to be feeling, but Charlotte wasn't fooled. Something bad was coming.

Let it come soon, and be over with!

They had breakfast in the oak-beamed coffee shop. Charlotte was grateful that they didn't have to go back into the dining room. If that waiter had been there, she'd probably have blurted out a confession just to end the suspense.

Arm in arm, they strolled just like normal tourists. No one would have guessed that one girl was a cruel mistress, and the other her cringing slave.

They bought sunglasses in an American-style drug store complete with a 1950s soda fountain and a portrait of a naked Marilyn Monroe. Then they headed into a maze of twisted side-streets.

'Look at the name of that lane,' Veronica giggled. 'Rue Marquis de Sade! We absolutely must explore.' She towed Charlotte up a narrow cobblestone passage, so darkly shadowed by overhanging buildings that it was suddenly chilly. 'And look what's at number 69! Just my kind of shop.'

There were piles of the painted wooden block manacles in the window, but mainly the ominous doubles, not the innocuous single ones that were really just junk jewellery. And these certainly weren't junk.

Most of them looked hand-carved. Some were decorated with intricate inlaid designs in silver or ebony. The wood was worn smooth in places, and looked ancient.

'It's a sort of antique store,' Veronica exclaimed. 'A store full of antique instruments of punishment. Look, there's a whip with an ivory handle. You can't buy ivory anymore. And a scold's bridle, and thumbscrews. Isn't this delicious, Charlotte?'

'I'm cold. Let's keep moving.'

'Don't be such a spoilsport. It's not all antiques. I can see rubber and latex – or is it vinyl? And look at that vicious dildo with all the ridges. Can you imagine? Come on, Charlotte, let's go in and browse. Who knows, I might even buy you a present.'

'I don't want to, Veronica. This place scares me. I'd like to go back to the hotel. Please?'

'Damn you for a snivelling coward. Very well, you go back on your own. I'm going in. You realise that this means another black mark, don't you?'

'No, Veronica! Please? I'll go in with you, if you want.'

'No – too late. The mood you're in, I don't want you around me. Go on back and polish your stolen salt cellar. I'll meet you for lunch and show you what goodies I've bought. Cross your fingers it's not that scold's bridle. That would certainly put an end to your incessant whimpering!'

Charlotte kicked a crumpled cigarette packet into the gutter and trudged back to the hotel.

Veronica didn't show up for lunch. Charlotte ordered from room service, so as to avoid the dining room, and resolved not to worry. It was just like Veronica to disappear for a few hours, just to upset her. Charlotte decided to take a long beauty-bath and not even think about her stepsister.

The bubbles disappeared. The bath water went cold, and there was still no sign of Veronica. Bitch!

Charlotte should just call a taxi and leave. Leave the hotel and leave the country. But then, if she did, she'd forfeit her inheritance.

No, she'd stick it out for the full month. Then when there was nothing to hold her to her sister, she'd go away and never see her again.

Or she'd find a way to get revenge.

She'd never thought of revenge before, no matter what Veronica did to her. That showed she'd changed, didn't it?

Veronica still hadn't shown up by five. Charlotte put on fresh sensible underwear, including a bra, comfortable

46

jeans and a checked shirt. Then she took the lift down in order to go for a walk. She wouldn't be around when Veronica got back. Let Veronica do the worrying for a change!

Her feet just happened to take her back to that strange cramped street. Veronica couldn't still be browsing, could she? No matter how fascinating she'd found the things inside.

A bell tinkled as Charlotte pushed through the door. It was big inside, much bigger than she'd thought. It was full of things that she'd rather not recognise. That was a stocks, surely? And two pillories; the crossbar with the holes for wrists and head at different heights. There was another set of stocks that reminded Charlotte of the way Clothilde had been restrained. One wall was lined with iron maidens. Who would want such things? Bondage she could understand, but an iron maiden wasn't for bondage.

An iron maiden crushed and pierced, and maimed and killed.

A cat-o'-nine-tails was coiled on a peg. A display case held row after row of paddles and riding crops. There was an umbrella stand, holding a dozen or more old-fashioned canes with hooked handles.

It was a sado-masochist's paradise.

'May I help you?'

Charlotte spun. The woman was tall, more lithe than slim, and dressed all in black.

'I – er . . . My sister? She was in earlier – this morning? I – er – I . . .'

'An attractive young lady? Long black hair? Dressed in whipcord pants and a riding jacket?'

'That's her.'

'Then you must be Charlotte! Veronica said you'd be by. She wanted you to see something: a present for you, I believe.'

'A present?'

'Only if it fits. It's a remarkable piece – very old. It's supposed to be the original Clothilde's, but I couldn't prove it. It is old enough though.'

'I don't understand.'

47

'Come here then. I'm sure that when you see it you'll appreciate it.'

Charlotte followed the woman to a counter. The top was wooden, and had been drilled with those peculiar threaded holes that were becoming so familiar. The woman reached beneath the counter and brought out a cunningly carved pair of blocks. Or one block, for the pieces were made to fit together.

The woman laid one piece carefully at the edge of the counter with the wrist-grooves uppermost. 'Try it,' she encouraged.

Unthinking, Charlotte obeyed. The padded grooves fitted her slender wrists perfectly.

'The leather lining is new, of course,' the woman said. 'The originals rotted away long ago.' She took the second block and laid it on the first. 'Yes, it is a good fit. They could have been made for your delicate wrists. Have you seen how they're fastened?'

'Fastened? I hadn't thought.'

'Like this.' The woman took a wooden screw and began twisting it into a hole that pierced the wood between Charlotte's wrists. It went deeper than just through the two wooden pieces, though. Of course! There was a hole in the counter beneath.

Charlotte pulled, straining to free her wrists from the blocks. 'I'm sorry,' she said, 'but I have to find my sister.'

'And so you shall, in good time, my dear.'

'What? Let me go! You can't –'

'But I can and I have. Just try to relax, dear,' the woman said, soothingly. 'Accept it, just like your sister did. It's easier that way.'

'My sister? You have Veronica?' said Charlotte.

The woman did not answer her.

'Let me go!' hissed Charlotte, panicking slightly.

'As you wish,' the woman answered, coolly, and proceeded to loosen the screws securing the wooden blocks to the counter, without actually freeing Charlotte's wrists.

Charlotte paused, her initial relief tempered by confusion, which soon gave way to irritation.

'All right, Veronica,' she said, as calmly as she could, 'you can come out now. You've had your fun –'

The woman looked at her, quizzically.

'Veronica?' repeated Charlotte, edging away from the counter, as the woman walked out from behind it.

'It was her choice, her decision,' said the woman.

Charlotte shook her head in disbelief, letting her eyes settle on the ornately carved blocks once again. She found it impossible to believe that Veronica would even have tried the restraints for size, let alone have allowed herself to be locked into them and taken prisoner. This was yet another of her twisted games; it had to be. And yet –

'I want to see her,' said Charlotte.

Again the woman said nothing, but ran an idle finger over the wooden blocks.

'Now,' said Charlotte, decisively.

'You have the same choice,' said the woman. 'You could walk out of here now if you wished –'

Charlotte sighed inwardly. Damn Veronica. If this was her idea of a joke –. And yet she couldn't help but feel strangely uneasy.

'Take me to her,' she muttered, resigning herself, yet again, to whatever Veronica had in store for her.

The woman rummaged in a drawer under the counter, and retrieved what appeared to be a black velvet scarf. Charlotte stood passively as, standing behind her, the woman blindfolded her, placing the thick, soft fabric over her eyes, then gave her what she presumed was meant to be a reassuring hug, her breasts pressing momentarily against Charlotte's back.

'That's a good girl,' murmured the woman, taking Charlotte firmly by the arm.

'Now I can take you where your sister went.'

Her arm held firmly by the woman, Charlotte allowed herself to be led out of the shop and into the street, the door slamming shut behind them as she was half-guided, half-bundled into the back of a car.

49

Five

Charlotte had no idea as to how far she had been driven, or of how long the journey had taken. It was probably safe to assume, given how small a country Steinreich was, that the driver had followed a deliberately tortuous route in order to confuse and disorientate her. Neither was she sure as to exactly when, exhausted and with her nerves in tatters, she had dropped off to sleep, nor at which point her blindfold had been removed.

When she finally awoke, she found that it was morning, and that she was in a comfortable bed. She yawned and stretched, scanning the room in vain for any sign of Veronica, and realising that she wasn't back at her hotel.

'W–who –?' she stammered, suddenly registering a naked girl standing in the corner.

'Good morning, ma'am. Are you ready for breakfast?'

'Where –?

'It's the castle, ma'am. *Schloss Steinreich.* You are a guest here.'

Bemused, Charlotte let what the girl had said sink in. The emphasis that she had put on the word guest had sounded ominous – no – terrifying.

'Breakfast, ma'am?' the girl repeated.

Charlotte focused on her. She, at least, didn't seem threatening. She was young, slender to the edge of fragility, and very pale. Her close-cropped hair was so white that it was colourless, and yet sparkling. If someone had put liquid diamonds into a candy floss machine, what spun out might have been a lot like the girl's hair.

She wasn't albino, as Charlotte had thought at first

glance. Her downcast eyes were exotically feline and intensely green, but framed by translucent crystalline lashes. An ashen mouth pouted, full and sulky. It was the sort of mouth that demanded a slap across the face, or a crushing kiss, or having its lips forced apart by an invasion of thrusting rigid flesh.

The girl's body was boyish, with breasts like the gentle swelling of unborn waves on a calm sea. Each was tipped by a crisp little nipple, so delicate a frosty pink that if her skin hadn't been incredibly white they'd have been invisible. There were hollows beside each sharp hip-bone; shallow indentations that might have been made to fit the balls of a big man's thumbs.

When freshly fallen snow lies like a clean new sheet, it urges you to walk on it, to scuff it, to mar its purity. The girl was like that. Charlotte felt an almost overpowering urge to reach out with pinching fingers or clawing nails, and leave deliciously livid weals on that temptingly untouched, pristine, almost virginal skin.

And she wasn't completely naked, as Charlotte had first thought. What she was wearing was much more shockingly erotic than mere nudity would have been.

Charlotte felt the beginnings of a warning tingle at the very edges of her sex-lips, and at the tip of her clitoris.

A black silk plaited cord had been looped around the girl's narrow waist. There was a black enamelled ring on one end. The other end had been threaded through the ring, and dragged down to pass between her legs, and within the groove of her sex.

One pale plump lip bulged down either side of the wicked cord. It was centred over her clit, compressing it against her downy mound. Each step the girl took must have chaffed – or perhaps not. The silk was smooth. Perhaps the friction wasn't so unpleasant.

The girl must have noticed Charlotte's eyes widen, and to where they were fixed. She turned around slowly, to display her rear. Her buttocks weren't boyish, not at all. Not unless the boy had been some much-prized catamite from ancient Greece. Her buttocks were high, round, succulent, deeply dimpled, and made to be prised apart. The cord emerged from deep within the crease between them. It was tied in an incongruous bow where its other end passed behind her sleek back, and a second glossy ebony ring dangled freely.

There would be a reason for that second ring, Charlotte was sure. An erotic reason; but she couldn't think what its purpose might be.

The girl turned back to face Charlotte with a sly smile on her sulky lips and one hip cocked provocatively. 'Breakfast?' she prompted.

'No! What I want is out. You can't hold me a prisoner! I'm an American subject. I've a passport. I'm a rich woman, or soon will be. And my sister! Tell me where my sister is!'

'Miss Veronica got here before you, ma'am. I'm sure that the Mistress will let you see her, when she decides.'

'Mistress? You mean the duchess?'

The girl frowned, as if confused. 'Duchess, ma'am? Oh no. There is no duchess, nor duke – not until the installation. There's a regent for now. But the Mistress is just – just the Mistress. She's in charge of the servants, like me, and the training.'

'Then take me to her. Get me my clothes.'

The girl frowned again. 'Do you think you ought to, ma'am?'

'Ought to?'

'Your clothes?'

'Fetch them, damn you!'

Her clothing had been laundered, and her jeans ironed for the first time since she'd bought them. When Charlotte was dressed she strode to the ornately carved door and tugged. It didn't budge.

'Unlock this door!'

'I can't, ma'am. It's locked from the outside. They won't let us out – either of us – until you put these on.' She held out the antique double-block that the woman in the shop had tricked Charlotte into.

'What? Never!'

'Very well, ma'am.' The girl just stood there.

Charlotte strode to a window and threw it open. Far below her was a flagstone courtyard. A banner flapped level with her eyes, at the top of a tall mast. It bore a golden stiletto on a field of green, with a single ruby drop at the dagger's point. Green and gold; the Steinreich colours. And the stewardess and steward had worn ruby drop pins.

'It's symbolic of our country's founding,' the girl said over Charlotte's shoulder. 'Just like Rome – two brothers who argued. Leopold the First had a dagger hidden under his jerkin, so he became our first ruler.'

'You people are proud of a fratricide?' Charlotte sneered.

'Cain and Abel? By the Bible, we all have a brother-killer in our family tree. It's a tradition with us, ma'am. Steinreich is proud of the passion of its rulers. Our noble families have always been hot-blooded. They've fought with passion, and loved with passion.'

'Each other?'

'Who else would be worthy?'

'Thanks for the history lesson. Now let me out.'

The girl held out the blocks, mutely.

'No!'

'Please, ma'am? I'll be punished if you don't.'

'I'm sorry about that, but if you think I'm going to willing make myself helpless, think again.'

'But you already are helpless, ma'am. You can't get out. If we don't go, eventually the mistress will send someone, and they might not be gentle.'

The girl made sense. A place like this would probably have thugs on hand. It was a country, after all. Even Switzerland has an army.

Charlotte held her wrists out.

'No, ma'am. Sorry. You'll have to turn around.'

Charlotte swallowed the lump in her throat, squeezed her thighs together to try to contain the purring sensation that the act of being bound always seemed to evoke, and turned. The leather was cool and smooth over a harder

53

padded core. Once the wooden screw had been tightened through the two blocks, her wrists and lower arms were totally immobilised. The girl led her to the door, which miraculously opened easily, and into a wide corridor.

'We'll take the lift down, ma'am.'

'Where to?'

'To the Mistress's training room, ma'am.'

Well, at least the girl hadn't said, 'To the dungeons', though a training room sounded ominous enough.

The lift was modern, and lined with grey silk *moiré*. It wasn't at all what Charlotte would have expected to find in a medieval castle. The Mistress's training room wasn't what she expected, either.

It was somewhere between a stately home's drawing room, a gym, and a torture chamber from the Spanish Inquisition. It could also have come from one of Charlotte's wettest and wildest dreams. The dreams she never let herself think about.

There was too much in the room for Charlotte to take it all in at once. There were wall bars, a vaulting horse, rings hanging from a high ceiling, and a triple row of blunt hooks along one wall. There were also three or four heavy black leather sofas, and footstools that weren't exactly footstools, and more, much more.

'Welcome, Charlotte,' a voice said. The husky resonance of it plucked a responding chord from Charlotte's clitoris.

The woman might have been tall. It was hard to tell when her boots had six-inch spiked heels. Charlotte couldn't tell how high those glossy boots rose on the woman's legs. They disappeared under a dramatically tapered black mid-calf skirt. Her white blouse was tailored, crisp, and straining to contain the largest pair of breasts that Charlotte had ever seen standing without support or a trace of sagging. Their lack of support was obvious. Even at this distance Charlotte could see dark brown halos through the fine fabric; halos and nipples. The buds were ripe chocolate-covered strawberries.

Charlotte licked her dry lips.

'Come here, child. No one's going to hurt you. Pain is

54

available in the castle, but only for those who choose it. There are always choices in *Schloss Steinreich*, aren't there, Blanche?'

The naked servant girl bobbed a little curtsey, and said, 'Yes, Mistress.'

Charlotte said, 'I want my stepsister, and I want out of here, in that order.'

The woman smiled, exposing white, biting, teeth. 'There's no rush. Your sister is busy at her lessons. If you decide to leave us, I'll show you the way out myself, in due course.'

'Lessons?' Charlotte asked. 'Veronica?'

'Let me demonstrate the way choices work here, even for the lowest of the low. Blanche, you have been tardy in bringing our guest to me, and she is inappropriately dressed. Discipline is called for. You are quite tiny, aren't you? I think a spell at number two would remind you of the virtue of prompt obedience. Do you agree?'

'Yes, Mistress. Number two. Thank you.'

Charlotte turned and watched with stomach-churning fascination as the girl padded barefoot to the wall with the hooks. She pulled the bow in the small of her back loose, and turned with her hands fumbling behind herself. Backing up, on tiptoe, she hitched herself high, and then stood with her hands by her sides. Her heels still raised clear of the floor, she faced into the room, her upper body tilted slightly forward.

Charlotte winced. Number two? That had to mean the middle of the three hooks. With the ring on the cord placed over that hook, at maybe a foot or eighteen inches higher than the girl's waist, the loop around her tummy was drawn cruelly tight. The girl's own weight dragged it down into a vee below the dimple of her navel. Where it ran lower, across the softness of a tender young belly, it cut a groove.

And the cord went between the lips of her sex, didn't it? What did it feel like, pressing cruelly against her flesh where it was most sensitive? Charlotte wondered if the height had been precisely calculated to allow the servant, were she to maintain that straining raised position, to feel acute discomfort rather than actual pain. She'd chosen the punishment, hadn't she? She'd agreed to it. As an alternative to what? Hook number three? That would have lifted her a foot higher. Hanging that high, she'd have been suspended by the cord that slotted the groove of her sex.

Charlotte had wondered what the ring was for. Now she wished she hadn't found out.

And she was the one who'd caused the delay. She had insisted on putting her clothes on. The girl had warned Charlotte that she'd be punished. What the poor child was suffering was all Charlotte's fault.

'I am to blame,' she said. 'If anyone is to be punished, it should be me.'

'You wish to take Blanche's place? What an interesting idea. I'm afraid that isn't permitted, but if you wished to shorten the length of her ordeal?'

'Of course I do!'

'Well, it's too late for you to undo your tardiness, but the other offence that she was guilty of could be rectified.'

'The other?'

'Bringing you to me clothed. We could take care of that.'

'And then you'd let her down?'

'Why not?'

Charlotte braced her shoulders and looked the mistress straight in the eyes. 'Very well. Undo my wrists and I'll undress. Can we hurry, please? The girl must be in agony.'

'The girl has a name. You might do her the courtesy of using it. And no, I will not release your wrists.'

Charlotte shrugged helplessly. 'Then how am I to undress?'

The Mistress opened the rosewood drawer of a Louis Quinze chest and produced a pair of tailors' shears.

Charlotte cringed. 'No. You can't do that. My clothes! What would I wear? How could I leave?'

The Mistress laid the shears aside and shrugged. 'Very well. It was your idea, wasn't it? I'm perfectly content to let Blanche hang. She's been well trained, you know. She won't save herself, not even if she collapses. Can you imagine what it'd feel like?'

Charlotte looked back at Blanche, still balanced on the tips of her toes, the strain beginning to show on her face. Her thighs were trembling. If she was to stumble, or droop? Yes, Charlotte could certainly imagine what it'd do to her.

'Very well,' Charlotte said. 'Do it.'

'Do what?'

'Cut my clothes off.'

'Was that a request? To me?'

'Cut my clothes off, please? Please, Mistress.'

'Well? If that's what you really want?'

'Please, please, please, Mistress?' Charlotte whined.

'Your attitude is improving. Given time I think I could make something worthwhile of you.'

Slowly, deliberately, the Mistress picked up the shears and stroked the long steel blades. Charlotte bit her lower lip. The damned woman was trying to provoke her into some display of impatience. It wasn't going to work. Charlotte refused to be manipulated.

That was ironic! She'd just begged the woman to humiliate her and destroy the only clothing she had with her, and she wasn't going to allow herself to be manipulated?

The tight skirt and the incredibly high heels on her boots restricted the Mistress's pace. She walked almost as a geisha does, if a geisha were to dawdle, and roll her hips voluptuously with every tiny step.

It seemed to take her forever to cross the room. Charlotte would have gone forward to meet her, but she was frozen in place by the dread of what was about to be done to her.

It wasn't just the imminent destruction of her clothing. It wasn't that her flesh was going to be bared. It was more than that.

What was happening was like a rite – a ceremony. There was something symbolic about it. She'd asked to be stripped of all her clothes. She'd volunteered. She was bound, and soon she would be naked. Both by her own choice!

She'd come into the world unclothed. Now her clothes were going to be cut away from her body. It was almost like a rebirth.

57

The Mistress laid the shears vertically in the valley between Charlotte's breasts, indenting the cloth of her shirt.

Charlotte flinched.

'Keep perfectly still,' the Mistress commanded. 'I don't want to mark your skin – not now – not this way.'

'You are going to let Blanche down,' Charlotte reminded, 'and you are going to take me to my stepsister, and release us both.'

'I always keep my word. I expect the same of others.'

The points of the shears traced a shivery line down to Charlotte's waist. They twisted into the gap between the lowest buttons. Metal touched Charlotte's skin.

Snip! A button fell. Snip, snip. Two more. The Mistress lifted the blades away a fraction. She'd reached Charlotte's cleavage. The blades cut. And cut. The Mistress brushed the two sides of Charlotte's shirt aside.

'What an ugly brassière. This will be a pleasure.'

The lower blade turned and slipped under the elastic strap that joined the two padded cups of Charlotte's bra.

Snip.

Charlotte didn't really need a bra, except to conceal her unnatural nipples, as her breasts weren't large. She'd been told that they were firm. She'd been told that they were beautiful, but they weren't as big as her stepsister's, and Veronica never wore a brassière.

The strap dangled, but the cups clung. Charlotte braced herself for the touch of the Mistress's fingers on her breasts. It didn't come. Instead, the woman took Charlotte's shoulder and turned her around. Fingers tugged her shirt from the band of her jeans.

This time it was a long slit, dividing the back of Charlotte's shirt from hem to neck. And then the shears clipped through Charlotte's bra-strap at the back.

The shears nudged to either side. The ruins of Charlotte's shirt and bra were pushed aside, to her shoulders. Long slices divided first one sleeve, and then the other. Rags fell to the floor, leaving Charlotte naked from her waist up.

And then her belt and the waistband of her jeans were lifted away from her skin.

'You could unbuckle me,' Charlotte suggested.

'That wasn't our agreement.'

Snip. The jeans were suddenly loose. And looser. Charlotte sucked her belly in. The jeans slithered down her legs. She stepped out of them.

'Cotton!' the Mistress snorted.

A blade, reversed, found the crease between Charlotte's buttocks.

Snip.

Charlotte lifted one foot, and then the other, and kicked the remains of her panties off her ankles, along with her scruffy old trainers. 'Now I'm naked. You promised?'

'Blanche!' the Mistress said.

'Yes, Mistress.'

Charlotte turned. The girl was unhooking herself. Walking awkwardly, with her thighs held apart, Blanche came to them, retying the bow behind her as she did so.

The Mistress said, 'You may leave us. Go to the nurse. Have her put some salve where you're sore.'

'Thank you, Mistress.'

With the girl gone, Charlotte felt even more naked. At least she hadn't been alone in her nudity before. Now, with the mistress fully dressed, her own nakedness was emphasised and more shameful. Perhaps nudity loves company?

'My stepsister?' Charlotte asked. 'And you were going to release us?'

'I told you that your sister is busy. She's an adult. She makes her own decisions. When she is ready to go, she will leave. Meanwhile, I'll show you the way out of the castle.'

Charlotte looked down at herself. 'I can't leave like this!'

'There are no laws against public nudity in Steinreich. In any case, you too are an adult. You make your own decisions. Turn around. I'll release your wrists.'

'Release?' It seemed too good to be true.

'You will need your hands free if you are to leave.'

Charlotte rubbed her wrists, although there wasn't a single mark on her skin. The wooden restraints were most efficient.

A door at the other end of the Mistress's room led to a passageway, which led into a medieval chamber. So there was a dungeon. Charlotte felt betrayed. She whirled to confront the Mistress. 'You promised me.'

'This is the way out. Just go on into the next chamber.'

There was no electric light. The room was lit by flaring torches and a hundred flickering candles. The ceiling was high, groined and vaulted. Great iron-bound doors stood ajar at the far end, but between Charlotte and the exit was a sight that made her rub her eyes. It was a scene from hell, or possibly from one of the wax tableaux in the museum.

But these figures weren't made of wax.

There were two enormous wooden triangles. A man was fastened to one and a woman to the other. Their wrists were in blocks. Each block was chained to the apex of a triangle. Just like Saint Clothilde, the victims' legs were spread, but a refinement had been added to their torment.

Their ankles were also blocked, but the blocks weren't fastened to the triangles' splayed legs. Instead, ropes had been threaded through ring-bolts on each block. The chains ran through more ring-bolts, screwed into the wooden posts, and then at the end of each chain heavy stone weights had been suspended.

The stretching – the strain – was constant. The long muscles on the back of each naked thigh were pulled taut. Each back was elongated. Each arm was being tugged to its fullest extent.

'Who? What? Why?'

'Don't babble, girl. Who and why are irrelevant. They are just bodies. That is why they are masked. Here!' The mistress pushed a birch into Charlotte's hand. 'Here is your key. Once you have flogged them, both of them, to my satisfaction, you are free to go.'

'Flogged?' Charlotte found herself drawn forward, repulsed and fascinated. Closer, she saw that the man was wearing a half-mask in the form of an eagle's viciously beaked head. It covered his face to his nose, and hid his hair completely. From the fine down that covered the backs of his sculptured thighs, Charlotte took him to be blond.

The woman's mask turned her into a cat – no – a black panther. Both of them, despite their bondage, were magnificent. His muscles, even strained, lay on his body in massive slabs. There wasn't an ounce of fat. Peering round him, Charlotte saw a belly that was as flat and ridged as a sandy beach after the tide retreats. And his sex? How strange.

Charlotte would have thought it would be shrivelled from fear, but instead a scimitar curve of pale flesh was rearing up from between his thighs, its head reaching above his navel. A glistening purple plum had emerged as his uncut foreskin had retreated. There was a steady pulse that twitched his stem. His scrotum hung between his splayed legs like a rich man's purse.

The woman was slender, but not hard. Her breasts, a little larger than Charlotte's own, had darker conical nipples, and were lifted by her contorted position. But Charlotte could tell that, were the woman released, they would still sit high and proud above the delicate arches of her ribs. Her belly was flat, and tight-skinned. Beneath it, between the straining tendons of her thighs, her pubic hair had been trimmed and combed to a sleek pelt. The lips of her sex were slightly parted, as if in anticipation of a lover's kiss.

'Beat them,' the Mistress snapped. 'Make them beg for your mercy, and you are free. They want you to stay, so they will resist. It is up to you – a battle of wills.'

'And if I refuse?'

'That is your choice.'

Charlotte ran her fingers over the birch. It had a handle of wrapped leather thongs. The supple wood had been split into two dozen or more long thin slivers. A blow from it would sting, but with only her meagre strength behind it, it would take a score of blows before it did any real damage.

Charlotte tapped the man's tightly clenched left buttock.

'Harder!' the Mistress demanded.

Charlotte beat him once more, harder. His skin flushed where the birch landed. Something trickled down the inside of Charlotte's thigh. An insistent pulse beat deep inside her sex. Its lips tingled.

Was she actually enjoying this terrible thing she was doing? The thought of taking pleasure this way was unbearable.

She threw the birch aside.

'You choose not to?'

Charlotte shook her head and clenched her fists. Her shoulders shivered.

'Very well. If you will return to your room, I'll have these two released.'

Defeated, head bowed, Charlotte slowly made her way back the way she had come.

The door to her room – the room they'd put her in – opened at a touch. The first thing she saw, on top of an antique serpentine chest of drawers, was the salt cellar.

Her heart in her throat, she tugged at the door she had just closed, seeking escape. It was locked. In that split second, without making a sound, someone had locked it.

The bed creaked. Charlotte whirled. The servant girl, Blanche, was standing on the bed, with her back to Charlotte. Her belly was pressed against the weird floor-to-ceiling headboard.

Then Charlotte noticed that the girl wasn't actually standing. She was fixed to the wood. They'd put blocks on her wrists and ankles, and screwed them to the headboard. Spread-eagled, her limbs were stretched so taut that her face and the soft swellings of her nascent breasts were mashed against the harsh wood.

At least the mattress under her feet bore most of her weight, and she wasn't suspended by that dreadful black cord.

'What?' Charlotte choked out.

Blanche twisted her silver-haloed head. 'It's the nurse's instructions, ma'am. As it was me who got you into trouble, in a way, she says that you should be the one to punish me. And as it was you who got me into trouble, she says that you should be the one to apply the salve to – to where I'm sore. It's on the dresser, ma'am. If I may, I think I'd like to take my punishment first. That'd save you doing the salve twice.'

Charlotte swallowed, and wet her lips. 'Punish you?'

'Whatever you think right, ma'am.'

'But I don't want to punish you.' And it wasn't a lie, not entirely. But the two strokes she'd given the man in the dungeon had affected her, hadn't they? And Blanche had such a nice, plump, white bottom. There was a deep dimple in each cheek, bracketing the indentation of her spine. The skin there was almost transparent. Charlotte fancied that with a gentle brush of her fingertips she would be able to electrify the endings of Blanche's nerves.

'Let me help you down, you poor thing.'

Blanche cringed away as far as she could. 'Oh no, ma'am! If you don't do it, it'll be much worse for both of us.'

'Then we'll simply pretend. You scream and I'll hit a pillow with something.'

'They'd know, ma'am. Really they would. Please do it. Just a spanking will do, if you like. There's a hairbrush on the dressing table, or you could use your hand.'

'You really want me to?'

Blanche's eyelids seemed to melt over the green glints of her eyes. Her lips pouted. A tip of pink tongue flickered between them, briefly. 'If you would, ma'am. Yes. Yes, please.' Her back arched. Her bottom lifted.

Charlotte made one last attempt to avoid something that she wasn't quite sure she wanted to avoid. 'Aren't you still sore from what happened downstairs?'

'There's lots of salve, ma'am.'

'Very well, if you insist?' Charlotte climbed on to the bed, intensely aware that the action exposed her naked sex, even if Blanche couldn't see. Thank goodness she couldn't. Even without looking, Charlotte knew the state she was in. When she was aroused, not only did she run with her juices, but the outer lips of her sex engorged, flushed a deep crimson, and puffed up.

Rob had thought it funny. He'd joked that it made her look like she'd just spent the night in bed with a football team, and that was before he'd so much as touched her. Her sex always reacted with indecent speed.

63

'Ma'am?'

Charlotte looked at Blanche's pert, upturned rump. At least, if she concentrated on that, she wouldn't have to think about the salt cellar and all that its presence implied.

She spread her legs for a firmer footing, and hung on to the headboard with her left hand. Her right hand rose, and fell.

'Harder, ma'am. That won't do. Not for them.'

Charlotte slapped, with a cupped palm.

'Ahhhh. That's – that's better, ma'am. That one stung!'

Charlotte wrapped her arm around the girl's shoulders. 'I–I'm sorry. I didn't mean . . .'

'More, ma'am! Please? They'll get impatient.'

Charlotte slapped again, and again. White skin flushed pink, and then the fresher marks of Charlotte's hand showed livid white on that rosy-tinted background.

The palm of Charlotte's hand became sore, but she hardly noticed. The insides of her thighs grew slick from the lust that wept from her sex, but she didn't notice that either.

Even though Blanche was clenching her buttocks, they still wobbled if the slap was hard enough. Charlotte was panting. She found that she could strike from the side, and send a shockwave of ripples across the softer layer that covered the muscles below. She could crouch a little and slap upward at an angle, and that imparted a different jiggle; if she actually brought her hand up between Blanche's legs, so that she was partly slapping the protruding split bulge of the girl's sex, there was a new sharper sound, because of the wetness.

'I–I think that's enough, ma'am. They'll be satisfied now.'

And a back-handed slap, using just the tips of her fingers, left marks that were shorter but more intense.

'Ma'am! Please, ma'am?'

Charlotte's hand paused in mid-air. 'What? Oh, are we done?'

Blanche grinned through her tears. 'I reckon so, ma'am. Look.' A backward nod indicated the dresser mirror, immediately opposite the bed. 'I think you did very well, ma'am, for a beginner, if you don't mind my saying so.'

Charlotte was appalled. Blanche's body was mottled pink and white, and turning red in places, from just above the backs of her knees to almost her waist. 'I did that?' she gasped.

'You certainly did, ma'am.'

Charlotte was almost as shocked by her own reflection. Her hair was a sodden mess, matted close to her head and clinging in rat-tails to her neck and shoulders. Perspiration beaded her upper lip, and ran in slow trickles between her breasts. The insides of her thighs gleamed. That was perspiration too, wasn't it? Her face was flushed, and heavy with lust.

And her arm ached. And her hand was sore.

What had she done? What vile hunger was there inside her, to make her do a thing like this?

'Did you wish to release me now, ma'am? The salve?'

'Of course.' Charlotte knelt to unscrew the wooden pegs at Blanche's ankles and then she dealt with those at the girl's wrists. She had to do it left-handed. The palm of her right hand was too tender to grip the sharp-threaded wood.

Released, Blanche flopped face down on the bed. Her buttock cheeks seemed to glow up at Charlotte.

'Can you start with my bum, please ma'am? I don't think I can roll over till it's done.'

'I'm sorry,' Charlotte said huskily.

'Oh no, ma'am. It's what I'm here for, after all.'

'What?'

'To give you pleasure, ma'am. It's quite a privilege, ma'am. When the Mistress told us to prepare for you, and showed us girls your picture, we almost had fights over who was to serve you.'

'When – when was that? When was it you were shown my picture and told to expect me?'

'Oh, it'd be about six months ago, ma'am.'

'What picture was it?'

'A nice one, ma'am. You were on a beach, in half a

65

bikini. You looked very sexy ma'am, but not as nice as the real you.'

Six months ago? A beach? In half a bikini? The only time she'd ever gone topless on a beach, was when she'd been on holiday at St Moritz. But she'd been alone in a secluded cove, and the beach had been deserted. How had they done it? Had someone been spying on her for over a year? She deserved explanations! She'd demand explanations, when she saw that Mistress again.

'My bottom, ma'am? The salve?' Blanche reminded her.

The jar was large, and unlabelled. Charlotte sniffed. It was aromatic; eucalyptus or cloves perhaps? She dipped in the fingers of her left hand and started with small circular motions just below the small of Blanche's back, where touching her was relatively safe.

'Oh yes, ma'am! That feels good. Lower, please ma'am? My cheeks?'

Trembling with eager reluctance, Charlotte's palm smoothed salve across burning skin. One tight-skinned glowing buttock was coated, and then the second. Blanche's skin was hot. Her flesh was solid, but it wobbled under Charlotte's palm. Her fingers kneaded, savouring the firm-under-soft texture. They closed on satin skin. There was a fold of delectably tempting flesh between her finger and thumb.

Blanche flinched.

'Sorry. Did I pinch you? I'll soon be done.' And then she salved the first smooth mound again, just in case she'd missed a spot, although she knew that she hadn't.

Blanche moaned and let out a breathy hiss from between her teeth. Her left cheek twitched under Charlotte's fingers.

'Did I hurt you again? Does the ointment sting? Was I too rough?'

'It's your right to hurt me, ma'am, if you wish. It doesn't sting exactly, but it does tingle.'

Charlotte tried a dab on the bruise-flushed palm of her right hand, where the pulse was hot and close to the surface of her skin. It did tingle. It felt like low voltage liquid electricity, soaking in and healing as it penetrated. It must

66

have been very soothing for Blanche, on her poor flushed buttocks. Soothing, and yet stimulating.

Blanche moved for the first time since flopping on to the bed. Her arm reached out for a pillow. She lifted her hips and tucked it under her belly, and then took a second pillow. Her rear was raised up, but the girl still kept it at an upturned angle. A wriggle, and her thighs fell apart. Charlotte could see, or was being shown perhaps, where her punishing fingertips had flicked Blanche's sex and engorged its lips to a succulent puffiness.

Had she been a man, she'd have mounted Blanche instantly. But she was a woman, and the sight of a naked girl didn't affect her, did it? Did it?

'Could you do that later, please ma'am? After my legs?'

Charlotte gave a tiny jerk. Her hands seemed to have minds of their own. She hadn't meant to slip the tip of one finger into Blanche's sex, had she?

With brisk efficiency, she scooped out a cool palmful of salve and applied it to the backs of Blanche's thighs.

The little slut groaned with pleasure. Her legs fell even further apart.

Charlotte hurried through her chore, not even thinking of the skin she was touching, not even aware of its silkiness, and certainly not noticing the way Blanche was sighing and crooning.

'I think that does it,' Charlotte said finally, in a perfectly normal voice.

'Yes'm. That's the salve all over where you spanked me, ma'am. There's just the other places now from my other punishment.'

A pulse twitched across the base of Charlotte's right thumb. Her fingers trembled. A quivery feeling fluttered through her belly and made a muscle deep inside her vagina spasm, just once.

'If you'll excuse me a moment, ma'am, I'll show you where it hurts.'

The jar of salve thudded to the floor. Charlotte managed to stand up. She looked towards the dresser, but the mirror was there, and she couldn't look at the headboard where

Blanche had been fastened, and if she looked the other way the salt cellar would accuse her.

'Are there any marks, ma'am?'

Charlotte was forced to turn around and look. Blanche had rolled to the edge of the bed. Her legs would have hung over the edge, except that she had hooked her hands behind her knees and pulled them up and apart, higher and wider than Charlotte would have thought possible.

'The mistress likes us to keep supple, ma'am.' Blanche was smirking, as if she'd read Charlotte's mind.

'So I see. Yes, there are marks.' Charlotte, suddenly moved, fell to her knees. 'You poor thing! There's an angry groove . . .' She didn't know how to tell Blanche where. The impression of the cord ran across the pink softness, where the flesh was thin over the underside of the girl's pubic mound. It marked a direct route from the opening of Blanche's vagina to the tip of her clitoral hood. Or perhaps it ran the other way?

Blanche raised herself yet higher, curling her belly and lifting her bottom off the bed. 'My bum, ma'am? Right in the crease? It really cut into me, between my cheeks.'

There was an imprint from the lowest part of her sex to the pucker of her anus. Charlotte fumbled for the jar of ointment, felt the salve's coolness on her fingertips, and touched Blanche half-way between the two entrances to her body.

A ripple convulsed the girl, curling her knees to the height of her head and thrusting the cusp of her body almost into Charlotte's face. Shocked, Charlotte instinctively gripped. Her index finger found the slippery slot between Blanche's thighs. The ball of her thumb indented the girl's anus, almost penetrating, but not quite. Charlotte snatched her hand back.

'I'm here for your pleasure, ma'am,' Blanche whispered. 'My punishments have made me more sensitive to touch. Once this little job is done, perhaps . . .?'

'Does this feel better?' Charlotte asked, in a business-like tone.

'It goes right from my tailbone, ma'am. If you were to start there. And then rub it in slowly, down across my arse

68

and then my pussy. Yes! Oh yes, ma'am. Deeper, ma'am, please?'

'It can't have hurt you inside your – er . . .'

'Arse, ma'am? Inside my arse? No, ma'am, it didn't, but when you put the tip of your finger up inside me, like that . . . like . . . Oh, Yes!'

Charlotte smiled a secret smile. She had no doubt that the little minx had been deliberately teasing her. Well, teasing only works when the victim resists. Once Charlotte decided to do some teasing of her own, the power became hers.

The finger at Blanche's anus probed, and palpitated. Blanche squirmed at it, creasing herself at her slender waist, but as she sought to impale herself further, the finger retreated.

'Ma'am?' she coaxed.

'Keep perfectly still,' Charlotte ordered. 'I have to be careful to apply this ointment where you need it the most.'

Blanche grinned up. 'Yes please, ma'am.'

'You're enjoying every minute of this, aren't you?' Charlotte asked.

'Of course, ma'am.'

'And that makes you . . .' Charlotte paused. She'd been about to say 'a randy little whore'. Even as the words formed, she heard her sister's voice saying the same, or similar, to her, a thousand times. But then this was different, wasn't it? She wasn't like Veronica, surely? She was a victim, wasn't she? She wasn't the instigator. She wasn't a free agent. She been forced – tricked – into this situation. She wouldn't normally spank a young girl until her bottom was livid, and then use her fingers to probe into her rectum. And get pleasure from both obscenities. And be thinking about other even more depraved possibilities.

Angry with herself, and with Blanche, she thrust her stiffened finger into Blanche's hot dry rectum as far as the second knuckle.

Blanche gasped and arched her back.

Her fingers suddenly strong and hard, Charlotte dipped her free hand into the pot and slathered salve lavishly between the gaping lips of Blanche's sex.

The slut humped at Charlotte's hand.

'Is this what you want?' Charlotte demanded, folding three fingers together and stabbing. In reply, Blanche rotated her hips and jerked. One hand released her knee. That leg stretched, reaching for the ceiling with pointed toes. The freed fingers found the hood of her clit, and pressed. A pink seed-pearl popped out.

Blanche's index finger joined Charlotte's hand where it delved into her sex, and scooped out a smear of salve. She dabbed the ointment on to the head of her clit, arched her neck, and burying her head in the soft mattress, and gurgled a strangled sigh of lust. A finger and thumb pinned her clit in place. The greasy pad of her index finger strummed.

'Damn you for a lascivious little bitch!' Charlotte lurched to her feet in a paroxysm of jealousy – jealousy for the lust that Blanche was enjoying. The girl was totally uninhibited. She'd surrendered to her own sensations and was riding them unreined, these runaway horses of joyful delirium.

If only she could bring herself to join in that mindless ecstasy!

At least she could stoke it, heat it to its inevitable explosive end. She could allow herself to participate to that limited extent.

The fingers of her right hand spread across the cheeks of Blanche's bottom, except for the one that wriggled deep inside it. Blanche's sex was greasy with the salve, almost as slippery as her own became when lust crept up on her.

'Yes, yes, yes,' Blanche yelped. The frotting finger at her clit blurred. She released her other knee. Both legs strained wide and up, unsupported. With a second hand free, Blanche pinched at one pale crisp nipple, and then the other, her hand darting between them.

Charlotte felt the muscles deep in the heat of Blanche's rectum spasming on her finger. The walls of the servant-girl's vagina contracted and convulsed. The straining tendons that stood out at her blue-veined groin twitched. The muscles in her folded belly rippled into hard ridges.

Blanche's buttocks flexed in Charlotte's palm, and flexed again, tensed into hard knots, and suddenly relaxed. Blanche's legs fell and flopped one to each side of Charlotte's hips.

Blanche lay so limp she looked moulded to the bed.

Charlotte raised an open palm. 'Damn you for a whore.'

Blanche smiled up at her, lazily. 'More spanking, ma'am? Or would ma'am prefer me to give her a little head? I'm not an expert, but I am enthusiastic, and Mistress always says that counts.'

Charlotte wanted something so badly the sensation was almost tangible, but she didn't dare think about what it was that she craved.

'Get out!' she spat.

Blanche gave a deep sigh, rolled over, and writhed off the bed. 'Something else, ma'am? If you wanted me to spank you I most probably could, though it'd feel strange.'

'Get out!'

Blanche pouted, but she didn't slam the door. Charlotte considered trying to open it, but somehow she knew it would be locked again before she could cross the room.

How did they do that? And how was Blanche so sure that they would know whether Charlotte punished her or not?

There could only be one answer. The mirror faced the bed, didn't it. The mirror was fixed flat to the wall. Like a window, almost.

Charlotte took a sheet from the bed and draped it over the mirror frame. Immediately, a voice from nowhere said, 'That is not permitted. If we cannot see you, you won't be fed. It is your choice.'

Charlotte pulled the sheet off, ran to the bed, and buried herself in the a foetal position under a tangle of bedclothes. It wasn't until the salve on her fingers made the lips of her sex begin to tingle that she realised exactly how she was seeking to comfort herself.

Six

Charlotte was woken by the distinctive aroma of dark-roasted coffee. Blanche plumped up her pillows for her and set a bed-table across her lap. The coffee was steaming hot and came with a cream jug and a bowl of unrefined crystallised sugar. Beside it were two soft-boiled eggs under knitted cosies, and two slices of lightly toasted wholemeal bread, smothered in butter, and cut into soldiers.

It was Charlotte's favourite childhood breakfast. She hadn't had it since she'd left England. Someone knew a lot about Charlotte. That was scary.

Defiant, Charlotte sat up and let her bedclothes fold down to her waist, just as if being bare-breasted in front of a naked servant was an everyday occurrence. She wasn't going to let *Schloss Steinreich*'s erotically charged atmosphere intimidate her. Nor was she going to let it seduce her. She'd conduct herself the way she'd have conducted herself at a nudist camp, if ever she'd visited one. Nakedness was perfectly natural, right? If servants here were routinely reprimanded by having sexual torments inflicted on them, then Charlotte was perfectly capable of accepting that, without showing any signs of shock, wasn't she?

'Bath or shower, ma'am?' Blanche asked, her emerald eyes focused on Charlotte's erect nipples.

'Shower.'

'How hot, ma'am?'

'I'll take care of it myself, thank you.'

'Very well, ma'am. I'll bring some nice warm towels when you're done. Is there anything else you'd like before you shower? Some personal service I might perform for

72

madam?' The little slut licked her pallid lips, slowly and lasciviously, in unnecessary emphasis on the nature of the services she was offering.

Two could play that game. 'How's your bottom this morning?'

Blanche turned and presented her rump. It was mottled, but healing. 'Did madam wish to . . .?' She slapped her own buttock to demonstrate.

'No, thank you.'

'Some oral service, perhaps? My tongue is at madam's disposal.'

'Get out!'

'Yes, ma'am. Later perhaps?'

Damn the girl! Damn this place! It was as close to her personal hell as she could imagine. For years she'd been fighting her own perversity, and now temptation was all around her. She was in a mink-lined prison, and her own worst enemy. One more slip, like the disgraceful way she'd let herself succumb yesterday, and there might be no escape for her. She'd find herself wallowing in an orgy of sado-masochism, a slave to her own most debased appetites. Well, it wasn't going to happen. No matter how they tempted her, or abused her, she would prove herself too strong for them; whoever they were. Charlotte would present a cool calm exterior, whatever they did, or offered.

The eggs were brown, and free-range. She'd almost forgotten what real eggs tasted like. When she stepped out of the glass cubicle Blanche was waiting with three fluffy warm towels.

'You'll be wanting to make your face up before you go down,' Blanche said as she patted Charlotte's breasts dry.

Charlotte snatched the towel and rubbed herself vigorously. 'Go down?'

'To see the Mistress.'

'Why would I want to?'

'I thought madam wished to leave?'

'Of course! You mean I'm being let go?'

'That's not for me to say, ma'am, but you won't be allowed downstairs until you are properly prepared. And I

73

don't think you want to spend the rest of your life in your suite, do you ma'am?'

'The rest of my life?' Charlotte sank on to the padded stool in front of the bathroom's vanity unit. Could they? Whoever they were, they had to be highly connected in this stupid little country. Would the US Embassy demand extradition? Did they even know she was there? She should have checked in with them, but she hadn't. There was no one, apart from Veronica and the lawyers, who knew where she was. It seemed that Veronica was a prisoner, just like her. As for the lawyers? What would they do for a foreigner, in their own country?

Perhaps it was the inheritance? This could all be a plot to swindle her and Veronica out of their birthright.

Somehow, she had to get out of the castle, and the first step was to get out of her suite.

Blanche laid cool hands on Charlotte's naked shoulders and massaged. 'Will you do your own make-up and hair, ma'am, or shall I do them for you?'

Charlotte almost snapped back that she'd see to her own damned toilet, thank you, but she swallowed her words. If she was going to escape, it'd be by craft. Her best bet was to appear compliant.

'You do it for me, Blanche. I think I'd enjoy that,' she said.

'Thank you, ma'am. I'll enjoy serving a beautiful mistress like you.'

The girl tied Charlotte's hair back with a ribbon and began with a facial massage, using a subtly scented lotion. Delicate sensitive fingers smoothed coolness on to Charlotte's brow, massaged her temples, caressed her cheeks, and stroked her neck. Despite herself, Charlotte found herself relaxing. She leant back a little, against the naked skin of Blanche's thin legs and the softness of her bare belly.

She could feel Blanche's sex-splitting cord against her spine. Lower, there was moist heat; the girl's sex pressing in the small of Charlotte's back.

Soothing hands stroked lotion under Charlotte's chin, down her neck, and to her shoulders. It was so good that

74

Charlotte squirmed like a kitten. Her arms fell limp by her sides. Her hands brushed Blanche's calves. Muscles moved under her fingers, tempting them.

Why not? She'd already been intimate with the girl in a shamefully depraved way. And it might be wise to make her a friend. Charlotte let her fingers wander up, and tickle the sensitive taut skin behind Blanche's knees.

Blanche pressed closer. She poured out more lotion, applied gentle palms to the upper curves of Charlotte's breasts, and stroked down and under, to cup one in each palm as if testing their weight.

'I do envy madam her nipples,' Blanche purred.

'You do?'

Oily fingers rubbed soft tantalising circles around Charlotte's aureoles. 'Oh yes, ma'am. Mine are almost invisible, and so small. Yours are lovely and big, and so responsive. Look! I've not even touched them yet, and already they're growing.'

And they were. Charlotte watched herself in the mirror through hooded eyes. Her breasts' peaks were engorging, turning a deeper pink and hardening to stone-solid cherries, part-way embedded in her flesh. When Blanche's fingers wobbled them they felt brittle enough to break. When soft pads oiled those cylindrical nubs, almost masturbating them, Charlotte had to suppress a groan of pleasure.

She snuggled back and closed her eyes to concentrate on the teasing sensations. Both nipples were pulsing now, throbbing with lust. Blanche must have felt their feverish heat, for she dripped lotion first on to one, then the other. The cold liquid drew rippling shockwaves up through Charlotte's breasts, almost as if two lovers were suckling on her at once. In response, she hooked her hands and drew her fingernails up the backs of Blanche's thighs. Blanche gasped and parted her legs, wriggling the wet splay of her sex on Charlotte's back and humping at her.

'Your pardon, ma'am. I got carried away for a moment.'

'I'll forgive you if you pinch my nipples.'

'Of course, ma'am.'

It was an exquisite pain. Charlotte felt the strength ebb from her body. She let herself fall back into Blanche's arms. The girl backed away a few inches, allowing Charlotte to arch backward on her stool. Charlotte's naked back slithered down Blanche's bare front. The servant lowered her gently until the stool was under the small of her back and the back of Charlotte's head was between her thighs.

'Oh ma'am!'

Charlotte turned her head sideways. Her lips felt the smooth skin on the insides of Blanche's legs. She kissed, and nibbled, and nipped.

'Ouch!' Blanche's fingers closed on Charlotte's breasts, massaging them deeply and hard enough to feel the glandular nodules beneath the smooth softness.

Charlotte circled Blanche's legs with her arms. Her hands gripped the girl's plump buttocks and she dragged her head higher. Her face was in Blanche's groin; she could smell the sweet heady musk. The plaited cord was an obstacle, but Charlotte's tongue forced it to one side and stretched high, to the nectar that was already flowing.

'May – I – use – my tongue on you in return, ma'am?'

'Mmmm.'

Blanche arched over Charlotte and supported her weight on Charlotte's thighs. There was a hot wet squirmy feeling in Charlotte's groin, and then her sex's lips parted of their own volition. The wriggling probe slithered into her sex, lapped, trailed back up, and found the head of her clit.

'Would madam like an orgasm?' Blanche panted, her hot breath scorching Charlotte's skin.

In answer, Charlotte spread her thighs wider. The tormenting tongue found her clit again. It felt as if its tip was trying to work its way under her hood.

Blanche drooled with pleasure. Saliva dripped on to Charlotte's mons and trickled into her groin. The tongue's tip followed, lapping the moisture back up before returning to the glowing nub to flick it in a slow hard rhythm.

'Faster!' Charlotte demanded.

Blanche obeyed. Charlotte released one buttock to claw

up at the girl's body and find one small firm nipple. As she twisted it, she pulled herself even higher, bending her head back. The inside of her lower lip slithered over the smoothness that lined Blanche's sex. It found the girl's clit and rubbed it. Her tongue curled. Its point felt a rigid and slippery nubbin. Charlotte wagged her tongue from side by side like an erotic metronome.

Blanche choked on a sob of rabid lust. Her tongue went into a frenzy, swabbing at Charlotte's sex, circling inside her labia. It stabbed deeper and then retreated to flick at her clit again. Tiny sharp teeth nibbled at Charlotte's succulent lips, gripping and stretching first the left and then the right, before sucking on them both together.

'Do me!' Charlotte groaned into Blanche's sex. 'Make me come.' She almost warned the girl about how wet she came, but Blanche was just a servant. Why bother. The little wanton would have to take what she got and like it.

Charlotte's pussy-lips felt as if they were buzzing. Her vagina clenched. Her clit was a fuse, burning with urgency. The fire hit her core. Something deep inside her vagina imploded softly, juddered, and clenched. The sweet gushing release flowed, rinsing out the lust that had clogged her.

Blanche spluttered. Charlotte burrowed her face into the girl's sex, relentless and demanding. She was rewarded by a sudden clamping of her thighs, a vibration through her tendons, and then an abrupt relaxation.

'Would madam like more?' Blanche whispered. 'Or may I dress her hair now?'

Charlotte swung herself upright on the stool. 'That will do for now, Blanche.'

The girl busied herself brushing and combing Charlotte's long golden hair, but the flush in her cheeks and the shortness of her breath betrayed the intensity of her reaction to Charlotte's loving. She wasn't completely back in control of herself until she'd applied the final touches to Charlotte's face.

'Isn't that a bit overdone, for the morning?' Charlotte asked.

'I've made you up to the Mistress's specifications,'

Blanche explained. 'She said she wanted you to look sexy, but not like a total slut; not today.'

'Not a slut? I'd say you've made me pretty close. I've never worn golden eye-shadow before, and that lipstick is downright whorish.'

'I'm just following orders, ma'am. Just one last thing and you can go down.'

Before Charlotte could frame a question, Blanche had left the bathroom and returned.

'Hands at shoulder height, please ma'am.'

Charlotte bit her lip, but obeyed. Blanche guided her wrists into position. The day's restraint was even worse than the double-block that had held her hands behind her back. It was two planks, about thirty inches long, jointed together at one end and with three leather-padded holes; one for her neck and one for each wrist. Fastened by a wooden screw again, it was like a portable pillory or a yoke.

Ancient peoples had used yokes on their prisoners to show their total submission. Very well. Perhaps Charlotte had no choice but to wear the vile thing, but she could at least carry her head high.

Blanche clipped a short chain to the ring set at the yoke's front. 'I'm instructed to lead you down, ma'am. Not the lift – the stairs.'

'Like some docile damned pet?' Charlotte demanded.

'The way the Mistress put it was, "Like a bitch that's in heat", ma'am.'

Seven

'Are you ready to submit yourself to instruction?' the Mistress demanded.

Charlotte drew herself up with all the dignity that she could muster. She was naked, her face made up like a trollop's, and her hands and neck were clamped into a wooden restraint. 'I submit to nothing. I demand that you take me to my stepsister and let us both go.'

The imperious woman put her fists on the voluptuous hips of the clinging black jersey pants that, with glossy black boots and belt, were all she wore. 'I had hoped we had made progress. Those were yesterday's demands. You were given your chance to leave, and refused it.'

The woman's magnificent breasts, each one as large as Charlotte's head and crowned with deep brown nipples the size and shape of overripe berries, intimidated Charlotte more naked than they would have covered.

She cleared her throat. 'I had no choice.'

'No choice? All you had to do was inflict a little pain on two people who mean absolutely nothing to you. It was your stupid idea of virtue that stopped you. You are weak, Charlotte. You should be grateful that I am willing to teach you to be strong, but the choice, as always, is yours. Accept my instruction, and you will see your dear stepsister very soon.'

'And if I refuse?'

'Do you?'

Charlotte took a deep breath, clenched her shoulder-high fists, and said, 'I do.'

'Then I must proceed with my duties, and I can't have you underfoot, getting in my way. Take her away, Blanche.'

Charlotte expected the girl to lead her back up to her suite, but it was a series of long stone-floored passages she was forced to stumble along. She passed ornate suits of armour, standing like insectoid sentinels, and under portraits of handsome men and beautiful women, painted in styles that reminded her of Rubens and Goya. She passed a striking nude that could have been by Gainsborough. Charlotte recognised a pair of portraits, of the duke and duchess from the *musée*. He was shown against a forest background, hawking, though the hawk on his wrist was disproportionately large. The duchess had some sort of black animal on a leash, but time had blurred her pet into unrecognisable shadows.

There was one painting of Saint Clothilde; of her naked head and shoulders, wearing an expression of transcendental ecstasy. Religious rapture, or the throes of an orgasm? Charlotte couldn't decide.

There were weapons on the walls; swords, halberds morning-stars and vicious-looking barbed hooks.

They passed the open doors of a library and of a stone-walled room that was hung with an assortment of whips and had three pillories grouped in the middle of the floor as some sort of nightmarish centrepiece.

Finally they came to a dimly lit room, bare except for an enormous wooden box; an eight-foot cube of age-stained oak.

Charlotte felt a tingle of fear creep up her spine. 'What is that?'

'It's for storage, ma'am. Lucky it's empty right now, seeing that I'm to put you somewhere that's out of people's way.'

'No!'

'Sorry, ma'am. Even if you were to change your mind about taking the Mistress's instruction, she'll be busy now.'

'You can't put me in there!' The tingle of fear was worse now. Now it was climbing up her rectum. She clenched her sphincter, but it was too late. The dread was already inside her, gnawing away.

Blanche unhooked the leash. 'Yes I can, ma'am. Now just you be a good girl.'

The box's door was three inches thick. A weak glimmer barely illuminated a high shelf with a deep rectangular slot. Blanche pushed Charlotte inside, manipulating her yoke so that it fitted into the slot exactly. Wood slid on wood. Charlotte strained, but her yoke wouldn't budge. The shelf had been designed to lock on to the wooden restraint. Charlotte was now standing securely in the exact centre of the box, unable to sit, stretch or move, or even feel the sides.

'Don't leave me,' she begged.

'Sorry, ma'am.'

The door clunked shut. There was darkness, absolute velvet darkness, and not even a declaration of total submission was going to get Charlotte out now. Her prison was soundproof, as well as lightproof.

She wasn't going to scream. She wasn't. No matter how long they kept her in that awful place, she wasn't going to scream.

And then she did.

Eight

Light glared. Charlotte straightened out of her exhausted half-dangle, half-slump and blinked.

'You are supposed to beg,' Blanche's voice told her.

Charlotte squinted at the girl's slender silhouette and croaked, 'Beg?'

'Beg to be let out. Beg to be allowed to submit to the Mistress.'

'How long? How long have I been in here?'

'No questions, ma'am. You are supposed to beg first, before anything.'

Charlotte braced. 'And if I don't?'

The door started to swing closed.

'I beg! I beg! Please, Blanche? Please? I'll do anything. I'll be good. I'll obey. Anything you want.' For a moment it seemed to Charlotte that she was reliving the past again; she was back in the attic, and it was Veronica's cruel hand that was closing the door. 'I'll lick you,' she promised. 'I'll lick you anywhere you like. I'll let you do bad things to my body. I'll be as naughty as you want me to be, I promise. Just let me out!'

'Thank you, ma'am,' Blanche sneered, 'but it's not me you have to please. Are you ready to obey the Mistress now, no matter what?'

'Yes, yes, yes. No matter what. I'll beat those two poor people, if that's what she wants me to do.'

'That was yesterday, ma'am. I doubt that option is open to you now.'

'Yesterday? It's still today then?'

'Isn't it always?'

'I mean the same day that you shut me in here?'

'That's not for me to say, ma'am. Here.' Deft fingers released the yoke. Charlotte staggered forward, almost collapsing into Blanche's arms.

'It's back to your suite for you, ma'am. A nice hot shower and a good meal will make you feel much better.'

'Thank you. And then?'

'Then the Mistress will see you.'

'Blanche?'

'Yes, ma'am?'

'What day is it? What time is it?'

'You'll have to ask the Mistress, ma'am. In *Schloss Steinreich* it's whatever day and time she says it is. The sooner you learn that, the easier it'll go for you.'

There were no windows along Charlotte's route back to her suite. When she got there, there were wooden shutters over the window. Her watch was missing from the dresser, but the salt cellar was still there.

After her shower it felt like morning, but a shower can do that. The meal was a clam chowder and lobster salad sandwiches on wholewheat bread; it was more like brunch than breakfast. But that didn't mean much. They might have served her bacon and eggs at midnight, cereal for lunch or roast beef at breakfast time, just to keep her confused.

Refreshed and naked, but without that horrible yoke, Charlotte was led downstairs again. The Mistress was waiting. She wasn't alone.

The man in the eagle mask and the woman in the panther mask were there, standing against a wall like mere furniture. They were still naked, except that the woman's feet were now shod in stiletto-heeled ankle-strap sandals. Both of them were restrained, but not by those demeaning wooden blocks. Broad black leather belts now circled both of their waists and their wrists had been tethered to them by short steel chains. The man's penis was also confined. A leather band circled its thick base, tight enough to restrict circulation slightly, with a thin chain that ran up across his muscular belly to his belt. His erection was rampant and glistening, as if intense foreplay, or even intercourse, had been interrupted by Charlotte's arrival. She felt an irrational twinge of guilt at having spoilt his pleasure.

The Mistress was still naked to her waist, but instead of black jersey it was now ebony spandex that sheathed her statuesque legs; it made her look as if she'd waded through oil.

'You are now ready to accept instruction?' she asked.

Charlotte lowered her eyes. 'Yes, Mistress.'

'Very good. I use old-fashioned methods, Charlotte. I believe in the carrot and the stick. Do well, and there will be some nice treats for you. Fail me, and you will suffer the consequences. I will keep a daily record of your behaviour. My book has two columns: credit and debit. At the end of each day I make a tally. My book has to balance. For every credit you earn, you will be suitably rewarded. For every debit, you will be punished. That way you will start each day fresh, neither owing nor owed. Do you understand?'

'Yes, Mistress.'

The Mistress snapped her fingers. Two girls entered, one a golden-bodied sloe-eyed Eurasian from similar stock to the girl Charlotte had noticed in the town. The other one Charlotte guessed to be a Filipino by her milk-chocolate skin, high cheekbones and enormous liquid black eyes.

Their delicate little bodies were naked apart from the plaited cords that circled their willowy waists, and the pendants that hung from those cords. These were not single strands such as Blanche wore. Each girl wore two, parted into the shape of a 'v'. They were attached about eight inches apart at the top, and followed the creases of the girls' groins to disappear between their thighs. Whereas Blanche's cord crossed her clitoral ridge and ran between the lips of her sex, these girls wore theirs spread apart, the gap narrowing as the cords crossed their bald mounds. The cords were no less cruel than the one Blanche suffered. The delicate lips of each girl's sex had been spread wide and tucked under the cords, exposing the shocking pink of their inner labia. The girls were naked beyond mere nudity. Their most intimate parts were on blatant display and infinitely available.

'Get on with it,' the Mistress snapped.

The Eurasian knelt at Charlotte's feet. She flinched, but held fast. The Filipino laid delicate fingers on Charlotte's breast.

'Excuse me, ma'am.'

Charlotte stood and quivered as the kneeling girl measured her feet, lifting each one in turn to check the length from toe-tip to ball, the depth of her arch and the circumference and height of her instep.

The second girl lifted Charlotte's breast to a tiny mouth, circled her nipple with a soft lips, and sucked. The pulse in that nipple pounded. The girl's cheeks hollowed as she drew harder. Despite herself, Charlotte felt her sex begin to moisten, and then the mouth was removed. Charlotte's nipple was dabbed dry on a square of cambric. The girl produced a pair of callipers and, to Charlotte's puzzlement, proceeded to measure both the circumference and length of her distended nipple.

The Eurasian ran her tape around Charlotte's calves and thighs, jotting notes on a pad. The Filipino sucked on Charlotte's other nipple.

The Eurasian then made a second thigh-measurement, only higher up, close in to Charlotte's sex. The back of the girl's hand brushed throbbing lips. Charlotte squirmed in embarrassment, certain that her sex was leaking on to the girl's skin.

'Would you stand astride, please ma'am?'

Charlotte obeyed and suffered more intimate measuring; the exact length of her pussy's lips, and their thickness; the distance between their lower juncture and her anus; and the space from there to both the base of her spine and to the small of her back.

The other girl, with the exact dimensions of Charlotte's erect nipples recorded, proceeded to check the distance between them, as well as the circumference of each individual breast.

It was a humiliating process. Charlotte felt that she had been reduced to the status of an object; she had been calibrated and noted, with no consideration of her humanity or femininity. She stole a sideways glance at the masked man. His presence made her ordeal so much more shameful, and so much more exciting.

His erection was oozing clear fluid. Charlotte licked her lips.

'We're done, Mistress,' the Eurasian said.

'Then about your duties. Send Nurse in. Charlotte, you have displeased me by delaying, but have since demonstrated an acceptable attitude. You have earned one debit and one credit, so far. Now you have another choice to make. I require that your sex be depilated. Would you be plucked, shaved or waxed?'

Charlotte swallowed. Her pubic hair? She'd been stark naked ever since the Mistress had cut her clothes off her, but there had always been that slight protection. Her sex had been veiled, in part, by the soft golden curls that decorated her mound. The plump lips of her sex, and their betraying moistness, had been – if not invisible – less visible. Bald, her sex would be on permanent display. Her every shameful reaction to sexual stimulus would be obvious. Having her pussy hairless would be like opening up her soul for public inspection.

Her choice? One of the three options, or refusal? And what would refusal bring? A return to that horrible black box, or perhaps worse, if there could be anything worse?

Charlotte coughed. 'Er – wax, please Mistress.' Waxing would be less painful, and faster than plucking. Shaving would mean that the humiliating process would soon have to be repeated. Of the three options, wax was the least repugnant.

'Here's Nurse,' the Mistress announced. 'Wax, please, Nurse. Here's her chit. Take her away.'

Nurse was a fortyish red-head, with freckles, a snub nose and a wide generous mouth. She was as voluptuous as the Mistress, but softer. Her abundant curves were tightly sheathed in an abbreviated white uniform that was

86

stretched to bursting across her jiggling bosom. The top three buttons were unfastened, displaying an incredibly deep soft shadowy cleavage. No real nurse would have dressed like that. She looked as if she had just stepped out of a French farce.

'Come with me, dear,' she said with a trace of an Irish brogue in her voice. A strong but gentle hand took Charlotte by her bare arm.

So she was to be removed from this strange room? Her depilation wasn't going to be watched by the Mistress and the masked couple. That was some comfort, Charlotte guessed.

Or was it? Was there a part of her that wanted her courage to be observed? Was she taking some sort of perverse pride in her total subservience and her ability to endure pain?

Not that it would be particularly painful, would it? She'd had her legs waxed. There'd been jolts of pain, when the sheets of hard wax had been ripped away, but they'd soon passed.

Her sex wasn't the same, was it? The skin of her sex would be more sensitive – much more sensitive.

'In here, m'darlin'.'

The room was black and white: white tiled walls and floor, black leather furniture. There was an examination table and a chair with stirrups, like the ones her gynaecologist used for her annual check-up.

'You get a choice again,' Nurse said. 'It's all blessed choices here, for you young trainees. That's her way, the Mistress. Strict but fair, she is.'

'Trainees? Are there – have there been a lot?'

'Ask me no questions and I'll tell you no lies. Now, which is it to be; chair or table?'

'What's the difference?'

'The table's for good brave girls who can keep still while I work. The chair's for the others. I strap you down in the chair.'

The words, 'strap you down' made the lips of Charlotte's sex tingle, but she said, 'Table, please Nurse.'

'Table it is then. Hop on up.'

Charlotte laid herself flat, arms and legs pressed close.

'Spread your legs, love. Give a body room to work.' The woman's hands eased Charlotte's thighs wide, dangling her legs from her knees down over the edges.

'This won't take long. You've little more than peach-fuzz. Hold still a minute.' She draped a white cloth across Charlotte's belly and two more over her thighs, leaving just a triangle of vulnerable pink skin exposed. Charlotte closed her eyes and tried to think of something else.

There was the sound of a match striking. Charlotte's eyes opened. Nurse had a candle, a tall beeswax candle, and she was lighting it.

'I – I thought there'd be special wax,' she blurted.

'The old ways are best,' Nurse said. 'The ladies of the *schloss* have been waxing their pussies this way for over two hundred years. What was good enough for the duchesses should be good enough for the likes of you, dear. Ready? Here it comes.' She tilted the burning candle. Liquid wax spilled. It splattered, two inches above Charlotte's clitoral ridge. Charlotte's abdomen convulsed, and she half sat up as she gasped from the searing heat.

'You want me to strap you in the chair?'

Charlotte tried to relax. 'No. No, it isn't so bad after the first shock.'

'Good girl. Spread wider, dearie. I'm going to do the left side next and I want to be sure to get right into your groin.'

With one semi-scalding drip at a time, it seemed to take an eternity. Charlotte bit her lip and let out an occasional groan, but she endured the discomfort.

'That's a nice smooth coating, though I do say so myself,' Nurse said. 'Almost done. All we have to do now is . . .'

She ripped the wax. Charlotte screamed.

'There! It all came away in one piece, and now you're as beautifully bald and soft and clean as the day you were born, dear. You'll be a mite sensitive for a while. Would you like some salve?'

Charlotte blinked her tears away and nodded. Nurse

poured lotion into her palm and cupped it over Charlotte's mound.

'Is that better then?'

Charlotte nodded. The hand squeezed gently, compressing Charlotte's mons in from the sides, and then flattened and pressed. It rotated, wobbling the firm pad of flesh beneath. Charlotte felt her clitoris respond, thickening and lengthening. Nurse pressed harder, grinding the heel of her hand on to Charlotte's ridge.

'Um!' Charlotte bit her lip, but not against pain.

'I see you're a wee bit needy,' Nurse said.

'What?'

'This.' Nurse's hand lifted, exposing Charlotte's shameful reaction. Her clit's head had crept out, pink and glistening. A single finger eased Charlotte's hood further back. 'The poor wee creature wants some loving, does it not?'

Charlotte was silent.

'Well, we'd best get your debits attended to then, so's we can take care of the mite's needs at our leisure. Turn yourself over, dear.'

Her mind foggy from the day's emotional battering, Charlotte rolled obediently on to her belly.

'The Mistress's chit just calls for three strokes,' Nurse said. 'That won't take but a moment.'

Three strokes! The meaning of Nurse's words sank in. Charlotte opened her mouth to protest but the swish of the cane cut her words short. There was a numbing impact, and then pain sparkled into her buttocks. Swish again. Another line of fire. It was so unfair.

Charlotte had trusted Nurse. Nurse had seemed so kind, even though she'd been the one to pour hot wax on to her pubes. That'd been almost a medical procedure, necessary pain, for Charlotte's benefit. Nurse ought not to be the one to beat her!

A third swish, and a biting agony sank deep, clawing pain down into Charlotte's bones.

It wasn't the pain that made Charlotte start to sob. It was the betrayal. And then there was more salve, tingling into the fiery lines. She was pulled up as Nurse hitched herself on to the table and lowered her again to nestle Charlotte's head into a cosy plump lap.

'There, there, dear. Let Nurse comfort you. Here.'

Charlotte blinked teary eyes. Nurse was fumbling the buttons of her uniform open with one hand and drawing out a massive pillowy breast. Its nipple was huge, a dark brown nodule the size of a man's glans. It nuzzled against Charlotte's lips. They parted and sucked.

Nurse rocked. 'There, there, my baby. Suck tit, sweetling. Nursie'll make it all better for you. Suck hard, darling. Nursie likes it when you suck hard.'

Charlotte's mind drifted into contentment as her mouth remembered its infantile instincts. The rubbery thing in her mouth wasn't smooth. Her tongue felt tiny soft bumps, and a sponginess that underlaid the skin. So rapt was she with her sucking that she didn't notice the palm that cupped her sex, at first. It wasn't until the firm palpitations coaxed her clit's head further from its sheath that Charlotte realised that a need was growing inside her. It wasn't urgent; not then. It was a warm feeling that soothed her more than it stimulated.

But the hand grew insistent. It milked at her mound, compressing and relaxing, compressing and relaxing. Charlotte's thighs fell apart. Her pubis lifted against the massaging pressure, pushing back.

'Not so fast, sweetling,' Nurse whispered. 'Suck Nurse's teat good, dear. Nurse can come from a good strong suck. Pull on it, my little one.'

Charlotte drew as hard as she could, relaxed, and pulled again. Nurse's fingertips brushed Charlotte's mound; she tested its new texture, pinched its ridge and tugged gently, drawing its hood back, leaving Charlotte's clit-head fully exposed to the air. Nurse's touch was so gentle that it soothed Charlotte even as it aroused. It was almost hypnotic, holding Charlotte at a point one degree below inflamed lust.

It was so nice being rocked, whilst sucking and being fondled. Even the stinging of her buttocks was fading to a pleasant warm tingle. Charlotte snuggled closer.

'Sleep soon,' Nurse crooned, 'but first . . .' She licked her finger and laid its wet pad directly on to the head of Charlotte's clit. It rotated slowly, then faster. Charlotte felt as if the lining of her vagina moved; it didn't clench, but crept. Something trickled inside her. Nurse's finger vibrated, pressing hard.

'Give it to me,' Nurse demanded. 'Make it nice and wet, little one. Here in my hand. Fill my palm with your sweet young essence.'

Tantalising fingers cupped between Charlotte's thighs and squeezed. There was no choice. Charlotte was a sponge, filled to saturation. The pressure started the flow. Somewhere high up inside Charlotte's vagina something suddenly relaxed. A barrier dissolved. There was no clenching, no spasm, no gut-wrenching convulsion. Charlotte simply let her orgasm pour out.

Two fingers folded up between her sopping lips and delved, forcing entry through flaccid wet folds, to stab and probe, stab and probe and twist.

'Now bite my teat!'

Charlotte bit into hot rubber flesh.

'Yes! Yes! Now wasn't that nice? Now it's time for bed, dearie.'

Nurse must have carried Charlotte up to her suite, for the next thing she knew she was between starched sheets and it was dark. She heard a soft sobbing from beneath her bed, which struck her as strange, but she hadn't the energy to investigate.

Nine

Charlotte woke rested, hungry, and warmly wet between her thighs. She'd probably had one of those dreams that she was always careful not to remember come morning. This time, though, she seemed to recall being on public display as a sex object, and sucking on an enormous nipple while strong fingers manipulated her sex into a strangely soft orgasm.

Charlotte fondled the firm pad of her mound, half-thinking about a quick wake-up masturbation, and found satin-smooth skin where there should have been silken down.

The waxing! Nurse! The Mistress! The two naked servant girls. The muscular masked man, and his lithe-bodied companion.

For a few seconds Charlotte's emotions boiled; fear and lust bubbling together, quivering in her belly as they inflamed her sex. Before she could calm herself enough to think coherently, she was interrupted.

'Breakfast!'

Charlotte took a deep breath and stretched her body beneath the covers, forcing herself to return to reality. 'Time?'

'I told you, ma'am, breakfast time.'

That was right. It was whatever time the Mistress decided it was.

Blanche served steaming coffee, a fresh green Smyrna fig that had been burst open in a microwave and slathered with clotted Cornish cream, and a small glass of pulp-rich freshly squeezed orange juice.

'A light breakfast today, ma'am, I'm afraid. The Mistress's orders.'

After her shower, and after Blanche had given her a thorough dusting with perfumed talc, Charlotte discovered why she hadn't been given much to eat. Once the girl had brushed Charlotte's hair, and made her face even more seductively whorish than before, she said, 'If you'll lay on the bed, ma'am. I'll help you into your new things.'

The things were a pair of boots, a pair of gloves, a corselet and a choker. All were black. All were soft glossy leather. Both the corselet and the choker were decorated with brass rings. Charlotte blushed. They were the sort of blatantly fetishistic garments that had featured in some of her more shameful fantasies.

She rubbed a glove between her fingers. It was as thin and supple as silk, with just a little give to it. Leather like that would stretch to fit, and then keep the flesh within subtly compressed.

'Made from the skin of a newborn chamois,' Blanche told her with obvious pride. 'The late duchess had a whole family move from Seville to live right here in the *schloss*, just to process that leather.'

'I can't possibly wear those boots. Those heels must be all of six inches.'

'Of course you can, ma'am. The Mistress requires that you do.'

'No choice? I thought there were always choices.'

'Yes, ma'am. In this case the choice is the boots or the bastinado.'

'Bastinado?'

'It's a frame that holds your feet soles-up, so that they can be caned. The idea is to teach you to learn to walk nice and elegant, on your toes. When your soles and heels are bruised and tender you don't have much choice in how you walk. I'd try the boots, ma'am. They were custom-made for you.'

'When?'

'During the night.'

So that was why the Eurasian girl had taken such pains measuring her feet. It was flattering, in a way. They'd gone to the trouble of having some poor bootmaker work through the night, while she'd slept, just to have these boots ready for her in the morning. Service like that was so luxurious it was almost obscene. Caliphs and eastern despots commanded that sort of service, not modern young western women, even if they were heiresses.

Schloss Steinreich was a world apart, where there was absolute domination and total servitude, with nothing in between. For some reason that thought was incredibly sexy, though given the choice, Charlotte wasn't sure which aspect aroused her the most or which role she would play: mistress or slave.

But she had no choice, had she? In *Schloss Steinreich* she was nothing but a lowly slave, to be used by others for their pleasure. Resistance was futile. She'd learned that. Very well, she'd obey for now.

She stretched out flat on her back and pointed the toes of her right foot. 'I'll try them.'

Blanche dusted Charlotte's foot again, even though it'd already received one coat of talc. A firm hand took her instep and steered her toes into a dainty toecap. Once her toes were properly fitted, Blanche took Charlotte's foot and bent it like a bow, pushing down on her toes and heel with her fingers while her thumbs pressed up into Charlotte's arch. The boot's waist was fitted up into that taut curve and Charlotte's heel slid snugly into its rigid heel.

So far, so good. The two sides of the boot's throat were drawn up over her instep and almost together. Blanche smoothed fine leather up Charlotte's calves, to her knees. She produced a long silken plaited cord, folded it in half, and looped the bend over the first two hooks – the ones positioned at the base of Charlotte's toes. Deft fingers zigged and zagged, threading the cord through four more pairs of hooks, and then pulled the cord tight.

'Too tight!' Charlotte complained.

'It's up to you, ma'am, but with these heels, and you not used to them, if there's any give you'll likely fall off your heels. The Mistress is really strict about clumsiness. She might lose patience altogether and send you back to the box.'

Charlotte shuddered. 'Very well. Get on with it.'

The leather was tightened over Charlotte's straining instep until both creaked. Blanche continued lacing as far as Charlotte's knee and then paused. She tied the lace off with a quick bow and massaged Charlotte's calf.

'It has to be perfectly smooth,' she explained. 'Like a second skin.'

There were still eight inches of boot to go. That was caressed on to the skin of Charlotte's thigh, worked snug, laced, tightened, smoothed, retightened and retied.

'I won't be able to bend my leg,' Charlotte observed.

'Yes you will, ma'am. Not much, but some. The boot suits you, ma'am, if you don't mind my saying so. You've the leg for it. Very elegant, if I might make so bold.'

Charlotte pushed up on her elbows to look down at herself. Being compressed to permanent *en pointe*, her size-four foot now seemed to have tapered away to almost nothing. The curve of her arch was now dramatically erotic. Her ankle, always slender, now looked fragile enough to snap at the least strain. Her calf and her thigh were both compressed to the point that she almost expected to see the leather pulse with the beat of her heart.

Above where the boots ended, less than three inches below the crease of her groin, her flesh bulged just enough to show off its soft vulnerability. Had that thigh been someone else's, Charlotte would have found pinching it almost impossible to resist.

She turned her foot so that she could see her boot's stiletto. It was a thin spike, vicious as a dagger, extending her leg past her heel to a needle point.

She lay back. 'The other boot. Get on with it.'

When both of Charlotte's legs were sheathed in erotic ebony evil, Blanche helped her sit up.

'The choker next, ma'am, then the gloves.'

There was no discomfort in the choker, but it was broad enough to serve as a constant reminder that Charlotte should keep her neck extended and her chin high. The gloves came almost to her shoulders; they were as tight as the boots, and thin enough for her to make out the cuticles at the bases of her nails.

'You'd best stand for the waspie, ma'am.'

Blanche swung Charlotte's feet around, off the bed. She took her charge's wrists, and tugged her erect. Charlotte swayed uncertainly, suddenly very tall and insecure.

'Weight forward, ma'am, over your toes. That's the secret of it. Hold on to the foot of the bed and lean a bit.'

Charlotte tottered into position. Blanche circled her waist with a broad band of leather that was as supple as cling-film. It came down to within an inch of Charlotte's navel, and up to the delicate undercurves of her breasts. There was a stiffened reverse 'v' that projected up between her vibrant globes, emphasising their separation.

'Deep breath, ma'am.'

Charlotte gasped as leather gripped and squeezed her midriff.

'Hold it, ma'am. Just a minute more. One more inch.'

A small hard knee dug into the small of Charlotte's back. Blanche tugged and rested, then tugged again. 'There.' She tied a bow. 'You can turn and see yourself now, ma'am.'

The Charlotte that she saw in the mirror was a woman she had never seen before. This was a succubus, a creature from Hell's most debauched whorehouse. Her face was an invitation: hooded glossy-lidded eyes and a mouth that seemed ready to melt. She was taller and more slender, but with strident curves that blossomed out of the severest throttling constriction. Her skin was as pale as death, except for the pink that tinted the imperious turrets of her nipples and the urgent ridge of her clitoris. This woman was capable of any depravity; totally wanton. She was ambivalent. Kneel to her, and she would demand total subservience. Bend her to your will and she would eagerly obey your most depraved commands.

Eventually Blanche said, 'It's time to go down, ma'am. The Mistress is waiting to start your education.'

Calves and thighs tense, belly quivering, Charlotte stalked after her servant.

Ten

The Mistress's cane cracked against Charlotte's naked left buttock. 'Head high! Shoulders back! Back straight. Walk proud, but with your eyes down. One-two, one-two. Halt! Now, Charlotte, we are going to try moving a little faster. I want you to trot, and with each step you will bring your knees high. Your thigh should be horizontal at the top of each stride. You will keep your toes pointed towards the ground. I want to see a pretty pony prancing, understood? Then begin. One-two, one-two, one two.'

The cane whipped up, stinging the underside of Charlotte's left thigh. The thin leather of her boot cushioned the blow, but not much.

'Up, up. Get those knees up, girl. One-two, one-two. Back straight, I said. Halt. Blanche! Cords and a rod, please.'

Charlotte stood still, but quivering and panting. Trotting around the room wouldn't have been so strenuous an activity, but that it was hard to breathe deeply with her waist so cruelly restricted.

She was intensely aware of the presence of the masked couple, both still bound as before, but allowed to sit on a bench and watch as she was made to perform. Their eyes were hot on her body, particularly on her naked heaving breasts. Even behind their masks, Charlotte could sense that. The man's interest was more obvious. His leather-bound cock was straining with his lust. His lust for her body. Charlotte jerked her shoulders back, twitching her breasts, and was rewarded with a responding twitch of his staff.

97

Blanche fetched cords and a three-foot ebony rod. The Mistress took them and turned Charlotte to face the seated couple. Strong hands pulled Charlotte's wrists behind her and corded them to the ring on the back of her corselet, with the rod between them.

A dozen turns of cord around her forearms tugged her elbows together, lifting her breasts even higher and separating them even wider. A slip-knot secured the cord, which was then run up and looped around the rod once more, and threaded through the ring on the back of Charlotte's collar. The Mistress pulled. Charlotte's nape pressed back against the rod.

Her back was straight, straighter than it had ever been. The rod dug a vertical groove between her shoulder-blades. Her breasts were now higher, and prouder. And she had no way to protect them, did she? They were totally exposed and temptingly uplifted. Anyone could do anything they liked to them, anything at all.

The Mistress looked deeply into Charlotte's eyes. 'Your body is a treasure,' she said. Her palms smoothed over and under Charlotte's breasts. 'These are lovely. Why would you slump and let them sag? Always consider your posture, Charlotte. Walking, standing, sitting or lying down, be aware of how you present yourself. You are judged by how you look and what that says about how you see yourself. A plain woman, who walks proudly and thinks well of herself, will draw more attention than a beautiful one who slouches. Be taut. When dressed and at liberty, decide for yourself just how much of your body, and what parts, you will display, or seem about to display. The body of a woman who is in conscious control of how she looks is a potent weapon. Can you remember that, Charlotte?'

Confused, Charlotte mumbled, 'Yes, Mistress.' The lecture had been delivered in the same way a doting mother might lecture her daughter on right and wrong, except for the cynical content.

'A strap,' the Mistress said to Blanche.

A leather band, three inches wide, was buckled around Charlotte's thighs just below the tops of her boots and drawn tight enough to clamp her thighs together. Now she was not only held rigidly erect, but she felt that the tiniest touch would topple her over to sprawl shamefully on the floor.

'Walk,' the Mistress said, tapping the clenched left cheek of Charlotte's bottom.

Her knees and thighs pressed tightly together, mincing from her knees down, Charlotte tottered on her impossible heels. The only way she could walk was by moving each knee around the other with every step. The only way she could keep her balance was by holding her head high and swaying her hips. It was uncomfortable. It was precarious. It looked, and felt, incredibly provocative.

That was the point – the Mistress's point, wasn't it?

Her sex was squished tight between her thighs. Each step squeaked the oily inner surface of one sex-lip against the inner surface of the other. After ten paces she was oozing. After twenty, the insides of her thighs were coated.

'You are doing well,' the Mistress conceded. 'Do you think you could still walk like that if I was to remove the strap?'

Charlotte looked at the glossy toes of the Mistress's boots and whispered, 'Yes, Mistress. I'll try.'

'Then we shall give you a test. Remove the strap, Blanche.'

The girl kneeled at Charlotte's feet. Charlotte tensed. That close, Blanche had to be breathing in the musky aroma that had leaked from her sex. Was that shameful, or something to be proud of? Charlotte didn't know.

The strap was removed, and a small rubber ball was pushed up between Charlotte's thighs, tight in the triangle below her pussy.

'Now walk again,' the Mistress ordered, 'but don't let the ball drop. If you do you'll pay a forfeit. Start walking while I think of something suitably amusing. Lessons shouldn't be all work. Go!'

The cane slashed across Charlotte's rump, just beneath her bound hands. She jerked. The ball moved, but the swift clamping of her thighs caught it.

99

Walking with the ball held between her thighs rolled Charlotte's walk even more. It had a slightly rough texture, thank goodness, but its upper surface dragged against her pussy's lips, tugging them left and then right, which stimulated them in a gently teasing way. Despite herself, Charlotte found that her sex was weeping even more copiously than before. Her juices trickled down, coating the ball, making it slippery. As she turned, upon reaching the wall, Charlotte felt the ball begin to slither. She caught it an inch above the tops of her boots, but every subsequent step moved it forward. She rolled one leg around the other and pressed, trying to force it back. On the third tiny pace after that, it popped out and bounced away.

Charlotte stood trembling, waiting to discover what forfeit might be demanded of her.

The Mistress strode up to Charlotte, and past her. She stopped in front of the masked man. Her silk-gloved hand took his rigid shaft and squeezed up its white length, as though she was milking a cow. A dewdrop of clear fluid extruded from his cock's eye.

'You've been very patient,' she said. 'I think you deserve a reward. Would you like me to have Charlotte suck on your cock for you?'

The man nodded.

'Charlotte? You've done this before?'

'Yes, Mistress,' she admitted.

'Are you good at it?'

It seemed wiser to say nothing.

'Your modesty becomes you. Very well, we shall see, shan't we. You've been teasing this man, with your provocative ways. Sometimes you have to pay off that promise. Come here, girl.'

Blanche helped Charlotte kneel between the man's thighs. The Mistress pushed Charlotte's head down, almost toppling her, for she was held stiff from waist to neck. Charlotte rested her cheek on the man's muscular thigh, his hairy balls an inch from her lips, and waited dry-mouthed for her instructions.

'We are going to see how quickly you can bring him to

100

orgasm,' the Mistress announced. 'When I say, "go", you may start. I will be encouraging you with this.' Her cane swished through the air. 'Go!'

Charlotte writhed up and fell forward to butt her forehead on the man's firm abdomen. She opened her mouth, and slid her face down. The head of his cock passed between her lips and slithered across the flat of her tongue.

A line of fire sizzled across her bottom's right cheek.

Charlotte gulped, swallowed, and worked her tongue. Another streak of pain seared into the top of her right thigh, just beneath her buttock's crease.

Charlotte's cheeks hollowed. Her tongue slathered frantically.

The third blow from the Mistress's cane caught the pendant edge of Charlotte's pussy-lip. Agony bloomed through her sex, igniting her clit. She jerked. Her lips slurped up the man's shaft. He thrust up at her face.

Sucking alone wasn't going to bring him to climax. Charlotte remembered that the few times she'd given a man oral sex, it hadn't been her mouth that had done the real work. Her mouth had mainly been a receptacle, seductively waiting. It had been her hand, pumping, that'd had the greatest effect. She knew that some women were skilled enough to bring a man off with their mouths alone, but she hadn't achieved that level of expertise – yet.

Pain lanced across her bottom's right cheek.

Her hands weren't free. She couldn't masturbate him with her fingers. Her mouth would have to serve both purposes; welcoming his semen with its suction and stimulating his shaft with firm wet friction. How?

The cane stung once more. There was numbness that dissolved into tingling torment.

Charlotte pressed up with her tongue, pushing at the underside of the man's glans, forcing its glossy smoothness against the roof of her mouth. She couldn't nod, not with her neck tightly tethered to the rod. She could bob from her waist though. Charlotte was dance-trained. The abdominal muscles in her slender waist were toned and strong. She clenched them, lifting her head stiff-necked, letting her lips slither up the man's stem, and leaving behind smears of bright lipstick. Then she relaxed them, letting the weight of her upper body lower her. She flexed again, then lowered again. It was like doing reversed sit-ups, trembling her abdomen into ridges. The head of the man's cock slid from her hard palate to her soft palate, and back.

Pain crackled through her bottom once more, urging her to greater speed. The whole of her right cheek was glowing with it. It was still pain, but hot lascivious pain now. The burning tingle was a fire, and her sex seethed with the fierce heat. The juice in her pussy felt like it was about to boil over.

Charlotte shook her head as she bobbed. She growled lustfully, demanding that the man give her the sweet-sour essence that she needed, both to bring an end to her bottom's torment and to slake her thirst for man-milk. Her throat and the inside of her mouth were needful. Her pride too, sought proof of her ability to control a man's cock with her mouth.

It was something worth being proud of, wasn't it? Giving pleasure? Giving it so well that a man couldn't control his reaction? Her mouth was going to finish what her beauty and grace had started.

Sudden pain! A goad, electric and stimulating.

Did watching her being caned add to his pleasure? Of course it did! The Mistress had transformed her into something special, and that new seductive beauty was being whipped into this anonymous man's service. What man wouldn't be thrilled to have so gorgeous and exotic a creature kneel to him, and service his pleasure.

And she was beautiful, was she not? So much more beautiful now that her true inner-self had been exposed. Charlotte realised that she had now given up all thoughts of resistance. The person she had been as a young girl, the self she had denied all these intervening years, was the real Charlotte. Veronica had been right to call her a harlot, a whore, and a bitch-in-heat. That's what she was, and now she could face it, revel in it even.

The fire in her bottom was a glow that spread throughout her lower body. Her stomach ached with the strain of pumping her upper body up and down. Her tongue was tiring. The man's cock seemed to be growing thicker, hotter and stiffer, filling her mouth.

Whack! She heard the blow, but the sensation was slow to follow. Her skin was numbing.

Charlotte writhed and heaved up. Her body arched like a cobra. Somehow, she managed to lift herself high and swoop down. Her throat opened to its invader. His cock's head lodged. Charlotte gargled on it, twisted on it, strived to impale her throat with it, and then withdrew with a long slow deliberately noisy suck.

Yes! Thick warm liquid, sweet and salt and very creamy, filled her mouth. She hadn't felt it arrive. It was just suddenly there! Charlotte swallowed and swallowed, delighting in the man's deep groan as she drew out the last few dribbles from the eye of his cock, and then sucked some more; she wanted to suck him dry.

'Four minutes and twenty-eight seconds,' the Mistress said. 'Next time you will do better. Very well, Blanche. It's time for lunch. Take her away and return her in an hour.'

Blanche released Charlotte's wrists and helped her to her feet. Caviar on tiny toast triangles and two small lamb chops waited in her suite, but before eating Charlotte was laid on her bed to have salve rubbed into her sore bottom.

'You were very brave,' Blanche told her.

'Thank you. That man?'

'Yes, ma'am?'

'Who is he?'

'No one, ma'am.'

'Will I –?'

'Will you what, ma'am?'

'Will he – will he be making love to me, sometime?'

Blanche massaged lotion into the swollen lips of Charlotte's sex. 'I'm sure I couldn't say, ma'am, but the Mistress is fair. She knows what you want better than you do yourself. Perform well, and who knows? He might be one of your rewards if you perform well enough to earn him.'

Charlotte raised her belly from the bed, pushing back at Blanche's hand. 'Do that more, Blanche; please?'

The hand was removed and wiped on a cloth. 'I'd like to, ma'am; really I would, but I'm instructed you are to be kept tense, for now.'

'For now?'

'Those're my instructions, ma'am.'

Charlotte turned over, despite the burning skin of her bottom, and pulled Blanche's face down to hers. 'A kiss, at least? That'd still keep me tense wouldn't it?'

'I – I . . .'

Charlotte's lips stopped her. Charlotte's tongue joined hers, inside her mouth. For three long breaths two tongues loved each other, wet and hot and squirming, before Blanche pulled back.

'Your lunch, ma'am?'

'It isn't food that I need.'

'I know, ma'am, but eat. You'll need your strength.'

When Charlotte hobbled back into the chamber below, the Mistress greeted her by pulling off a glove and exploring Charlotte's shocked sex with two fingers. Charlotte stood and swayed, hardly daring to breath in case it should interrupt this sudden intense pleasure. The fingers twisted inside her, stiff and straight. Then they were still, buried to their second knuckles.

'You're very horny,' the Mistress said.

'Yes, Mistress.'

'Then show me. Look at me with naked lust in your eyes.'

Charlotte lowered her head and looked up at the Mistress through the bars of her sweeping lashes.

'Not bad. Let your mouth go slack. Make it inviting. Good. Sway a little. Move your hips from side to side. Droop one shoulder towards me now. Yes, you are learning. Very well, now you may fuck my fingers.'

Fuck her fingers? No one, not since Veronica, had talked to her like that. If only someone had! If either one of her two immature lovers had been given the insight to treat her like the slut she was, she might have found happiness years before.

Charlotte spread her legs. Her belly rippled. She pushed her hips forward, driving the Mistress's fingers deeper, and then pulled back, dragging on them until only their tips were inside her eager sex. The fingers thrusted again. Charlotte skewed her hips, swivelling into the thrusts, faster and faster. Stiff fingers. Lovely stiff fingers. Fingers to fuck; to get off on; to bruise her most delicate membranes on; to use, use, use.

Charlotte went into a frenzy. Sweat soaked her ringlets, turning them into sodden hanks that whipped her shoulders and the upper slopes of her breasts. She shimmied her shoulders even as her hips drove her, swinging the divine weight of her breasts from side to side.

Damn! She needed those fingers to be deeper. Without thinking, she grabbed the Mistress by her wrist, braced her thighs, and – and the Mistress snatched her hand back, leaving Charlotte's pussy an aching void.

'I did not give you leave to touch me.'

'I'm sorry, Mistress. I couldn't help myself.'

'Exactly. That is what you should be ashamed of. Be proud of your lust, but hold it under strict control. Lust is power. Like all sources of power, without discipline it is useless. Very well. As self-control is what you need to learn, that is what I shall teach you. Blanche? Prepare her.'

Blanche tinkled a little silver bell. The two tiny servants wheeled in the strangest piece of furniture that Charlotte had ever seen. It was made of chrome, leather and wood; a five-foot semi-circle, three feet wide, on wheels. The outer rim was padded black leather. Radiating inward were jointed chrome rods, each ending in one of those leather-lined wooden blocks.

Blanche unfolded a padded chrome bar, from beneath the highest point, across the leather rim. 'Hop on up and grab hold, ma'am,' she told Charlotte.

Charlotte stood with her toes against the thing's base and stretched. Her fingers reached, but were a foot short of the bar. Without a word, the masked man left his seat, crossed to Charlotte, stooped, grasped her ankles, and lifted her effortlessly.

Charlotte grabbed hold and hung there, her body conforming to the quarter-circle circumference, her breasts flattened against it. Blanche unfolded two more metal arms, fitted the wooden blocks at their ends to Charlotte's wrists, and screwed them shut.

It felt uncomfortably like a whipping frame. Was that to be her punishment for giving in to her lust? Did the Mistress intend to cane her again? The right cheek of her bottom still glowed from the beatings it had endured in the morning. If she was to be subjected to further caning, Charlotte prayed that the blows would fall on her left cheek. The skin on her right was so tender that another session would be agonising.

Blanche touched Charlotte's boot beneath her right knee. 'Pull up, ma'am, please. Drag up and get your knees on the leather, with your bum pushed out. You have to kneel up on it.'

Straining, Charlotte obeyed. It was a ridiculous, shameful position. Kneeling up like that, her bottom jutted out. Then Blanche made it worse. She tugged Charlotte's feet apart, to the edges of the leather half-wheel, unfolded more chrome rods, and blocked her ankles in place. Now, not only was Charlotte's bottom stuck out and exposed, but her sex was on display between the tendon-stretching spread of her thighs.

Her belly cringed with her shame. Walking, trotting even, her bizarre costume had transformed her from a real person into a mere sex object, but a desirable, elegant one. Now her elegance had been stolen from her. Her position was awkward and, she felt, ugly. Her audience wasn't watching grace any more, just the lewdest possible display of her sex and her anus. Her rectum puckered, as if tightening her sphincter was her last defence.

Wasn't the lesson supposed to be in how to pose seductively? Her position wasn't seductive. It was blatantly obscene.

Part of her lesson? Walk in a sexy way – display your

body proudly – and then, then there came a time when the veneer should dissolve and the rabid slut was let show through? Didn't animals go through elegant mating dances and then, when the time came, the females would crouch and present their vulvas, shamelessly displaying their need?

Was that what she was being taught?

The Mistress reached between Charlotte's thighs. Silk-covered fingers manipulated the lips of her sex. 'Still wet,' the Mistress remarked. 'She really is a horny little slut, don't you think?'

'Yes, ma'am,' Blanche replied.

The fingers rubbed. Against her will, Charlotte felt herself ooze. The Mistress smeared Charlotte's seepings over her vulva, then probed between her lips to coax still more viscous liquid from her depths, and spread that too.

Two hands took Charlotte's lips and pulled them wide apart, everting them. Pressed to the puffy sides of her sex's bulge, they stuck. Charlotte's most intimate flesh had been opened like the petals of some overblown tropical flower. Parts of her that were internal, that should have been secret from any gaze but that of a lover, were now on public display.

The Mistress's wet fingers caressed one of the tender ridges that her cane had raised across Charlotte's right buttock. Charlotte gasped. The touch was almost painful, but not quite. In a strange way, it was exciting.

'You!' the Mistress said.

Charlotte twisted her head sideways. The diminutive Eurasian came closer and moved beyond the range of Charlotte's sight, to her rear. Charlotte braced for whatever was to come next.

A tickle. A soft wet tickle. Charlotte squeezed on the bar she was holding. The pretty little girl was licking the weal on her bum with just the point of her tongue. The touch was so light that had Charlotte's skin not been beaten into extreme sensitivity, she probably wouldn't have felt it. Her belly knotted. If she hadn't been clamped into position, she'd have twisted her bottom away from that tantalising stroke.

She couldn't move. She had to endure it.

'Again,' the Mistress said. 'Her vagina is pulsing with pleasure again. I can see a vein throbbing deep inside her.'

Charlotte felt her face burn with shame. The Mistress was observing – scrutinising her internal reactions! Charlotte had been reduced below the rank of a mere sex object to the status of a sexual guinea pig.

Imperious, the Mistress called, 'Next.'

Charlotte squeezed her eyes shut. This wasn't happening. She wouldn't feel what they did. She wouldn't react.

Another tongue flicked a welt across the top of Charlotte's thigh. She knew it was another tongue because she could still feel the first one, running up and down the other weal.

Fingers snapped. A cool hand rested on her bottom's left cheek, tugging it gently away from her right. It wasn't enough that they had exposed her sex's insides, now someone was peering at her anus so closely her tight knot could feel hot breath.

Hot breath – and wetness. God! A tongue was rimming her anus. Three tongues were teasing her. One, she knew, belonged to the Eurasian. The other two? She couldn't even tell whether they were female or male. It could be the man who was torturing her thigh's wound with forbidden pleasure; or worse, it might be his tongue that was now prodding gently, squirming its wet way through her sphincter.

No one had ever done that to her, not even Veronica, when the two stepsisters had been steeped in depravity. It was so shameful – so disgusting – so incredibly exciting.

Fingers, they had to be the Mistress's because they felt like wet silk, toyed with her pussy. Charlotte gripped the metal bar until her knuckles ached. It was so unfair. She'd been faulted for displaying her reaction to sexual stimulation, and her punishment was more caresses, more intimate touches than she had ever experienced; she knew that any reaction on her part was bound to bring punishment.

Two slippery fingers squeezed the head of her clit, squeaking it between them like an orange pip. A husky voice whispered in her ear, 'Don't come. Don't you dare have an orgasm. Control yourself, Charlotte. Show us how strong your self-control is.'

Charlotte bit her lower lip. Fingers manipulated. Another tongue, wriggled into the gape of her pussy, slavering on the smoothness inside, sucking at sensitive inner surfaces, drawing out their moisture.

How could she not react? How could she remain still and outwardly calm, when two fingers and four tongues were deliberately driving her into a state of sexual delirium?

Four tongues? There was the Mistress, but it wasn't likely that she'd pay oral homage to her victim. That left Blanche, the two other servants, and the masked couple. Five people. The odds were that one of those tongues belonged to the man; but which one? If only she knew. If she did, that would be the tongue she would concentrate on. Whichever one it was, its caresses would somehow be less shameful. His loving would be less humiliating to endure, to enjoy, to relish.

The fingers were urgent. Should she surrender? Should she allow herself to come? Was that what they wanted? Did they want her to have an orgasm, but not show any outward sign?

Yes. That had to be it. Very well, focus on the sensations. Let them all work their erotic magic, but don't scream, don't writhe, don't show any sign of pleasure.

It was building. Her vagina was twitching. There were goosebumps on the skin of her tummy. Her breasts were heavy, her nipples were like flint. Another few seconds and she would feel that ultimate relaxation and her insides would melt and flow.

Suddenly it stopped. It all stopped. A swish. Agony again. Her left buttock this time.

'I told you not to come.'

'I – I didn't.'

'You were close. Control yourself, girl. Right! Let's start over.'

A tongue touched her new welt. Another flickered over the inside of the left lip of her sex. A third slavered the crease below her left buttock. Fingers gripped her clit once more.

It was early evening, she judged, when the Mistress finally ordered that she be released. Her bottom bore six new stripes, and she hadn't come. She trembled with frustrated need, but they hadn't let her reach orgasm.

Charlotte had known lust before, what she had considered all-consuming lust, but this was beyond that. In the past, she had just felt lust. Now she personified lust. She was no longer human. Outwardly, only the trembling of her limbs showed how much she ached. Inside, she was screaming.

The Mistress balanced her books, by having the Filipino girl ravage Charlotte's mouth with a thick musk-and-spice tongue at the same time as she, the Mistress, pinched one swollen lip of Charlotte's sex between vicious fingers.

Blanche helped a quivering Charlotte back to her suite, stripped her of her leather garments and soothed her smarting skin with lotion. Then she hand-fed Charlotte lamb stew that was heady with Greek wine, and left her.

Charlotte bathed gingerly, in lukewarm water. Dressed in a fluffy comforting robe, she laid on her belly, across the bed. She needed sleep, but was still desperate for an orgasm. Should she masturbate beneath the bedclothes? Would they somehow know, and punish her? Worse, would someone burst into the room at the crucial moment, and stop her? Punishment she could take. One more aborted orgasm would drive her crazy.

She lay, squirming her thighs together, torn between her need and her fear.

A sob came from beneath her bed.

Charlotte rolled off her bed directly on to her knees. Her buttocks were stiffening. Standing would have been painful.

On all fours, peering awkwardly under the high bed, she could make out a darker oblong shadow against the wall beneath the bed's head. The whimper was coming from there. Gingerly, she flattened out on to her belly and wriggled closer. It was an ornate iron grille: an air vent. When she touched it, it moved. There was a bolt at each corner and they were loose.

'Hello?' she whispered. 'Who are you?'

There was the sound of a moan being swallowed. 'Charlotte?' Veronica's quavering voice whispered from the darkness.

Eleven

Eleven

Even if her room was being watched by hidden cameras, they wouldn't be able to see what she did under her bed. And they couldn't watch her every single moment, could they? Charlotte rolled out from under the bed, arranged her bolster under her bedclothes to make a dummy, and scurried back to the vent.

'The bolts are loose on my side,' she called softly. 'How about yours?'

'Mine too, but the hole isn't big enough to wriggle through.'

Charlotte's fingers twisted at a bolt. 'Nevermind. At least we'll be able to hold hands. How long have they had you prisoner?'

'I don't know. What day is it?'

'Don't you know either? They don't let me see out. I don't even know if it's day or night.' The first bolt came out. Charlotte started on the second.

'Me neither. There was a woman in that shop . . .'

'Tall? Slim? Dark?'

'That's her. I should never have let her bring me here.'

'And when you didn't come back to the hotel I went looking for you. And when she said she'd take me to you – I couldn't just have left you, could I?'

'And since then?' Veronica asked.

The second bolt fell. 'It's been . . . They've done some terrible things to me, Veronica.'

'Made you wear kinky outfits and perform sex-acts for them? Made you into a sex-show, of the most depraved kind?'

112

'You too? Oh, Veronica, how are we ever going to escape?'

Veronica's voice became a sardonic drawl. 'Are you sure you want to?'

'What do you mean?'

'Isn't this like one of those games we played as girls, but for real?'

Charlotte laid the third bolt aside. 'I suppose it is, but the "for real" frightens me.'

'You enjoy fear.'

That was too close for comfort. Charlotte concentrated on the last bolt. When it came loose, the iron grille tumbled into her hands. 'My side's open.'

'Just a minute. Yes – mine too. Can you reach?'

Charlotte fumbled through the hole and found Veronica's hand, stretching from the other side. They clutched each other's fingers.

'Have they beaten you, Veronica?'

'Just with canes. I've had worse from lovers.'

Charlotte digested that. 'You? You, Veronica? I thought ...'

'That I was the one who always did the beating? Usually, yes. Always with you, but not always with my other lovers. Inside every sadist there's a masochist lurking. Haven't you realised that by now?'

Charlotte thought about the other side of that coin: that inside every masochist there is a sadist.

'My bottom's sore,' Veronica complained. 'I didn't show enough humility today. I was punished for that with a beating, and worse.'

'Worse?'

'You don't want to know. Take my advice, if they want you to abase yourself, do it.'

'I'd already decided to be obedient, no matter what.'

'That's wise, but it may not be easy, even for you.'

'Is it that bad?'

'It was for me. How sore is your bum, Charlotte?'

'Very. I can hardly move.'

'Shame I can't kiss it better for you. Move up, Charlotte. Get your bum close to the vent. Perhaps I can comfort it.'

113

The tormenting lust that had been subsiding reared up again. Putting her bottom against a hole in a wall so that Veronica could soothe it with her fingers seemed such a perverse act that the thought of it made the inside of Charlotte's sex quiver. She shouldn't succumb. She knew that, and yet to refuse would seem churlish, and – and she was desperate for a loving touch.

Charlotte turned on to her other side and wriggled into position. A cool fingertip touched her hip, trailed down her rump, and paused at the first tender ridge.

'Does that hurt?' Veronica's voice sounded husky through the vent.

'No – yes – some.'

The finger stroked, leaving a trail that felt as if it sparkled. 'Shall I stop?'

'No.'

'You like this, don't you.'

'It's – comforting.'

The finger withdrew for a moment. When it returned it was wet. 'Is this comforting?' Veronica's finger pushed between Charlotte's clenched buttocks. 'Relax. Let me.'

Despite herself, Charlotte let her muscles soften. The damp fingertip rimmed her sphincter, coaxing it open.

'Don't, Veronica,' Charlotte pleaded, belying her own words with a backward squirm.

'Did the Mistress have the masked man bugger you yet?' Veronica asked.

'No.' Suddenly jealous, Charlotte asked, 'You?'

'Oh yes.'

'Was it – was it painful?'

'At first.' Veronica's finger forced its way through the tightness of Charlotte's knot.

'And after?'

'It was like this.'

The finger straightened and pressed. Charlotte clenched on it, and then surrendered. The humiliating probe slid deeper, withdrew, then eased in again. Charlotte submitted. Her stepsister's finger was violating her anus, delving deep into her rectum. Elastic walls gave way to it. Charlotte felt that her most intimate and internal self was being profaned. Her body had been breached. She was open in a way that she had never been pierced before, and the obscenity of it was absolutely delicious.

'I'm fingering my own arse as I do this to yours,' Veronica said. 'We are sharing this, Charlotte. We may not be sisters by blood, but we are truly sisters in this, our depravity.'

'I'm not depraved,' Charlotte protested, wriggling on the full length of Veronica's finger.

'You aren't? But it's in your blood.'

'What do you mean?'

'You remember I told you I'd spied on our stepfather, with my mother? He was sodomising her, Charlotte. He was big – long and thick – and he was pounding into her arse, and she loved it. You know what he was telling her, as he used her bum? He was telling her about doing the same thing to his first wife – your mother. He was comparing how tight each one was, and how hot inside.'

'No – no.'

'Hump at my finger, Charlotte. Skewer yourself on it. Do like your mother did, with our stepfather.'

The mental image was unbearable. Gathering her will, Charlotte twisted her body, dragging her rectum off its invader. Flat on her back, she drew a deep breath and searched for the right words with which to curse her stepsister. Before she found them, Veronica's fingers discovered her weeping sex. Two fingers hooked between Charlotte's sopping lips, and a thumb flattened her clit against her pubic bone. It squeezed and wobbled, driving shards of hot lust into Charlotte's body. She splayed her thighs almost reflexively. Her hands grabbed Veronica's wrist to push it away but at that point a nagging thob began inside Charlotte's body, compressing her very being.

Ever since her arrival in this dreadful place she'd been subjected to arousal after arousal, and had usually been denied release. There'd been that time with Blanche, and the dreamy one with Nurse, but never enough. The pressure of her accumulated need was too great for her to fight.

Instead of pushing Veronica's fingers away, she drew them in tighter, forcing her stepsister's fingers deeper and squishing her clit harder against that damned insistent thumb.

Hot wet velvet tore inside her. Her entire being unfolded. Just as she melted into nothingness, she heard Veronica's voice from what seemed like a long way off.

'Goodnight, sweet Charlotte. Till tomorrow.'

Twelve

Charlotte slid the shower door open. She stepped over the sill and emerged from a billowing cloud of perfumed steam with her knee high and her bare toes extended and pointed down; she had been taught that 'pretty ponies' pranced this way. The Mistress had schooled her to always be conscious of how she looked, and to take pains that her pose should always be as erotic as circumstances allowed.

She turned her thigh inward coyly. An arm was folded modestly across her bosom, concealing one flushed breast but accidentally allowing the nipple of the other to peep saucily through the crook of her elbow. Of all the lessons that the Mistress's cane was implanting, the joy of posing was the most fun. Being body conscious was becoming second nature to her.

She paused for a long moment, to let Blanche get the full effect of her sensuality. That orgasm the previous night, at her stepsister's hands, had gone a long way towards restoring her sexual self-confidence. However confused she was about the exact nature her erotic needs, there was one thing she was sure of. She was desirable. Many men, and a few women, had pursued her. Her own inner turmoil had kept her from taking lovers, except for those two inept boys. She now realised that she had chosen them for their blandness. Insipid was safe. Insipid was all that her stepsister, Veronica, wasn't.

Here, in the *schloss*, there was no such safety. She felt she was finally beginning to come to terms with the suppressed volcanic power of her own sexuality. She would use it. She would use her body's beauty. Charlotte decided

117

that she would turn the full heat of her desirability on everyone she met. She would seduce her way out of this Sybaritic prison, person by person if that was what it took, starting with the nearest: Blanche.

'Dry me,' she said, lifting her arms in high graceful curves. Charlotte knew what that ballet pose did for her. It lifted her breasts. It flared her ribcage. It slimmed her waist, and twisting sideways a touch, the way she did then, narrowed it even more. She was sure that the sight of her lithe body, plus the proximity and intimacy of the service that Blanche was about to perform, would lead to an embrace at least, if not an intimate caress. The thought of Blanche's fingers parting her, and her tongue delving, made a delightful tremor run through Charlotte's tummy.

Blanche, blank-faced and totally impersonal, patted Charlotte's body from her toes to her face, and fitted a stiff leather collar around her neck.

'No blocks today?' Charlotte asked, trying to sound sardonically aloof, as she held her pose.

Blanche clipped a heavy plaited leather leash to Charlotte's collar. 'Today you are just a pet animal. Down on all fours, please ma'am.'

'Why not wait until I get downstairs?'

'Orders, ma'am. I'm to beat you if you don't obey.'

Descending the stairs was the worst part. The carpet was coarser. Crawling head-down made Charlotte feel that she was constantly about to topple on to her face, particularly when Blanche tugged at her leash. And it was so undignified. A pet on a leash has no chance of posing provocatively. There wasn't even any point to her wriggling her hips, with Blanche leading her.

The Mistress said, 'I won't have time for her until later. Tie the bitch up over there, out of the way.'

Charlotte crawled at heel and was secured to the wallbars. So much for seducing her way to freedom. So much for the power of exuding eroticism. Another lesson? That some people were immune, even if they enjoyed your seductive posturing?

'Keep a good posture; back straight and horizontal;

118

head up,' Blanche advised her, perhaps confirming her suspicions. 'She'll notice if you slouch and it'd be the worse for you.'

Charlotte composed herself as best she could, very conscious of her nudity, and especially aware of the way her coral-tipped breasts hung beneath her. Those lush fruits should have drawn the attention of hungry fingers.

Charlotte sucked in her stomach, and tried to emphasise the sleek lines of her body. Kneeling there, gorgeous, naked and vulnerable, she should have been the focus of attention.

They just ignored her. She found that more humiliating than anything they had done to her before. She had only just discovered the power of her body. Then, when she tried to use it, they showed her how weak her power really was.

It was so unfair!

The Mistress sat in a leather armchair, sipping tea. She wore a tight ribbed jersey sweater, boots, and nothing else. The couple sat opposite on a hard bench, also drinking nonchalantly from bone china, as if people routinely shared mid-morning tea with half their faces covered by grotesque masks and their bare bodies criss-crossed by tight leather straps. When Charlotte had first seen them, they'd been victims in a hellish torture chamber. Yesterday, they'd been mute slaves. Now they sat with the Mistress, almost as equals. It was very confusing.

The Mistress glanced across at Charlotte. She stiffened in anticipation. A beckoning finger brought the Filipino girl, naked except for a frilly little apron and a perky white cap, to the Mistress's side. The Mistress gave soft instructions. The girl poured tea and milk into a saucer and carried it to Charlotte.

Charlotte looked down between her hands at the saucer. She could ignore it. She could pick it up and drink from it. Neither was what was required. She knew that without being told. Meekly, she dipped her face to the saucer and lapped, trying to curl and flick her tongue the way a dog or cat might do. A few drops of tea splashed on to the carpet.

'Naughty!' the Filipino snapped.

Charlotte flinched expecting a blow, but none came. Perhaps that was beyond the girl's authority. What the girl did do was worse. She simply fetched a sheet of newspaper, lifted the saucer, and slid the paper beneath it. Not only was Charlotte a mere pet, but she wasn't even properly house-broken. The shame of it flushed her cheeks and breasts.

A familiar clinking told Charlotte that the tea things were being cleared away. She dared not turn her head to stare, but she watched from the corners of her eyes. The Mistress hitched herself further back into her chair and spread her thighs to hook one booted knee up over each leather arm. She beckoned with both hands and pointed. The masked couple scurried to her; the woman to kneel on the floor before her and the man to stand close by her side.

The Mistress pointed again, at her own sex. The cat-woman obediently bowed her face and started licking. Charlotte saw that the man's cock wasn't trussed in its usual harness. Without so much as a glance, the Mistress reached out and idly ran the backs of her fingers up its undercurve, as if vaguely curious as to its skin's texture.

Her other hand stretched towards Blanche, who was standing in waiting. The chalky-skinned girl handed her a riding crop.

Charlotte flinched as the Mistress used the man's cock to pull herself forward, and slashed down with the crop across the cat-woman's upraised rump. The crouching woman jerked once and redoubled her oral attentions. Charlotte could hear the frantic wet sounds clearly across the room.

Apparently content with the woman's crop-inspired efforts, the Mistress sank back again, gently fondling the length of the man's stalk. He stood rigid, as his cock slowly grew thicker and longer under the Mistress's teasingly delicate ministrations. Before long his hips were swaying, slithering his hard flesh through the loose circle of the Mistress's fingers. She allowed that for a while, but as soon as his body stiffened and his thrusts became urgent, she squeezed, halting him in mid-stroke. A tug brought his glistening glans to her face. She lapped, once, across his purple dome. The man groaned. She held him still for a while, poised just short of his orgasm. When she judged that his lust had subsided enough, she resumed her stroking, but used only the trailing tips of her fingers. The sensations he felt were just enough to keep him on the brink, but never enough to allow him release.

The Mistress told the cat-woman, 'Faster! Harder!' A quick gasp signalled her climax. Her boot shoved the cat-woman sprawling. A tug on his cock told the man to take her place. As he began his licking, the cat-woman writhed to her feet and took up position next to the chair. Her slender thighs were already parted, ready for the Mistress to explore her sex should that whim take her. It did.

The man had to be encouraged twice with the crop before the Mistress gasped once more. By that time four of her fingers were buried between the petals of the cat-woman's female flower and she was panting with lust.

The man was allowed to lick the woman's essence from the Mistress's fingers before all three walked over to Charlotte; the Mistress took imperious floor-stabbing strides, the man almost loped, and the cat-woman was sinuous and feline.

'She's a fine little bitch, but untrained, as yet,' the Mistress said. 'You may touch her if you like. Try the texture of her skin – it glides under your fingers like oiled silk. It takes a beautiful mark, as you'll see if you inspect her rump.'

The masked woman petted Charlotte's head, as if she was a pedigree dog. The man smoothed a palm over her flank, lingering on her weals as if he was reading Braille. The Mistress lifted a booted foot and rested its toe on the wall-bars' third rail, directly in front of Charlotte's face.

Charlotte gazed up past the knee, along a statuesque thigh, to the Mistress's sex. It was her first really close look. Swollen pendulous lips clung together, still glistening with her slaves' saliva, and her own spending. The ridge of her clitoris was unnaturally long and thick. Its head, half-exposed, was the size and shape of an acorn, sitting in a wrinkled cup.

'Suck my heel.'

The words didn't sink in for a moment. Before Charlotte could react, the cat-woman had knotted her hand into Charlotte's curly blonde tresses and jerked her face forward.

Charlotte opened her mouth and let the narrow black spike slide between her lips. She tasted steel and polished leather. A harshly metallic point threatened her tongue. The Mistress wriggled her heel impatiently. Charlotte sucked.

'Nice lips,' the Mistress remarked, 'but they'd look even better swollen from a little bruising. You!' she tapped the man's shoulder with her crop. 'You know what to do.'

The heel slithered out. Charlotte blinked. His feathered mask loomed inches from her face. His eyes, soft to the point of sadness, gazed into hers. One big hand wrapped the back of her neck and the other gripped her throat through its collar. Sure that he was going to kiss her, Charlotte let her mouth go slack.

It wasn't a kiss. It was a savage attack. He ground his mouth on hers, forcing her lips wide apart. For a few seconds she breathed in his hot breath and then his teeth closed on her lower lip. His mouth was as hard and as feral as the beak of the eagle's head he wore. He tugged at her lip, twisting it from side to side. His teeth sank into her softness as hard as they could without puncturing her skin. She gasped. He chewed, nipped and chewed again. Relinquishing her lower lip, he snapped at her upper one, holding it between his incisors, and tugging on it viciously.

It would have been more bearable if he had growled or made some other animal sound, but, despite the ferocity of his attack, it was cold-blooded and planned. As each part of her lip was chewed until it started to swell, he moved on to the next section, to gnaw on that in its turn. Once her lips had been violated to the point that she was moaning her pain into his mouth, he paused, and mashed his mouth full on hers. His tongue stabbed, but with no more tenderness than the Mistress's heel. He used her mouth, as though he were drinking from it, exploring it, mastering it.

He sat back to inspect his work. The Mistress reached down to take Charlotte's lower lip between cruel fingers and turn it out. She scrutinised its inner surface, twisted it, then let go.

'Satisfactory,' the Mistress said. 'Don't you think these swollen lips would look nice, wrapped around the stem of your cock again? You enjoyed her clumsy efforts last time, didn't you?'

The man nodded twice, quickly.

'Perhaps we should continue her oral lessons then.' She snapped her fingers. The Filipino girl brought a plastic container of liquid honey. Blanche and the Eurasian dragged her leather chair up to the wall-bar. The Mistress sank into it. 'I'd like to see if you two have learned your lessons. I will watch. You two take over. Show me how well you can teach.'

The man grinned, wrapped his hand around his shaft, and pulled his foreskin back. The cat-woman stooped, honey in hand. Taking careful aim, she squeezed a sticky drop precisely into the eye of the man's cock.

The Mistress said, 'You – the bitch – lap it. Use just the very tip of your tongue.'

Charlotte stretched her tongue out. The man retreated. She craned her neck. He backed away. It wasn't until she was straining forward at the full length of her leash, trembling with her neck and tongue fully extended, that he allowed her to reach him. The very tip of her tongue felt the stickiness, squirmed in it, and drew a golden strand from his cock's eye back into her mouth. Honey had never tasted so good.

The cat-woman poured again. Honey coated the man's glans like toffee on a toffee apple. He didn't move any closer. Charlotte strained against her leash until it seemed her collar would choke her. The Mistress, still sprawled in her chair, extended an arm. Her crop flicked the tip of Charlotte's right nipple. It didn't hurt, but the threat was obvious. Perform well, or be subjected to intense pain.

123

Charlotte elongated her tongue until its roots ached. The man held fast. The end of Charlotte's tongue flattened on golden-coated glossy skin and laved in tiny hard circles.

Damn the man! The half-dozen times she'd paid men the compliment of using her mouth on them, they'd gone crazy with grateful lust. This man – the bastard – was teasing her with his cock. Now it was she who was desperate to get his cock into her mouth, not the other way around. Damn him to hell! She resolved, then and there, that the time would come, before she escaped this dreadful place, when she would make him crawl on his hands and knees, begging her for the ecstasy her mouth could give.

The Mistress's crop flipped up, lightly stinging the underside of Charlotte's dangling breast. Her thoughts had distracted her. For just a moment she had been less avid in her slavering at the man's plum-head. Goaded, she lunged against her leash, disregarding its throttling tightness, and fitted her lips to the head of his cock. She sucked, hard and long, as if his cock's eye was a straw through which she could draw out his spunk by sheer willpower.

A single droplet of spicy fluid rewarded her.

'She's an avid little bitch, isn't she?' the Mistress drawled.

Charlotte became aware of how ridiculous she must look, posed like a retriever straining to point out game. They'd treated her like a bitch-in-heat, and she'd abetted her own debasement by acting like one, snuffling and scrabbling to get at the nearest cock.

How quickly she'd fallen. A few short days before, she'd been an elegant young heiress, *en route* to her inheritance. A few implied threats, a couple of dozen blows from a cane, and she'd been reduced to the status of a lust-crazed grovelling animal.

So be it! If they wanted her to be an animal in heat, then that was what she'd be. She growled deep in her throat and pressed her swollen lips on his dome, frantic to make him react.

Suddenly the Mistress said, 'Lunch time already? Come on. We'll continue this afternoon.'

Charlotte let her leash pull her back on to her haunches. Her mind reeled. Lunch time? Debased and demeaned or not, she'd been so deep into her role that she'd been half-hypnotised with lust – and they were going to break for lunch? Had she had that little effect on them?

She blinked herself back to sanity and found that they were gone. She had been alone for perhaps five minutes, wallowing in self-pity, when the Eurasian girl returned with two dog bowls and set them before her.

'Am I to . . .?' Charlotte started.

The girl picked up the Mistress's discarded crop and whacked it across Charlotte's bottom. 'Naughty little bitch-dogs don't talk,' she snapped in an accent that Charlotte might have found charming under different circumstances.

Charlotte dipped her head. The contents of one bowl looked like dog food, but her nose told her it was boeuf bourgignon. The clear pink liquid in the other bowl sparkled. A dip of her tongue told her it was rosé wine.

A leashed bitch she might be, but at least she was a spoilt one. Even though she had been left alone, she lowered her head to eat and drink. It wasn't that she feared being observed. At that point, it didn't even occur to her that she could have raised the bowls to her mouth.

They resumed after lunch. The Filipino girl dabbed away the food strains from Charlotte's face with a warm wet perfumed cloth. Charlotte watched as the Eurasian climbed to kneel on a low bench. The Mistress arranged the girl's naked limbs with little taps from her crop.

Was this girl to become another dog? Was Charlotte to be taught to perform tricks by following her example?

The Mistress untied Charlotte's leash from the bars, dragged her across the floor, and half-lifted her to kneel up and set her hands on the bench's edge.

Charlotte found herself staring straight into the crease of the girl's arse. Blanche's palms parted plump golden buttocks. There, near the base of the crease, was a tiny brown puckered hole. The cat-woman reached over with the honey bottle, put its narrow neck to the girl's anal sphincter, rotated it until half a tapered inch sank in, and squeezed.

When the bottle was plucked out, a single sweet droplet oozed out to cling to the raised rim of the tiny flesh crater.

The Mistress dragged on the leash, thrusting Charlotte's face between the girl's cheeks. 'Lap, bitch!'

Charlotte felt sick. Anilingus? It had to be the most debased, the most demeaning, of all sexual acts. Not only was the act itself unthinkable, but this girl was the lowest of the low; she was at the bottom of the *schloss*'s pecking order.

No. Charlotte realised her error. The slave girl, who went naked, had her sex held open by cruel thongs and was available for anyone to use in whatever way took their fancy, was not the lowest in rank here. Charlotte was. She had been demoted to the status of arse-licker to slaves.

But someone had done it to her just the day before, hadn't they? And she'd enjoyed it? Was that the lesson? If you give someone pleasure, there is no other morality, no other rank? It was so confusing. Sometimes it seemed that there was a rigid hierarchy at the *schloss*, and everyone knew their place. Except Charlotte.

Blanche served her, had been spanked by her, but also commanded her. The slaves and the mysterious masked people had all been made to service Charlotte sexually; and now, it seemed, she was expected to repay those intimate attentions. Only one thing seemed definite: the Mistress commanded all. But there had to be someone higher still, didn't there? Did the Mistress grovel in her turn, before whoever had ultimate command? The thought was strangely satisfying.

A hand pushed at her nape. Something swished behind her. She felt the wind of its passage and then sensed a second swish. Pain crackled across the backs of her thighs. The crop's impact drove Charlotte forward, mashing her face between the girl's buttocks. She gasped, sucking in the musky aroma of the girl's sex. Swiftly, before the Mistress decided to strike again, Charlotte lapped. Her tongue tasted honey, licked it up, and then stiffened and sought its source.

126

The buttocks that were squished against her face twitched and trembled. Her tongue was doing that? Her simple probing lick was giving the girl that much pleasure?

Charlotte pressed left and then right, easing the girl's buttocks further apart with the pressure of her face. She pursed her bruised lips into a tiny tight circle and then fitted them to the girl's tinier, tighter one. Pushing forward as hard as she could, Charlotte spread her lips, forcing the Eurasian's anus to open for her. She loaded her tongue with saliva and pushed spit into the girl's sphincter, following it with the folded and stiffened tip of her tongue. Honey dissolved into dewy nectar. Charlotte's tongue flicked the sweetness back into her own mouth, one drop at a time. The girl grunted with pleasure.

'What do you think, Blanche?' the Mistress asked.

'Like she was born to stick her tongue up the bums of slaves, Mistress.'

'I agree. The little bitch learns quickly. Blanche, Song-li doesn't need her buttocks held for her now. If you wish, you may caress her. Give her an orgasm if you like. She's been a good girl.'

'Thank you, Mistress.'

Leaving Charlotte to her anal duties, Blanche moved to face the Eurasian, Song-li. Stooping, she took her face in tender palms and gave her a long deep kiss.

With one tongue wriggling in her mouth and another squirming inside her bottom, Song-li shivered with delight. Blanche reached beneath the kneeling girl. One hand cupped and compressed a delicate pendant breast. The other trailed lower, over the soft curve of her belly, and found her sex, already held apart by cruel silk. Inquisitive fingers explored inner folds, found moisture and drew it back on their tips, to be massaged into a quivering clitoris' head.

Song-li sobbed into Blanche's mouth.

'You two may also play, if you wish,' the Mistress told the masked couple.

Charlotte stiffened. Would they choose to play with each other, or with her? And which did she want it to be?

No, that was dishonest. She wanted their hands and

mouths on her. She was half-kneeling, wasn't she? Would the man be moved to mount her? Was she finally going to feel that gorgeous long hard cock of his, sliding into her eager pussy? And if she did, was she going to be allowed an orgasm at last? At that moment Charlotte felt that she'd kill for one good gut-wrenching climax.

She twitched her hips encouragingly.

She felt lips, soft and wet on her bottom's right cheek. Whose? Fingers delicately traced the undercurve of her left breast, and finding her nipple, tweaked it. A woman's touch? A stronger grip milked at her right nipple, urging it to engorge even more than it already had. If only she could see who was touching her where!

Palms flattened on her buttocks and spread them. She felt a tongue – no – two tongues, one to each side of her bottom's crease. Two warm cheeks were laid on her buttocks. There was coarseness; surely the fabric of the masks. She couldn't tell fur from feathers, not by the feel of them.

Charlotte sensed, more than felt, that the two tongues were playing with each other. A hot wetness touched the sensitive rim of her anus. His tongue? Hers? Both of them?

The palms spread her even wider. She felt the tug at her sphincter. She clenched for a moment, and then relaxed. Something probed. Damn it! She couldn't tell if it was one tongue, two, or a moistened finger.

It was a wet finger. It was too thick, strong and round to be a tongue. It eased into her a fraction and then rotated, persuading her anus to open up for it. Something, a second finger, rimmed her puckered hole. Oh God! It was squirming in beside the first! Was one of them working two fingers into her, or could it be one finger belonging to each of them? How intimate that would be; to share in the violation of someone's arse.

The fingers tugged to either side. They were opening her wide, turning a pin-hole into a gaping funnel. Someone was staring right into her; right up the forbidden channel of her rectum. Wetness dribbled into her. Spit? Oil? She couldn't tell which, but it lubricated her enough that the fingers were able to invade even deeper, and were joined by another one, and then one more.

128

She'd read a short story once, in a book of erotica that Veronica had sent her for Christmas. In it, a sadistic butch-lesbian had fisted a masochistic drag queen, easing her entire hand into his anus. She'd dismissed it as an impossibility. No one could take a clenched fist deep into their rectum without suffering severe injury.

Could they?

An hour before, she'd have been sure that she wouldn't be able to take two fingers in there, let alone four, but now she was.

Were they preparing her for him to bugger her? Her virgin arse? Would she be able to stand it, if they were? Something deep inside her told her that she would, and more; she would even find that ultimate violation enjoyable. Sodomy. Being used. Being reduced to a mere thing; a living toy; nothing but a sex-object.

Where would the pleasure be for the victim of such an act? In being distended, filled, and stretched? In the achievement of enduring? In the knowledge that you were giving yourself, totally?

Four fingers, linked and entwined, pistoned into her rectum. Two hands, both firm now, milked at her breasts, dragging on their tips. Teeth nipped her buttocks. Mouths lapped at her weals. Tongues flattened, slavering on the tenderness of the ridges that the Mistress's cane had raised on her skin.

And Charlotte, stimulated almost to mindlessness, slobbered into Song-li's anus, mewing with animal lust.

She felt another hand, belonging to either the Mistress or the Filipino, on her sex. It clamped on her mound, squeezing her lips together, palpitating and kneading her flesh like dough. Charlotte felt herself squeeze out moisture. She was going to come! Thank God, she was going to come at last! A few more moments of this divine torture would do it!

Song-li squealed and slumped-forward into Blanche's arms, dragging her bottom off Charlotte's tongue. Charlotte blinked in the sudden light.

The Mistress barked, 'Freeze!'

All movement stopped. The fingers were still inside her rectum, holding her stretched open. The moulded palm still compressed her mound. The hands were still on her breasts, with her nipples pinched and elongated; they were all in tableau, as motionless as the wax figures in the *Musée de Sainte Clothilde*.

It was unbearable. A spasm of raging lust convulsed her. She screamed, 'No! No! No!' and thrust her body backward at the tormentingly immobile fingers.

They snatched away. The riding crop cut her buttocks; once, twice, three times. Their force flattened Charlotte on the leather bench. Pain exploded through her rump, igniting her sex. She squirmed her sex on the leather, desperate to find a seam to rub her ferociously demanding clit against. Her mouth made sounds, gobbling pleading sounds. Her swollen lips went slack. She felt dribble on her own chin and didn't care. Nothing mattered. At that moment, she'd have sold her soul to Satan for a single orgasm.

It was not to be. The Mistress dragged her from the bench by her hair. Charlotte sprawled on her back on the floor, legs spread, humping at thin air.

The Mistress said, 'Cool her off. We'll continue when she's regained her self-control.'

The masked couple grabbed one of Charlotte's ankles each. The Filipino and Song-li took her wrists. Kicking and screaming, begging for her orgasm, Charlotte was carried out of the room.

130

Thirteen

The water was cold enough to claw through Charlotte's bones to her marrow and forceful enough to distort and bruise her flesh. Where it drummed on her skin, a deep dimple vibrated. She huddled in the corner of the white-tiled room, trying to shield her face and bosom from the icy torrent. The jet pressed a frigid path down her body, to her sex. As she dropped a hand to cup a protective palm over her sex, the stream of water flicked up to pummel the undersides of her breasts.

She rolled over and curled into a ball. A piston of water pressed the cheeks of her bottom apart and jetted against, then into, her rectum. It felt as if her arse was being penetrated by a throbbing icicle.

She clenched, but the force was too strong. She felt as though her sphincter would give way to the insistent pressure, so she rolled again and took the full fury on the top of her head. The noise was deafening. Her brain started to numb. She'd have screamed for mercy, but each time she opened her mouth it was flooded hard enough to fold her tongue to the back of her throat and distend her cheeks.

Suddenly there was silence. Her ears rang with it. She huddled herself tightly, trying to calm the shivering down. Someone spoke, but she couldn't hear the words over the sound of her own teeth chattering. Her nipples were brittle icicles, stabbed deep into numb flesh. Her knuckles felt as if they were being crushed in the grip of frost-coated pliers.

A blanket-sized towel, warm and thick, enveloped her. Its comforting protection enabled Charlotte to emerge from deep within herself, where she'd been forced to hide.

'There, there, ma'am,' Blanche's voice soothed. 'You're yourself again, right? Under control?'

Charlotte nodded. She wasn't sure that she was herself, but to admit to doubts might bring the terrible hail of water back.

'I've got a nice hot bath ready. Let's get you to it. Best be quick, before the chill stiffens you.'

As Blanche soaped feeling back into the numb flesh of Charlotte's back she said, 'There's going to be more, you realise, ma'am? There's more to the oral lessons, and they are going to try to distract you. You won't lose control again, will you, ma'am? You mustn't let your own passion overwhelm you.'

'No,' Charlotte mumbled through lips that didn't want to work. Having been subjected to the man's abuse and then frozen by the frigid deluge, they felt as if they had been anaesthetised.

'Here. Drink.' Blanche handed her a steaming cup of bouillon that had been spiked with vodka. 'This'll make you glow.'

Charlotte was left, still clutching herself against the shivering, wrapped in a fluffy robe, under her bedclothes. How long for? Was she to rest for the night, or would Blanche be back for her at any moment, for her to resume her lessons? Was it day or night?

Restless despite her gritty-eyed weariness, Charlotte got up and went to the window. The shutters were solid and screwed in place. If only she had some tools.

Her manicure set was on the dressing table. Somehow it had been brought from the hotel. They probably had the rest of her things. They were efficient. They'd have booked her and Veronica out of their suite. Their hotel would have forgotten them by now.

There should be a nail file in the kit, but the green leather case sat just in front of the mirror, and someone could be watching her through it.

Charlotte sat herself on the stool and leant forward, as if checking her appearance. As her chest brushed the box, she raised an eyebrow, feigning surprise at discovering it.

She opened the lid and poked at the contents. Taking an emery board, she rubbed it across the tip of a nail. She acted as if the board wasn't enough. The nail file? Oh, there it was. A few strokes seemed to satisfy her, but instead of returning the file to the box, she put it down on the table. She leant forward again and pulled down a lower eyelid, checking her eye. Oops! Her sleeve brushed the file to the floor, but she didn't notice.

She got up, wandered around the room, and flinched at the sight of the salt cellar, still on top of the chest of drawers. She made her way back to the window, out of the direct line of sight of the mirror.

Charlotte dropped to her hands and knees, crawled across the floor, and retrieved the nail file. Now she had a tool.

It wasn't strong, and the screws that held the shutters were firm. Her inefficient tool twisted in her fingers. It took about twenty minutes, as well as she could judge, to loosen the first screw. She pulled it out and put her eye to the tiny hole. No light. Did that mean that it was night outside, or did it mean absolutely nothing?

She twisted the first screw loosely back into place and started on the second one. She was rebelling, and it felt good.

The door made a sound. Charlotte threw herself on the bed, thrust the nail file under her pillow, and waited.

'Are you rested, ma'am?' Blanche asked. 'Have a nice sleep? It's time to go back down.'

Charlotte rolled over and rubbed her eyes. 'Huh?'

'I told you – it's more oral today. You started on your lessons in anilingus. Now its time for more advanced cunnilingus and fellatio. Aren't you looking forward to getting a nice hot cock in your mouth again, ma'am?'

Charlotte nodded, and considered what the consequences might be if she bit down hard on the man's glans. Perhaps she'd better not. She could get her revenge more subtly; by tormenting him as much as they had tormented her. If she drove him delirious with lust, would he be the one to huddle helpless in the tiled room?

'Didn't I do that – fellatio? Yesterday? Earlier?'

Blanche dismissed the words with a wave of her hand. 'That game with the honey, ma'am? That was just a little treat, for you and him. Like kindergarten. You have to graduate from a much tougher school. By the time the Mistress is done with you, you'll be able to make a cock sit up and sing for you.'

For the third time that day, unless midnight had passed unmarked, Charlotte bathed. How long was it since she'd last slept? It seemed like more than a full day, but Blanche was talking as if it was less. That was part of their plan, wasn't it? Disorientate her? They did that when they brainwashed people. That and sensory deprivation, like that dreadful black box. They were deliberately erasing her personality so that they could imprint her with a new one.

Or were they stripping away a false one, to reveal her true nature?

Dripping, she emerged from the water, stood and let Blanche pat her dry.

'I really envy you, ma'am,' the girl said, kneeling to dab between Charlotte's thighs.

'Envy? Why?'

'Oh, lot's of things, ma'am. There's the training, for one. I still look back on my own lessons, though they weren't near as rigorous as yours. Those were exciting times. Then there's your passion, ma'am. I'm only a serving girl, I know, and I shouldn't make comparisons, but I really admire the strength of your lust, ma'am. You're a real fiery furnace, if you'll forgive me saying so.'

Charlotte thought about that. She'd never considered herself particularly lusty, and she'd never thought of randiness as a virtue. The values here, in the *schloss*, were different from those in the rest of the world. She'd always judged herself as a bit of an oddball, not quite fitting in. Was this hell-hole the natural habitat where she belonged?

'And, like I told you before, ma'am, I do so admire your nipples.'

'My nipples?'

Blanche's fingertip reached up to stroke beneath one

erect turret. 'Nice and big, and such a lovely deep colour. Mine are tiny, and too pale.'

Charlotte bent to peck a swift kiss on the tip of one pale pink little thorn. 'But pretty. Size isn't everything.'

Blanche stood and turned her back to Charlotte. 'Thank you, ma'am, but I have my points, so I'm told. I've been told that my bum makes up for lack of tits and nipples. What do you think?' She shot a dimpled hip at Charlotte.

'You have a very pretty bottom, Blanche.'

'I really envied Song-li, ma'am, when you were doing her bum so nicely with your tongue. I'm keeping my fingers crossed – for when the Mistress gives you your lessons in pussy-eating. But I think she'll want to keep that personal – between you and her.'

Charlotte swallowed. The Mistress's sex was so lush, so succulent, and had that incredible clitoris! Would she, if it was required of her, be able to cope? Could she do justice to that quintessence of womanhood?

'Collar and leash, ma'am. We have to go down.'

In the training room, Charlotte was laid on her back on the low leather bench, her shoulders to the edge. The Eurasian, Song-li, and the Filipino, Maria, pulled her limbs wide and down, and strapped them to the four legs. Blanche crawled underneath on her belly. She pulled on Charlotte's leash, tugging her head down and back until her face was virtually upside-down; she fastened the leash's loop somewhere beneath. Charlotte's blonde curls dangled to brush the carpet.

The Mistress laid a cane across Charlotte's ribs, just beneath her breasts. 'What a pretty sight. Just like a virgin sacrifice. Aren't you lucky that this is twentieth-century Steinreich, not ancient Greece? Anyway,' she continued, changing the subject, 'today we concentrate on your mouth.'

The cane stroked Charlotte's swollen lower lip. Without thinking, Charlotte parted her lips to the touch. The Mistress inserted the cane's tip and let Charlotte suck on it.

'That's it,' the Mistress hissed. 'Kiss the cruel implement that brings you your pain! Love your tormentor. I swear by the blessed Saint Clothilde, if you learn today's lessons well, and give me just three good orgasms with that sweet mouth of yours, you shall be rewarded.

'Maria! Kneel at her head. I want you to demonstrate exactly how your Mistress's pussy likes to be taken care of.'

Maria knelt, cheek to cheek with Charlotte. Charlotte waited, knotted with tension, as she listened to the sounds of furniture being moved. A second bench was pushed into place, not two feet from Charlotte's eyes. The Mistress sat her naked bottom on its very edge and lay back. Her thighs spread wide, allowing Charlotte to stare directly into her humid sex.

'Like this,' Maria whispered.

She nuzzled low between the Mistress's legs, almost at her anus. A long pointed tongue flickered, teasing the delicate skin between the Mistress's sex and her rectum. It trailed wetly, leaving a glistening track, up along the crease of the Mistress's groin.

Charlotte flinched. Two people, she could not see who, had knelt beside the bench she was strapped to. Two hands were laid gently on her belly. Fingers traced idle circles on drum-taut skin, infinitely tantalising.

Maria chewed at a pussy-lip, sucking it into her mouth and mumbling on it with lip-padded teeth. The Mistress's sex was pulled wide open. Charlotte gazed into a pulsating purple and pink slot, already florid and drooling droplets of liquid lust. The clitoris that crowned that oozy slit was growing, creeping from its sheath.

Then the Mistress croaked, 'Give my mouth your cock.'

So neither of the hands that smoothed the skin of Charlotte's belly belonged to the man. He had to be standing at the Mistress's head. Charlotte swallowed her disappointment and concentrated on what Maria's mouth was doing.

The girl had drawn her head back, pulling a loose lip with it, stretching the Mistress even wider. She craned across and started chewing at the opposite lip. Charlotte, her face lower than Maria's head and the Mistress's sex, was gazing up at both, and could see everything in close-up detail.

Small white teeth nipped hard enough to leave tiny dents in flaccid flesh. The Mistress gave a muffled grunt. Charlotte imagined the Mistress's lips wrapped around the base of the masked man's stem, her mouth crammed full with his throbbing flesh; she envied her.

Still keeping her eyes on Maria's mouth, she just managed to twist her head sideways and get her tongue to the inside of the Mistress's thigh. Perform well, and she'd be rewarded. She knew exactly what reward she'd choose, given a choice. An orgasm. Fingers would do. A tongue would be better. Best of all, the man's cock, hard and deep, pistoning into her with all the force his lean firm loins could deliver.

A fingertip stroked the shaft of her clit. She managed to lift her hips to it, despite the straps' restraint. A pointed nail tickled her ribcage.

Maria stood. Was she done already? No. She was just changing her position. She straddled the Mistress's body and dipped her head again. The glossy pink skin between the Mistress's clit and vagina was tight over her pubic bone. That gleaming stretch was Maria's tongue's target. Its point made little whorls, paused and tapped. Maria curled her upper lip back, exposing her teeth. With incredible delicacy, those sharp edges scrapped across sensitive skin.

The Mistress grunted again and twitched up. Maria lifted her head, spat, and pushed her closed mouth down. She spread her saliva with hardened lips, nuzzling it into smooth pink skin that showed a throbbing tracery of fine blue veins.

Charlotte couldn't see it, but the underside of Maria's chin had to be rubbing against the head of the Mistress's clit. Determined to participate, she found a tight tendon that ran inside the Mistress's thigh and laved it with the flat of her tongue.

The hands on her body moved. One hand's fingers drummed on the pouting dome of her sex. The other slid wetted pads up the length of her right nipple, drawing on it gently.

Maria lifted her head once more. She winked at Charlotte

and pressed her chin down on the Mistress's mound, forcing her clit even further from its protection. Maria's lips hardened into a beak and pecked at the head of the Mistress's clit.

Gobbling and slurping sounds came from where the Mistress's head had to be. The fingers that had been drumming on Charlotte's mound stopped. The heel of a palm pressed down, eased, pressed again, and found a tormenting rhythm. Charlotte could feel that each compression squeezed her clit out. Each relaxation allowed it to withdraw. Its movement, within its hood, was a fiendish form of masturbation. While that slow torment continued, the level of her lust was kept at a peak. Unless it accelerated, she could never achieve her climax. She humped up at the hand. It stopped, waited until her hips subsided, and then resumed, no faster and no slower than before.

Maria opened her mouth wide. The tip of her tongue flicked up and down to a slow steady beat for a few moments, and then wagged from side to side. Charlotte nodded her understanding. She was being shown what Maria's tongue would be doing when it was out of Charlotte's sight.

The mouth descended. The head of the Mistress's clit disappeared between its rigidly gripping lips. The Mistress's legs went stiff. Charlotte could visualise exactly what was going on inside Maria's mouth. Her lips were holding the Mistress's clit, clamped still, hood skinned back. That sinuous tongue was stroking, up and down, up and down. At the moment that the stimulation was just about to give the Mistress her release, it was pausing, waiting for a long moment, and then resuming its action, but from side to side.

Charlotte had never been given such expert oral lessons, but she could easily imagine what it felt like. It would be exquisite torture. A few minutes of that edging towards climax, and then being pulled back every time, and she'd have been screaming.

There were gulping and gargling noises from the Mistress, followed by a satisfied sigh and a loud licking of lips. For a moment Charlotte thought that Maria had erred, allowing the Mistress to tip over the edge. Then she realised that the sounds were those of a truly lascivious mouth, welcoming a man's hot cream. That too was a lesson. The few times she'd brought a man to climax in her mouth she had swallowed swiftly and silently. Perhaps, when consuming a man's fresh-spilled spunk, oral noises were not only permitted, but to be encouraged.

Maria began to hum.

The Mistress sat up and pulled the slave-girl's face from her sex. 'Enough, Maria. Let's see what the bitch can do with her mouth.'

Charlotte was amazed. What self-control! The Mistress had been held at the brink of orgasm for at least ten long tantalising minutes, and she was able to call a halt to it. All she'd had to do was lie still, or order, 'Do it!' and she could have enjoyed her release.

Charlotte was suddenly ashamed at her own weakness. A real woman was strong. A real woman could rejoice in her pleasure, but always under complete self-control. No wonder the Mistress had punished her. She'd allowed her lust to control her. She'd deserved every cut of the crop, every icy drop of the hose. Never again, she swore. Let them do their utmost, never again would she writhe and beg for release. Perhaps there was wisdom in that. A climax is a destination. It could be that the journey was more important than the arrival.

Then the Mistress said, 'Blanche, get this man's cock hard again. I can't stand having a limp dick lolling around. You, the bitch. Show me what you've learned.'

Someone pushed the benches closer. Charlotte's upside-down face was squished up tight into the Mistress's groin. Her nose was tucked between her buttocks. She snorted, deliberately blowing hot air against the woman's anus. Her tongue extended, sliding into humid sponginess, seeking smooth slick surfaces to lick. With her face reversed, there was no way she was going to be able to duplicate every caress that Maria had performed, and she didn't want to. Slavish mimicry wouldn't suffice. She'd learnt her lessons, but she'd adapt them to her own use, her own style.

She burrowed, squirming her face as far into the Mistress's sex as she could. She was determined to lick the Mistress in places deeper and more intimate, than anyone had ever licked before her.

It was delicious in there. It was sweet and salt, and spicy. There was a trace of brandy-glazed baked pears to her nectar. Charlotte snuffled and insinuated, deliberately letting the obscene animal noises her mouth made show just how much she was enjoying what she did.

The Mistress leant forward over Charlotte's body. Her fingers spread into fans that flickered the tips of rigid nipples.

Charlotte spread her jaws wide. Her mouth opened, further and further. The inside of her lower lip slithered over the glossy skin that coated the underside of the Mistress's pubic bone. Straining even further agape, Charlotte managed to get her lip to the head of the Mistress's clit. Her tongue twisted as it stabbed. Her lip trembled. She stopped, nipped left and right and centre, and pressed inward once more. She found smoothness, closed her lips on it, and sucked hard. This was exactly what she had done as a teenager, when a boy had requested a love bite as his neck's badge of honour. Leaving one on the Mistress's pussy, would be akin to leaving a flag atop Mount Everest; a sign that she had been where few, if any, had gone before her.

The fingers on her nipples held still, then gripped and tugged. Charlotte felt her breasts being lifted up from her chest. One breast was released. The freed hand spread on her other breast, pushing down. With her left breast flattened and its nipple plucked high, the strain on her flesh as it elongated was a delicious agony.

She lifted her head, deserting the Mistress's pussy, fumbled with her lips, and clamped on that oversized clit. It was big enough, and long enough, for her to treat it like a tiny cock. She sucked and relaxed, sucked and relaxed, drawing it in and releasing it, giving it head the way she would have done to a man. Her reward was the Mistress shifting forward on her bench, lifting up over Charlotte's mouth, and twitching down.

The Mistress's clit was fucking Charlotte's mouth.

Daringly, Charlotte clamped on it, threatening it with her teeth, and holding the Mistress still. She flattened her tongue and licked hard four times. Then she made her tongue into a point, circled the pulsating head, and then nodded up.

The Mistress grunted and jerked. She almost toppled forward, to Charlotte's delight. One hand flattened a breast. The other landed on Charlotte's mound. Both squeezed. Charlotte matched her mouth's tugging at the Mistress's clit with the Mistress's palpitation of her sex and breast. The Mistress soon realised what Charlotte was doing. The squeezing rhythm slowed, and so did Charlotte. It accelerated. Charlotte followed suit. It paused. Charlotte waited.

Squeeze, squeeze, squeeze, fast and furious. Suck, suck, suck, just as frantic. It was as if the compression by the Mistress's fingers was being transmitted through Charlotte's flesh to the Mistress's clit. She was masturbating herself, through Charlotte.

Faster and faster. Harder and harder. Just as Charlotte thought that her ploy had broken the Mistress's iron control, the woman stopped.

'That was excellent,' she said. 'You have earned the privilege of giving me an orgasm. Keep perfectly still.'

Charlotte froze. The Mistress swayed from side to side, dragging her flaccid open sex across Charlotte's slack lips. She counted down, 'Five, four, three, two, one . . . Now!'

Female essence gushed over Charlotte's face. It was incredible. The amazing woman had withdrawn from the physical stimulation that Charlotte had been giving her, and with no more contact than the slow wet drag of pussy-lips across Charlotte's mouth, she had willed herself into an orgasm.

What control! Not only could the Mistress resist her climax, delaying it indefinitely, but she could summon one at will.

A flood of understanding stunned Charlotte. This was what it was all about. If she could but master that incredible power, an infinity of sexual pleasure would await. A woman with that much control over her own body could make love for as long as she could stay awake, climaxing when it suited her, or letting stimulus after stimulus drive her level of lust to heights that mere mortals could only dream about.

Charlotte was still dazed by the revelation as they lifted her head and pulled the second bench closer, to allow her to rest on it. The Mistress straddled Charlotte's face and settled her sex down on to her mouth.

'That was one. Two more, and you will be rewarded. You may begin.'

Charlotte started to lick.

Fourteen

Charlotte rinsed the stiffness of the Mistress's dried spendings from her face.

Blanche, waiting meekly in attendance, asked, 'Are you sure there's nothing else I can do for you, ma'am? Short of giving you an orgasm, of course. The Mistress says that I'm not to, for now.'

'Nothing, thanks. Go do whatever it is you do. All I want is rest.'

'Very well, ma'am. More oral lessons later, right ma'am?'

Later? She meant tomorrow, surely. She was still keeping up the stupid game of 'Don't let Charlotte know what time, or day, it is'.

Charlotte could play games, too. She acted out her elaborate charade of settling down to sleep. In bed, she cuddled her bolster down under the covers, plumped it up, and slithered out from under the clothes on the side away from the watching mirror. On hands and knees, she crawled to the window, found her nail file, and set to work. Once the third screw was loose, she crawled back under her bed to perform her second act of disobedience. She whispered through the vent, 'Veronica? Are you there?'

'Charlotte, dear? Are you all right?'

'It wasn't too bad today. They didn't beat me much this time. It's mainly sexual frustration that I'm suffering from. The Mistress made me lick her until my tongue ached. She soaked me from my chin to my hair, but she still didn't let me . . . Could you – er – would you . . .?'

'You want me to do you with my fingers again, like before?'

143

'Please?'

'You really are a horny little bitch, aren't you? Here you are, the prisoner of a gang of sexual sadists, and all you think about is the itch in your damned pussy. Why don't you do it for yourself? You're under your bed, right? No one could see you.'

'I – I hadn't thought. I suppose I could, but it wouldn't be the same, would it?'

'Not dirty enough for your taste? Straight masturbation has become too normal for you? It has to be perverse in some way, for you to get off on it, right? Being diddled by another woman, your stepsister perhaps, is more to your kinky liking?'

'Please?'

'I did you last time. You think I'm not being made to suffer just as much as you are?'

'I'm sorry. I was being selfish. You're right, Veronica. I'm no good.' Charlotte stifled a sob.

'There, there. I understand. Be brave. I'll do it for you, dear, but be fair. Do me first.'

'Of course. Can you get your – get close to your side of the vent?'

There was the noise of Veronica moving. Charlotte stretched through the vent and groped. Nothing.

'Reach up, you silly goose!'

Charlotte bent her arm at her elbow and fumbled vertically. Her fingers brushed a curve of smooth hard flesh. The underside of Veronica's thigh? A mental picture formed of Veronica, leaning back against the wall and squatting down low, with her legs spread wide. That meant that the vent couldn't be under the bed, on Veronica's side, but it still had to be out of sight of whatever way they were peeping into Veronica's room. She'd have to ask her stepsister about that.

Fingers gripped her hand. From a muffled distance, Veronica said, 'Here.' The fingers steered hers, sliding their tips over satiny skin, to warm loose pulpy softness. She fumbled, found a puckered parting, and fingered the folds open. There was seeping wetness inside.

144

'My clit, you ninny! No time for foreplay. They could come for one of us at any time.'

'Sorry!' Charlotte flattened her palm on squishy flesh and cupped it. The heel of her hand pressed up, compressing Veronica's sex, pushing it into her body. Charlotte's curled fingertips touched a fine pelt of silk-smooth hair; so they hadn't depilated Veronica. She brushed her fingertips from side to side, feeling for a fleshy ridge or for anything that would indicate the presence of a clitoris. It wasn't so easy, searching blind. No wonder those boys, in the sagging backseats of cheap English cinemas, had seemed so clumsy in their adolescent groping. She'd been impatient with them then. Now she had more understanding.

'You're missing it,' Veronica hissed. 'Here.' A hand wrapped hers. A finger lay alongside her index finger. It guided Charlotte's digit, and there it was; a naked little nodule of hot flesh, wet and vulnerable under the pad of her finger.

'Do it then! Hurry up!'

Charlotte pressed and wobbled.

'More!'

Charlotte made her finger vibrate faster and faster.

'That's it, little stepsister! Do me good, fuck you!'

Charlotte paused. Veronica wasn't usually so crude in her language. What she was doing to her must have peeled away a layer of her civilised sophistication. Her finger was getting to Veronica, and that was gratifying.

Perhaps she should have been just as crude herself, when a man had been doing his best to please her body. It was a form of applause, and everyone works better when their efforts are appreciated.

She pressed harder and used two fingers, flickering them over the vibrant nub as quickly as her tiring wrist would let her.

'Yuh, yuh, yuh!' It was part-way between 'yes' and a grunt. Veronica was bobbing up and down on springy thighs, making it harder for Charlotte to maintain pressure on the exact spot. Then there was a long whistling sigh. Wetness seeped into her palm. She felt Veronica stand up, lifting her sex beyond Charlotte's reach.

'My turn,' she hissed through the vent.

'No time! They're here for me. Tomorrow.'

Charlotte went back to her lonely bed. Eventually she slept.

Fifteen

Charlotte thought the Mistress looked incredibly desirable in her mid-thigh boots, glossy black leather cache-sex and laced-up leather waistcoat. There were two sets of criss-crossed leather laces: the one that held her top together and the one that formed an open fly to the scrap of soft leather that was moulded to her pubes. Given permission, Charlotte would have loved to undo both sets, using just her teeth and tongue. Then, perhaps, she'd get her mouth on that lush body again. She would love to nibble and graze at it.

Her erotic daydream was interrupted when the Mistress said, 'This man's cock needs to be properly prepared. Here!' She tossed a tangle of leather at Charlotte.

'We don't want him coming too easily,' the Mistress continued. 'It's been a while since we allowed him to have an orgasm and he's spent the last few hours watching Maria and Song-li make love. Men find that sort of thing very stimulating. The state he's in, two good strong sucks and he's likely to ejaculate. We can't allow that. Put that on him to slow him down.'

Charlotte, nude except for a golden collar and massive gold chains around her wrists, waist and ankles, squatted to sort out the web of leather straps.

The masked man stood magnificently tall and proud, and waited with apparent indifference. He had an air of command about him, even though he was almost naked. He was wearing a collar around his throat. It was hard black leather, too thick to be flexible, too wide to be comfortable. There were brass studs all the way around it and

147

rings set into it at both sides and front and back. That was all he was wearing, except for his mask. His arms were bent behind his back and held there by a wooden block. Even so, he radiated serene arrogance. His deeply dimpled chin was raised high.

If he was a prisoner, he was the Man in the Iron Mask. If he was a slave, he was Spartacus. Perhaps he was Prometheus, chained for his audacity but still unbowed.

Despite the Mistress's words, he didn't look all that much aroused, sexually. His cock was impressive, but only half erect. It was a down-curved arc of flesh, thick but pliable. Its head was modestly concealed within a wrinkled hood.

Still, the Mistress was an expert in these things. Charlotte wasn't familiar with men's cocks that weren't engorged. The only times she'd ever seen her boyfriends' cocks had been after extended petting and foreplay, when they were up, stiff and throbbing. Most of her limited experience of cocks had been by touch, in the dark.

It seemed as if this poor man was being exposed to sexual stimulus of some sort or another every waking moment. No man could maintain an erection all the time, not even in the sexually charged atmosphere of the *schloss*, could he?

Part of the complex harness was a belt. That part's use was obvious. Charlotte looped it around the man's muscular waist from behind. Getting close enough to reach around his waist from the front would inevitably have brought some part of her body into contact with his cock. She wanted that, desperately, but wasn't sure how she'd handle the situation if he suddenly engorged and her face was just inches away. Her mouth might find the temptation too great.

'Get on with it!' the Mistress snapped.

There was a strap dangling over his belly, and three rings. The rest of the weird contraption hung to his knees. Three rings? Charlotte took a deep breath. She could see how they were to be used. All she had to do was bring herself to use them on him.

148

She took the limp length of his cock in her hand. It twitched in her palm, dry and burning hot, like a snake that had been basking in the desert sun. There was a mole on his foreskin, about a quarter of an inch back from his glans and just to the right of centre. The skin was like glazed suede, textured but smooth. As she tightened her grip, the living cylinder flexed. She'd better complete her task quickly. If his cock got thick and stiff it'd be harder for her to do with it as the Mistress required.

Charlotte pushed the top ring over his still-sheathed glans. It was a tight fit over the bulge of his cock's head, but once it passed the swollen part it slithered down his shaft to his cock's base fairly easily.

'Tighter,' the Mistress ordered.

Tighter? How? Oh yes. The ring was like a belt, with a soft plastic buckle. Using delicate fingertips, careful not to nip his skin, Charlotte pulled on the loose end. A little round tang slipped from one hole to the next. The man grunted, though Charlotte couldn't tell whether this was from pleasure or pain – or both.

'Two notches tighter,' the Mistress said.

Two? God, that'd strangle him, and he wasn't fully erect yet, though he was stiffening rapidly. That was the point, she supposed. Throttled like that, his blood could pump into his flesh, engorging it, but its exit would be slowed. He could get bigger and harder, but not smaller or softer. Would it be painful for him? She had no way of knowing.

Two sharp tugs adjusted the belt as stranglingly tight as the Mistress required. Charlotte crouched down, trying to ignore the slow strong pulse that throbbed through the thick vein up the underside of his now-wagging, vibrant cock. Averting her eyes was difficult, because now she had to deal with the other two loops, and the dangling sack of his scrotum.

How anything that hairy and wrinkled could be beautiful, she didn't know; but it was. Perhaps it was the knowledge of the rich liquid fruitfulness that was held within. Perhaps it was a natural feminine instinct to want to draw out the precious warm milk in any way she could.

There was pressure there. It needed release. That was a woman's part; to release the pressure in a man's testes. She could make it squirt into her own body, through her vagina; or she could stroke his cock with her fingers until it spat staccato bursts of hot seed into her palm; or she could use her mouth on it. She could suckle on him, like a baby at its mother's teat, and suck musky essence of man into her mouth, to let her thirsty tongue savour its flavour fully before allowing that sweet thick juice to trickle slowly down her throat.

Doing that would be like consuming him, wouldn't it? Literally eating him. Swallowing a man's precious seed gave a woman possession of him, or at least a part of him, forever. United. One flesh. Perhaps that was why men didn't like women to spit their come out. It was a form of rejection.

Taking the utmost care not to squeeze, she separated his balls inside their pendulous sack and guided one through each leather noose. Not waiting for the Mistress to give instructions, she tightened them both. His sex was divided into three distinct parts: a cock, and two balls. Each was gripped and constricted. Each had been restrained and enslaved by her. It gave her a peculiar feeling of ownership, of responsibility. His sexual parts had been conquered, captured and bound, by Charlotte. She owned them now. They had become hers. Their welfare was in her hands.

There was still more to the vicious contraption. A thong now dangled from behind his scrotum; a thong with an implement attached.

'Here!' The Mistress tossed her a long-necked plastic-bottle of oil. 'Turn him round and bend him over. Do it from behind. Oil it, and him.'

Yes, she would. She'd oil both the obscene thing and the intimate place it was going to be forced into. The more oil she applied, the less he would suffer, she hoped.

Her fingers touched the hard column of his thigh. Obedient to her signal, he turned his back to her and bent forward, thrusting the split of his backside at her face. Charlotte sat back on her haunches, unsure where to start.

He had such a masculine bottom. Two hard flat slabs, where she had twin rounded soft cushions. There were three faint ridges across his right buttock and two decorating his left. He too had known the sharp kiss of the Mistress's cane. They had shared that pleasure-pain. Somehow the knowledge made Charlotte feel drawn to him. They were fellow victims. The Mistress had abused them both.

Her nervous fingers lifted the plastic bottle. Its long soft spout nudged at his crease. How was she to gain entrance? As if sensing her dilemma, his bottom relaxed. His cheeks parted for her. She squirmed the nozzle, found the open core of a tiny wrinkled crater, and pushed. The nozzle sank in; a quarter of an inch; half an inch; a full inch. His sphincter spread wide over the cone of its tapered neck.

A sudden wicked impulse made Charlotte thrust. There was dragging resistance, but it gave. Three full inches of the soft pliable spout slid into the masked man's rectum.

Oh God! She'd enjoyed doing that, hadn't she! She'd taken glee in acting the masculine role; she was being the ravisher instead of the ravished. And now, like a man, she was going to squirt liquid into the body of her dear victim.

She compressed the bottle, jetting oil into his rectum. She pushed in another inch, and squeezed again. She went in further and pumped; withdrew a fraction and pumped again. Was what he was feeling at all like the sensations she had felt, when a man had climaxed inside her, filling her vagina with his hot wet come? Was it seeping now, permeating him? Could he feel that slow tickling trickle as it lubricated every internal crease and fold?

She steadied her bottle with one hand and put the heel of her other palm to its base. One good hard shove would show him exactly what she was; his Mistress and his owner. Her strength would stretch his flesh. She would do it to him for no other reason than that she could, and he couldn't stop her.

Her arm braced – and relaxed.

No. She was no rapist. Had he asked her to violate his anus, distend it painfully and pierce it to the quick, she would have done so with the utmost pleasure. He hadn't asked. He was helpless and bound. That was important. Inflicting pain was no sin if the person who suffered it wanted it. Strap and tie, beat and bite, tease and torment; all were permissible, with mutual consent.

Then how about her? She'd been bound and beaten, teased and denied release until her sexual need had been an unbearable torment. Had she, in a way, consented? If she had really demanded her release, struggled and fought, would they have let her go? Was she somehow a willing participant in all the indignities that had been heaped upon her? Had she surrendered, not because she had no choice, but because surrender was seductive?

Perhaps she had. Charlotte set the thought aside, though she wasn't sure why. Was it because the possibility that what she was enduring was an elaborate charade and was comforting; an assurance that she would never be really hurt? Or was it because acknowledging that she was a co-conspirator with the Mistress and her staff in her own humiliation and degradation would spoil the game?

Don't think about it. The answers are too complicated.

She plucked the bottle out. The rim of his anus gripped it for a moment, before releasing it with a soft plop. Charlotte squirted oil lavishly all over the obscene thing she held in her other hand and prepared to use it.

It was only five inches long; a flexible rod of black rubber topped by a hard ball as big as a plum. She could have taken it into her vagina with ease. An anus was different though, particularly a man's anus. Men are made to penetrate, women to be penetrated. What she was about to do was an unnatural reversal of that, which was why a part of her was gloating.

She set the slippery ball between his hard cheeks, nuzzling it against his puckered hole. Her thumb pressed. He eased open. For a second the ball was lodged half in and half out, like an egg in an egg cup. An ounce more pressure and it plopped in. His sphincter closed, gripping the slender shaft. It was inside him, stretching that strong tight channel. It was a foreign object, lodged inside his body. He

152

stood as though he felt nothing but he had to be supremely conscious of its hard invasive presence.

Charlotte pushed and pushed, easing five inches of flexible shaft inside him. Eventually, just the thong that was attached to its base dangled. Charlotte lifted it, found the ring at the back of his belt, threaded it through, pulled tight and tied off.

What did he feel? Now the strap from his belt was tightly anchored to the ring that throttled his cock. That ring, in turn, held the two other rings that divided his scrotum into two separate weighty sacks. From there the thong threaded between his thighs, was fixed to the invasive instrument that plugged his rectum and ran, still tight, up to the small of his back.

He straightened. Even that must have afforded him some discomfort, with his anus plugged. His cock was fully erect now, straining in a vibrant arc. Even as she watched, it darkened. Veins stood proud, transforming smoothness into gnarled complexity.

Everything that was sexual about him was restrained and under unyielding tension. If the man took so much as a single step, the harness would wag his cock for him, wobble his testicles, and move the distending lump that was lodged high inside his rectum. His whole being had to be focused on his sexual parts. He had to need release, desperately.

A man's erotic need, distilled. Part of Charlotte found that shiveringly delicious. Her hand reached out to caress the man's bottom, partly because she wanted to feel its downy texture under her fingertips, but mainly because she wanted to stimulate him even further. She wanted him to want. She wanted him to be crazy with desire for her. She let her nails prickle on his skin.

The Mistress stalked a circle around the man and Charlotte, inspecting. 'Very well, he is prepared,' she said. 'What are you going to do with him now?'

'Suck his cock, very slowly?' Charlotte guessed.

'In due course, yes, but don't be in such a hurry. Savour your power, Charlotte. Up to now you have been the subject of our exercises. You've been teased and tormented,

153

and punished when it has been necessary. This man has been one of my instruments in tantalising you, Charlotte. Now you have the chance to repay him for all those torturing licks and maddening caresses. The constriction of the strap around the base of his cock will delay his orgasm. Do you think that is enough?'

'I – I don't understand, Mistress.'

'Blanche, show Charlotte what I mean.'

The crisp-nippled girl opened a pot of white cream.

'It's a topical analgesic,' the Mistress explained. 'A local anaesthetic, if you like.'

Blanche made a fist around the man's painfully engorged shaft and pulled his foreskin even further back. She scooped up some ointment and smeared it over his purpling glans. Her palm massaged it slowly but insistently into the glistening skin of his dome.

'That will delay his orgasm even further,' the Mistress said. 'His cock's head will numb, and it is the stimulation of a man's glans that is the physical cause of his orgasm.'

'But . . .?'

'Yes?'

'If he's numb, Mistress, won't that kill his desire?'

'By no means. That's the beauty of it.' She touched a finger to her forehead. 'Lust is born here. That's why young boys have wet dreams. Girls too, but theirs aren't so obvious. This –' she tapped the side of the man's cock with her cane '– is simply the trigger that releases it. A man's lust doesn't begin in his cock. It ends there. With his glans deadened and his cock's shaft strangled, we will be able to drive him into agonising paroxysms of want. Only an incredibly strong stimulus will be able to overcome what we have done to him and grant him his climax. We are going to have fun with him, aren't we, Charlotte?'

The thought of the torment she was about to inflict had Charlotte close to salivating. 'Oh yes, Mistress. We will. I'll do my very best to make it unbearable for him.'

Blanche wiped the man's glans clean with a damp cloth.

'It has no taste,' the Mistress said, 'but we don't want to deaden your mouth when we get to that stage, do we?'

Charlotte stretched a hand towards the man's darkly rearing column. 'Shall I . . .?'

'Oh no. Not yet. Let's start with some nice slow foreplay. You! Man! Kneel for your Mistresses!'

Awkwardly because his hands were confined behind his back by the wooden manacles, the man knelt to one knee and then both.

'Kisses first,' the Mistress said. 'Teasing kisses. Let him taste your mouths. Maria – you first.'

The man was so tall, and the girl so short, that she didn't have to stoop far to take his face between her palms and bend her mouth to his. Charlotte watched in envious fascination as the diminutive Filipino extended her tongue. Its tip slid between one corner of his lips, and dragged across to the other corner. He opened his mouth wide, encouraging a deeper invasion. She curled the tip of her tongue up under his upper lip, slithered it across between lip and teeth, and then returned it, probing beneath his lower one.

He swayed towards her, but she leant back, denying him more than her tongue's point.

'Song-li!'

The Eurasian took the Filipino's place. She didn't use her tongue at all, but simply nibbled with small white teeth; the upper lip first, then the lower one, then back up again. The man made a little pleading sound, deep in his throat. It was the first noise that Charlotte had heard him make.

'Blanche! Your turn.'

Blanche used her supple pale lips. She fitted them softly to his, moaned into his open mouth, and brushed them from side to side. When his tongue darted out, she snatched her mouth back. As it retreated, she returned to her tantalising caresses. She licked her own lips, coating them with her saliva, and used them to paint his. Her mouth slid across the man's, letting him taste her but denying his tongue entry.

Blanche reached sideways, beckoning Song-li. The Eurasian bent her face close. Blanche turned her mouth from the man's and kissed the slave-girl, hard and deep, one hand drawing the girl's head closer as the other held the man's at bay.

Two pairs of feminine lips parted, very slowly, inches from the man's mouth. Extended tongues tangled. The man stretched his, straining to reach. As one, the girls turned to him, stabbed both of their tongues into his mouth, and snatched back before he could react.

Both holding his collar, they trailed their slack mouths across his cheek, to his ears. Blanche nibbled on a lobe. Song-li slithered her body around him, dragging the tips of her childish nipples across his naked shoulder, and crouched at his back. Vicious little teeth nipped between his shoulder blades. A hot tongue laved his spine, down to the small of his back and up again to the edge of his collar. The man shivered and groaned.

The Mistress said, 'His mouth is yours now, Charlotte.'

Charlotte hooked her fingers into the man's collar, getting a firm controlling grip. She looked into his eyes, silently promising him that she would outdo the teasing that he had already endured. Her tongue slid out and retreated; once, twice, three times. She flattened the palm of her other hand on his chest, with her fingers hooked just enough to let him feel the points of her nails. Her mouth brushed his cheek, touched the corner of his mouth, and planted a tiny kiss.

She raised herself, bringing her mouth to the level of his eyes. There she let it slacken and show the intensity of her oral lust. She pursed her lips as her mouth descended once more, blowing gently, caressing his cheek with her breath.

The man's breathing deepened. His face and chest flushed. He made kissing motions with his lips.

Charlotte darted, catching his lower lip between her teeth. Her own lips were still swollen from the ravaging his mouth had inflicted on her. Now it was her turn. She nipped, harder and harder. He moaned. His mouth was wet. Charlotte could taste his saliva. She sucked as she bit, drawing from the pool of his mouth. Her tongue flicked over the inner surface of his lower lip. She rimmed it inside and out before releasing it, to take a grip on his upper lip.

Charlotte chewed, deliberately vicious. The man's grunt told her that she was inflicting pain, delicious pain. Her teeth released him. Her tongue soothed where her teeth had bruised. When his mouth softened in response, she nipped again. Caress followed bite. Bite followed caress, keeping him in confusion, as pleasure and pain melted together.

Charlotte moved her body closer, brushing his chest with her rigid nipples. The hand that had been pressing his chest lifted to trail down his cheek, and across the stiff leather that circled his muscular neck. She dragged her nails down the slab of his pectorals, and dropped lower. The backs of her fingers touched the underside of his rearing male flesh. It was as hot as a fever, as hard as mahogany, and stiff enough to snap.

She made a fist around his shaft, delighting in the strong pulse that beat into her palm. Holding him, she looked into his eyes once more, reading his silent plea for her to stroke and squeeze; she smiled a denial.

Instead, she dragged his face to hers. Her tongue plunged into his mouth, writhing, wet and lascivious. He pressed against her, despite her grip on his collar. She pulled her tongue back. His followed. Charlotte's cheeks hollowed as she drew on his tongue, sucking it deep into her mouth. When she was sure that it was extended to its fullest length, she bit down, trapping it.

He gasped. She used her free tongue on his captive one. She tickled its upper surface, wormed around it, and tasted the sweet liquor beneath it. She sucked hard in a steady rhythm, pumping at it. It was her toy, her oral plaything. Charlotte was in complete control of the man's tongue. She could inflict pain on it, or delight it with tantalising pleasures.

Relenting at last, she kissed him fully, allowing his tongue free-rein, letting it explore her mouth. He was returning lust for lust, drinking and being drunk from.

He sighed into her mouth. She squeezed on the bulb of his cock, letting him know where she intended to torment him next.

The Mistress said, 'He is totally yours, Charlotte. Use him as you will. Make him suffer. The three servants will obey you for now, if you require assistance. Use anything you like. We have paddles and canes, if that is your desire. This chamber is amply furnished with restraining devices. You may stand him, bend him, stretch him, or whatever you wish. I place just two restrictions on you. His cock may not enter your sex, nor may you use him to achieve your orgasm. Apart from that, he is all yours.'

Charlotte stood, dazed by the wealth of possibilities. Her own human toy! The erotic power of the idea made her clench her vagina, squeezing out a few drops of moisture to coat the outer lips of her pussy.

'For how long, Mistress?' she asked.

'Until he climaxes. When he does, he is free of you, and I have plans for your torment, Charlotte, in which he will participate.'

It was fiendish! She was free to drive him mad with lust, and to prolong his agony for as long as she was able, but every moment that she did, she too would be further inflamed with desire. By torturing him, she was torturing herself, and at the end of it all, no matter how long she made him last, was the prospect of further erotic teasing for her. She had no doubts. The more she made him suffer, the worse he would treat her when her time came. She could postpone her own suffering, but only at the price of escalating it.

But, if she was merciful and gave him swift release, there was no guarantee that he would be equally kind. And did she want him to be? That was another of those questions she would rather not ask herself.

Charlotte came to a decision. She would enjoy her power while it was hers. What followed would follow.

First, how to restrain him? She wanted his body to be available from every direction. She wanted him helpless, and perhaps to suffer a little discomfort. There was so much to chose from. The wall bars? But then he'd have to either face them or have his back to them. Charlotte wanted access to his avid mouth, his cruelly plugged rear, and especially to his poor aching, tightly strapped cock.

There was the leather half-wheel, that she'd been forced

to crouch on, her bottom jutting out for them to use at their will. It'd be nice to pay him back that way, but with him kneeling, his cock would be less available. He'd be in an ideal position for her to cane or paddle him. She'd be able to reach between his thighs from behind, to tease him with her hands, but it'd be awkward to get her mouth to him. She decided to postpone that pleasure for another time; if there was one.

Blanche touched Charlotte's arm and pointed to the wall. Charlotte allowed herself to be led over. There were two wooden beams just above the wall bars, folded back. Blanche scrambled up the bars and demonstrated how the beams unfolded to form a triangle that projected out into the chamber, about seven feet above the floor.

Song-li and Maria each offered cords and straps. It was obviously up to Charlotte to show her ingenuity in utilising these restraints.

She gave swift decisive instructions. Her three assistants followed them. Within a few minutes the man was hanging, his ankles spread wide and blocked to the wall bars at points about three feet above the floor. His wrists were secured to the overhead beams. He sagged face down, his body an arc; a ship's figurehead projecting the rigid prow of his rampant penis.

Maria offered Charlotte a cane. She waved it aside. She wasn't quite ready for that, yet. Instead, she stood Song-li and Maria against the bars between his feet and within the wide splay of his thighs.

'Play with his bum,' she told them. 'Bite, pinch, scratch, whatever you like. Blanche – you may use his mouth. Tease him with your nipples, kiss him, use his lips for your pleasure. Do whatever you like to his mouth.'

'How about this, ma'am?'

Blanche did a little jump and caught the beams with her hands. Her arms bent. As she pulled herself up, first her mouth then her chest dragged across his lips. She paused when his face was level with her tiny breasts and wriggled. She flipped a nipple's thorny point on his lips.

No sooner had they pursed and begun sucking than she

lifted herself yet higher. His tongue slavered down her ribcage, over her navel, across her belly, and to her mound. She swung her legs up over his straining shoulders, and sat with her thighs wrapping his neck. With a squirm she squished the lips of her pussy on his mouth. He lapped, just as she let herself drop away from him. Flexing her thighs, she raised her body once more to allow his tongue fleeting access to her sex before it was snatched away.

Charlotte swallowed. 'That will do very well,' she allowed. 'And I . . .' She dropped to her knees, below and in front of him. There was his cock, in all its straining splendour, a few inches from her salivating mouth. He couldn't see her. Blanche's thighs and belly blinkered him. Perhaps he felt Charlotte's breath on his naked glans despite the combined deadening effects of the harness and the anaesthetic, for he lunged at her, stabbing blindly for her mouth with the lance of his cock.

Charlotte let his flesh graze her cheek. She was tempted to take him into the heat of her mouth, and she would, but she would make him wait. Ducking lower, she nuzzled against the inside of his knee. She moved in with soft lips first, and then wet-lipped, with a flattened tongue. Her humid kisses climbed slowly up the inside of his thigh, mumbling, nipping, teasing him with the tip of her tongue.

The tendon close in to his groin was wire-taut. She gnawed at it, flicking her tongue across its ridge, nibbling higher and higher until his scrotum was dangling in her hair. She moved her head from side to side, deliberately tickling him. Then she swung around on her heels so that she could tilt her face up between his thighs, and took one pendant testicle into the gaping wet oven of her mouth.

She did not close her lips on it, though. Open-mouthed, she breathed out hard, bathing his skin with humid air. Her tongue made a point, to trace barely touching lines on his skin. She could feel the tickle of his curly hairs and knew that the gentle caress was tormenting him as much as it did her.

Mouth stretched wide, she wobbled her lips around on his testicle. She crooned softly, letting the vibrations of her wordless song tingle him. Closing her mouth delicately, clamping on the stretched skin, she hummed. Her tongue buzzed on him.

The man gasped, though the sound was muffled by the softness of Blanche's thighs. Still mouthing his scrotum, Charlotte explored with a fingertip. His anus was blocked to her, but she was able to press on the base of the plug that stretched his rectum; to press and relax, press and relax; to slowly and gently sodomise him. A wet mouth closed over her fingertip as it palpitated the man's anus. She couldn't tell whether it was Maria's or Song-li's, and didn't care.

Her nails traced tantalising paths down the stretched skin behind his scrotum. He flinched with pleasure, wagging his cock above her head. Her palm stilled it. He froze in delight at that delicate touch.

The nails of her other hand prickled their way across his balls, to the constricting band that circled the base of his column, and then moved higher. The flesh she touched was burning, swollen and incredibly firm. Her nails closed on him like a pair of delicate pincers, dimpling his skin.

Charlotte withdrew her face from between the man's thighs, to inspect what she touched. The veins on his cock were like leafless vines now, entwined around a thick smooth branch. His skin was as glossy and smooth as hot wax, poured to coat an impossibly solid bar of flesh. The sheer masculine power of it took her breath away. She was torn between the urge to fall down and worship it, and the impulse to destroy it.

She could do both. That was woman's answer, since the time of Eve. Her act of adoration could dissolve its strength. Her physical love could drain it. It was part of the primeval power of women's bodies; to be able to strengthen their men, and to be able to render them helpless.

Glowing with the certainty of her special female magic, Charlotte turned her head sideways. Her mouth closed on him, clamping his shaft between her lips as if it was a cob of sweet corn that she was about to sink her teeth into. She hummed again, and shook her head from side by side, using her lips' grip to slide his foreskin up and down his shaft.

After a few shakes, she let her mouth slide higher by a fraction, to repeat the threatening caress further up his stem. Inch by inch, her lips ascended. His skin was so delicious in her mouth that she drooled. Saliva dribbled, leaking from her mouth, and ran down his fleshy cylinder. She let him feel her teeth nibbling his skin, growling on it. Then with a looser mouth, slobbering noisily, mumbling her way higher towards her goal, she reached his magnificent mushroom crown.

Her lips felt the knot beneath his glans. Charlotte pursed, sucking on it, licking through tight lips at its tender intricacy. She focused on that tiny convolution, hissed through her teeth at it, and drew on it.

His cock twitched, fighting the restraint at its base. Charlotte reared up, poised for a moment over his great glistening one-eyed dome, and swooped. Its glossy head glided across the flat of her tongue to butt hard, into the back of her mouth. She withdrew an inch and lunged back down again, battering it into her, thrusting it into the narrow constriction of her throat. Her mouth closed on it as close to its base as she could force it, and withdrew with infinite loving, lingering slowness. She gargled on it, making the most obscene animal sounds she could. Saliva bubbled in her mouth, popping against his dome. Her tongue pressed up beneath his shaft, forcing its head against the roof of her mouth.

She bobbed, faster and faster. As she bounced, her lips wobbled. She sucked and pulled back.

Oh God! It was so beautiful! A helmet of lust, pierced by an eye that led down deep to where his precious liquid seed waited, seething with its need to be released. Charlotte pursed her lips over that tiny opening. The tip of her tongue drummed into it, as if she could force it wider. She sucked, trying to draw his milk from him.

Arched above her, his body writhed in frustrated passion. His mouth groaned his need for her to bring him release. It was Blanche's sex he was moaning into, but Charlotte was the cause of that muffled plea. He was praying to her, his goddess of desire.

Very well. She wrapped his shaft in two soft hands, opened her mouth to him, and told his penis, 'Give it to me. Come in my mouth, damn you! Give me your hot cream to drink. Squirt into me!'

Pumping him, she lowered her head, stretched her mouth wide, and fitted it over his glans. She willed him to climax, and he did. Burst after burst of boiling spunk jetted out. It splashed against the roof of her mouth and flowed so fast it forced her to gulp and swallow as quickly as her throat could work.

'Very good,' the Mistress said. 'Why don't we all retire for lunch and return refreshed for Charlotte's next lesson – one in which she will be the happy victim?'

Sixteen

The damask-covered table was dominated by the tall silver salt cellar that Charlotte had stolen from the hotel's dining room. Nobody mentioned it. Nobody used it. It just sat there, a silent threat, reminding Charlotte that the Mistress could, if she wished, hand her over to the local authorities; that would mean the brutal man with the white-hot branding iron. The iron that would sear a shameful 'T', for 'Thief', deep into the delicate tissues of her breast. And then her body would be ugly forever!

She fiddled with a silk napkin under the table, running it through her trembling fingers. The fabric was as soft and as fine as the masked man's foreskin. But even that thought wasn't able to distract her from the silver phallus that stood accusingly between a bowl of fruit and an ornate silver cruet.

The Mistress devoured three bloody bacon-wrapped filets mignon; two gigantic black butter-fried Portobello mushrooms; a vast heap of Caesar salad; half a french loaf slathered with sweet butter; and the best part of a bottle of Beaujolais.

Charlotte nibbled at a simple garden salad with blue cheese dressing. It wasn't just the salt cellar that curbed her appetite. She didn't know what sort of contortions her body was going to be subjected to. It didn't seem like a good idea to face her coming ordeal with too full a stomach.

The masked couple shared the Mistress's menu, but in smaller portions. He was still plugged by the rubber dildo Charlotte had forced up his rectum. That must have made sitting uncomfortable for him; even more uncomfortable than she'd been, when she'd sat quivering in the hotel's dining room with the stiff salt cellar all the way up inside her tender sex.

Charlotte wondered what the seating arrangements said about the hierarchy. Did who ate with who indicate rank? Were she and the silent couple equals, above the servant, Blanche, and the slaves, Song-li and Maria? Or was the seating a deliberate abberation, meant to confuse her even further?

In medieval times, the lower classes sat 'below the salt', didn't they? The salt cellar was directly opposite her place. Her three companions all sat on the other side; the Mistress to her left, the cat-woman directly opposite, and the man to her right. Was that significant? If so, of what?

The Mistress laid aside her fork, half turned to the woman in the panther mask, drew her face to her own, and kissed her lips with cold ferocity while mauling one tender breast in a cruel hand. Soft white flesh bulged between crushing fingers.

Was this part of Charlotte's next lesson? Was this *Schloss Steinreich*'s version of table manners? Perhaps it was just the Mistress's impulse. Her mouth thirsted for a kiss, so she took one. Her fingers itched to torment a breast, so they took hold of the nearest.

That would be one of the advantages of owning sex-slaves, wouldn't it? Any caress that takes your fancy, you help yourself. There would be no obligation to discover whether or not the other party was in the mood; no commitment to follow one caress with another.

Foreplay wouldn't have to lead to intercourse, nor would intercourse require preliminary caresses. You could indulge your every erotic whim. If you had a notion to be licked in some intimate place, that service was instantly available. When you tired of that tongue, it had to withdraw and you owed it nothing. You could take what you wanted, from whoever you fancied, whenever you liked.

The other person's slavery liberated you from all responsibility. To be really free, Charlotte realised, you needed to own slaves.

165

The Mistress drained her glass, dabbed her lips, and stood. Two servants, a man and a woman who Charlotte hadn't seen before, scurried to clear away the table. They were dressed in full livery. Charlotte found that strangely shocking in a castle where everyone she'd seen had been half naked, except for Nurse. Even Nurse had been short skirted and had displayed an indecent amount of freckled plump cleavage. She'd been just as much a sex object as everyone else here, but in a different way.

In the *schloss*, the staff were part of the décor.

It was almost a relief when Charlotte noticed that the woman's heels were very high and the man's trousers fitted more snugly than would have been seemly in polite society. Both were handsome. Charlotte had no doubt that they were just as compliant and sexually available as Blanche or the other two girls.

The Mistress led them all back to the training room, where the three naked girls waited in a row, heads bowed. Without having to be told, they took the gold chains from around Charlotte's wrists and ankles. They had been briefed. Only Charlotte was kept in total ignorance.

'Now climb the wall bars.'

Charlotte obeyed.

'Hang from the top bar, face out.'

Charlotte turned and dangled, her bare heels precarious on the bottom bar. Hanging like that, with most of her weight on her arms, lifted her breasts to their highest. It fanned her ribcage. It stretched her waist. Her navel became a vertical slot.

She knew how desirable she must look, and relished their eyes on her. How she had changed! But a few short days before, being exposed like that, naked and with her body erotically elongated, would have had her blushing from head to toe.

No more. She knew that they all wanted her body, and she took savage glee in that. They were going to do things to her. There would be both pleasure and pain. She would welcome both. Acceptance was her strongest weapon.

The Mistress snapped her fingers. 'Blocks for her wrists.'

Maria and Song-li scaled the bars. Deft fingers clamped Charlotte's wrists into padded and lined blocks. The blocks were fastened to a bar. Charlotte released her grip and let the blocks take her weight. The two slave girls stayed on the bars, one to either side.

'I promised you a reward for good behaviour,' the Mistress told her. 'Nurse!'

Blanche moved a sidetable and set it close to Charlotte's right knee. The Nurse entered, laid a wrapped bundle down, and inspected Charlotte's breasts with a critical eye. 'I need her nipples to be stiffer,' she said.

Charlotte tensed, not knowing what to expect. She'd taken canings. Her bum wasn't that sensitive and had recovered quickly. Her breasts were different. Her breasts were an integral part of her body's beauty. Pain there, would be unbearable. The thought of having to bear scars on their loveliness was terrifying.

Song-li and Maria reached across her. Each took a breast in hand. Their heads dipped. A mouth closed on each of Charlotte's nipples, and sucked. Two hidden tongues fluttered on her peaks.

After a few moments, Nurse moved Song-li's head aside. She dabbed Charlotte's throbbing nipple dry. Charlotte knotted inside. Her nipple! Nurse was going to do something terrible to her nipple!

The woman unwrapped her bundle. She took a pair of pliers with circular jaws and fitted gleaming gold into them.

Oh no! Nurse was going to pierce her! Not that, please not that. Pleasure-pain she could take, but a piercing would be so damned permanent! Should she scream, kick, beg? Would anything she could do stop them? She was so helpless.

She'd been helpless since the moment she'd woken in her suite's bed, but there had always been that feeling that they wouldn't really hurt her, not in any permanent way. Spanking or caning were discipline. The pain passed. Weals faded. Maiming was different.

What a fool she'd been. She'd trusted these people with

the same sort of trust that she'd had in Veronica during their girlish games. No matter how perverse the things Veronica did to her were, there was that unspoken assurance that it would end, that real life would resume, with nothing to show for their depraved sport but fading bruises and deliciously shameful memories.

What an idiot – to assume that this would be the same!

Nurse pinched the tip of Charlotte's cringing nipple. She pulled on it, elongating Charlotte's breast into an obscene pink pear. The cruel pliers came closer, and closer. They fitted around the base of Charlotte's nipple. Nurse's knuckles whitened.

Charlotte closed her eyes. There was a clamping feeling, a compressing; a hard metallic pinching squeeze. She blinked and looked down. Relief almost made her swoon.

She hadn't been pierced! Her nipple was still whole; complete and undamaged. All that Nurse had done was cinch a glittering gold ring around the base of Charlotte's nipple, as tightly as she herself had buckled the strap around the masked man's shaft.

And it had the same effect. As she watched, her nipple darkened. The cylinder of flesh swelled up into a purple bead. She could feel her heart's blood throb in it.

'Nurse is an expert on nipples,' the Mistress said. 'Aren't you, Nurse.'

'Yes, ma'am. I used precise measurements. The rings will constrict just enough to keep her nipples permanently erect and very sensitive. They won't need taking off. The blood can flow just fine. All I've done is increased the internal pressure a wee bit. That's all it takes.'

Maria's mouth released Charlotte's second nipple from its suction. Nurse dabbed, stretched and clamped. Charlotte's breasts soon matched. Both nipples pulsed dark and bloated. They were prickly with their need to be touched.

'You'll enjoy this,' Nurse said. Her fingernail scratched a tip very lightly. Pleasure jolted through Charlotte's body, from nipple to clit. Her sex clenched and started to ooze.

Nurse took a strip of plum velvet and dragged it slowly across an aching nipple. Charlotte convulsed with ecstasy.

'I just knew you had the right sort of nips for this treatment,' Nurse said. 'And when I . . .' Her lips pursed. She touched them lightly to Charlotte's nipple. The gentlest suck drew the swollen hard nub into her mouth. Delicate teeth grazed with infinite care.

Charlotte sobbed and beat back against the bars with her bottom. The shock of that tiny caress had lifted her so incredibly close to an orgasm that she could feel the electricity sparking her clit and twitching the muscular lining of her vagina. If they let it continue for a few more moments, and perhaps let someone touch her clit, she'd be there! Her legs scissored the air, clamped together and scissored again. Almost anything would do it!

But nothing did. Nurse pulled back, leaving Charlotte in needful agony.

'You may thank me, and Nurse,' the Mistress said.

'Thank you, thank you, thank you.' Charlotte was babbling, truly grateful for the exquisite sensations, but thinking with her clitoris and nipples. What could she do to please them? How could she persuade them to grant her what she needed? She'd have grovelled and begged, had she been free to do so. She'd have done anything they required of her. Anything at all. If this was all some sort of elaborate plot to steal away her inheritance, they could have it. She'd have traded every penny of her birthright for the divine pressure of a finger or a tongue on her clit; or a big hard cock inside her sex, pumping, pumping, pumping.

Her hips bounced with the rhythm of her thoughts.

'I think she's ready for her next lesson,' the Mistress said. 'Her ankles, please.'

Maria and Song-li dropped to the floor. Song-li lifted Charlotte's left ankle, and extended her leg straight out from her body. She pulled it to the side, all the way back to the wall bars. Charlotte's hips twisted to follow. The two slave-girls clamped a block on Charlotte's ankle, anchoring it to the bar at the level of her hips.

'You've had ballet training, I believe?' the Mistress asked.

Charlotte nodded.

'And acrobatic dancing? Some yoga?'

Charlotte nodded again, nervously.

'Then you are limber? Able to do the splits?'

Oh no! Yes, of course she could do the splits; one leg forward and one back, or even a sinew-straining spread to either side, for a few moments. It wasn't going to be for just a few moments, though, was it?

The two naked girls took Charlotte's second ankle. She concentrated on relaxing. Resistance would make it much worse.

They drew her leg up, and out. The tendons that ran up the insides of her thighs protested, creaking and stretching. It took all of Song-li's weight, pushed against Charlotte's calf, to get her leg flat back against the bars on the opposite side. Charlotte bit her lip but a groan still escaped. Her hips felt as if they were on the point of dislocating. Her thighs were taut enough to vibrate. She felt her sex pulled wide open, its lips tugged in opposite directions. Cool air sighed into her vagina, strangely alien in a channel that was usually sealed.

Maria screwed the wooden peg home, locking the block and fixing Charlotte in place. She was inverted; more helpless and sexually available than she'd ever been before. Her entire body was pinned out waiting to be probed. And it wanted to be probed. It was desperate to be probed.

'Is that uncomfortable?' the Mistress asked in a soft, concerned voice.

Charlotte nodded.

'Is it agony?'

Charlotte nodded, then shook her head. It was painful, but not unbearable, not quite.

'Help her, Nurse. Make it easier for her.'

Nurse poured lotion into her palms and rubbed them briskly together. 'Relax, dearie,' she advised. 'Just let yourself go limp. You're safe as houses. You aren't going to fall now, are you.'

The lotion was cool on her drum-tight groin. Nurse's capable hands squeezed, massaging tortured muscles. She smoothed over and under Charlotte's thighs. Her fingers brushed Charlotte's sex's lips, sending jolts of pleasure through her.

'You're wide open, aren't you, dearie?' she asked, her mouth not three inches from Charlotte's left nipple. The breath of each word flirted with its tingling skin.

'Wide,' Charlotte managed to agree.

'If the Mistress was to let that nice handsome man fuck you, dear, he'd go in very deep, wouldn't he?' Nurse's eyes were hot on hers, feeding on her erotic needs. 'It's not just that he's big,' Nurse continued, 'but the way you're held. Your legs are out of the way, you see. He'd get so very close in to you. Your pussy is tilted as well. That'd help him get in even further. With the size and the length of him, he'd have no trouble filling you up, dear. Wouldn't that be nice?' Her hands were insistent now, pressing firmly into Charlotte's muscles.

Tears of desire filled Charlotte's eyes. The spreading of her thighs had opened her so wide and so deep, that all she wanted in the whole world was for that aching void to be filled; to be totally occupied by burning hot, rigid, forceful man-flesh.

Someone was making a breathless mewing noise. It took Charlotte a few moments to realise that it was her.

Nurse's finger tickled Charlotte's anus, playfully. Her palm slapped up at the underside of Charlotte's thigh.

'Well, you're done now, dearie. Doesn't that feel better?'

It did. Charlotte almost relaxed, but then she saw what Blanche was bringing to her.

Oh God!

The cushion was wedge-shaped and covered with black leather. No. It was impossible. She wouldn't be able to bear it. They were so unfair! Her body had adjusted to their unnatural demands. She'd stretched as wide as she could. She'd been good. How could they ask more of her?

Blanche put the hard wedge, narrow end up, against the bars beneath Charlotte. Its edge touched her skin. Blanche pushed up. The wedge forced its way behind Charlotte's bottom prying her away from the bars. Her tendons creaked. The wedge tilted her hips forward and up. The joints in her hips protested. The strain on the skin of her belly tugged on her clitoris' hood, retracting it, leaving a quivering and bloated nub fully exposed.

The heel of Blanche's hand hammered up at the cushion's lower edge, driving it higher. Charlotte knew that she was going to split; she knew it for a certainty. They'd overestimated her flexibility. There was no more elasticity in her groin. She had to tear apart. She simply had to.

And then Blanche stepped back, leaving the cushion wedged up behind Charlotte's buttocks.

She wasn't done, even then. She showed Charlotte two wide leather straps. 'These'll help,' she reassured. One strap went around each of Charlotte's straining thighs, half-way between knee and groin, and around the bar behind. Blanche had been right. With those straps taking part of her weight, Charlotte's discomfort was eased a fraction.

The Mistress said, 'Blanche, Maria, Song-li! Here. There's one for each of you. You know what to do with them.'

Charlotte stared, wide-eyed. The Mistress was tearing petals off a full-blown pink rose. What on earth was going on?

The slave-girls scaled the bars again, giggling and grinning. Perched to either side, hanging by one arm each, they reached across. Two petals, two incredibly soft smooth pink petals, caressed Charlotte's nipples.

She screamed. The savage pleasure of those gentle touches bit into her breasts. They boiled with lust. Her nipples imploded, exploded, thrummed with delight. They were as hard as diamonds, as heavy as lead; they were rooted deep in her flesh, but about to take flight.

There was an orgasm locked deep in her vagina, trembling with its need to be released. Lust crackled in her clit. Charlotte was a storm cloud, charged with erotic electricity. Anything, any stimulus at all, would enable her to discharge; to throw great jagged bolts of sexual lightning; to release the sweet aromatic rain that was saturating her sex.

She screamed, 'Touch me!'

And they did. As one, the slaves and Blanche touched Charlotte with rose petals, one to each nipple, one to her clit's head. They wrapped the triple triggers of her passion in smooth softness. Their fingertips held the petals in place while their nails' points stroked her through the delicate thickness of the petals.

Charlotte climaxed.

It was unlike any orgasm she'd ever experienced before. It wasn't that sweet relaxation, the unknotting of tension, the gentle flowing. It was volcanic, explosive, cataclysmic.

She arched, heedless of the strain on her limbs. She juddered and spasmed, and writhed. Perhaps she screamed. How could she tell, with the noise of her coming roaring through her entire being?

Eventually, she was drained. She hung, quivering for a while, and then slumped, soaked with her own sweat.

'That was nice, wasn't it?' the Mistress said. 'Are you ready for another?'

What a silly question! Of course she wasn't. She'd been emptied, totally. No one could climax with that intensity and still be ready for more.

Before Charlotte could summon the strength to reply, Song-li leant across her, to touch her lips with her tongue. Maria's tongue lapped at Charlotte's left nipple. Blanche's fingertips slipped into the squelchiness between Charlotte's thighs.

Fresh desire welled up as if it had been lurking, waiting for any excuse to rebound from its momentary quiescence.

Craving unfolded, consuming Charlotte once again. She croaked, 'More, please.'

'Then more you shall have. Give her another orgasm, girls. We are going to teach our Charlotte that a woman's lust is infinite. For a true woman, one orgasm is never enough. Sexual desire is our strength and man's weakness. A woman who is truly multi-orgasmic can enslave any man she likes. She is a challenge that no man can resist, nor overcome. Let us teach Charlotte something about her own power, shall we?'

She turned to the masked man, standing meekly to one

side. 'Watch closely, man! Witness the magic. You have ten times her physical strength, but when she has completed her training you will be as nothing to her power. Your lust for her will sap you. Her lust for you will defeat you. The war between woman and man has been continuing since Eve seduced Adam, and the delight of it is, no man has ever won a single battle, nor ever will.'

The man shrugged his massive shoulders, neither agreeing nor disagreeing, perhaps content that what the Mistress had said was self-evident and didn't dismay him one bit.

Charlotte jerked. She'd been concentrating on the Mistress's words. The two moistened fingers that Blanche wriggled into her rectum came as a total surprise. The slave-girls swung across her. Their mouths made circles that fitted to Charlotte's breasts, each ringing a nipple. They sucked rhythmically, palpitating her entire haloes. Blanche's mouth descended. Her tongue's tip traced the crease of Charlotte's left groin. It drifted up, to draw a line across the curved white plain of her belly, lap into her navel, and trail down. Sharp little teeth nibbled at the shaft of her clit.

Three naked and beautiful girls were servicing Charlotte's erotic needs, but her lust was greedy. She wanted them all to worship at the shrine of her body. Hadn't the Mistress explained that a woman's lust was magic? They should all be under her spell. Charlotte willed the masked couple to want her. She would have liked to have had power over the Mistress as well, but was sure that the imperious woman's magic was stronger than her own.

Perhaps the waves of lust that she directed at them worked, in part. Perhaps it even affected the Mistress. She pulled the masked pair to her, the girl low and the man to her breasts. Both unlaced her leather garments with feverish fingers. The waistcoat sprang apart, freeing her great white globes. The cache-sex slithered down statuesque thighs, to be kicked aside by a booted foot. The Mistress reached down to her own sex, pulled the hood from her enormous clitoris with forked fingers, and dragged the crouched girl's face close.

174

The girl's lips clamped on it. The Mistress knotted her fist in the hair at the girl's nape, and thrust with her hips. She used the girl's mouth, fucking it.

Charlotte was distracted for a moment. The lips and tongues at her nipples and pussy were working such sweet magic, she could feel the intensity building; the dam was nearing its bursting point.

She looked down at Blanche and barked, 'Drink me, slut!' Urgent, but under complete control, she allowed herself to flow. Her spending gushed; filling Blanche's thirsty mouth, it overflowed and ran down her cheeks, dripping from her chin to splatter on her pale childish breasts.

The pressure of lust momentarily lessened, Charlotte looked up. The man had left the Mistress's bosom, though the swollen state of her left nipple and the toothmarks that ringed it told a story. The Mistress must have instructed him, because he was tightening the buckle of a strap that clamped the cat-woman's elbows behind her. While she suffered, as her helpless mouth was ravaged by the Mistress's thrusting clit, he took up a rattan paddle.

The swish of its passage through the air sent a delightfully cold chill through Charlotte's sex. The whack of it revived her lust.

Tied, spreadeagled and totally helpless, Charlotte commanded, 'Song-li, take Blanche's place. Eat me good or it'll be the worse for you. Blanche! Up here. Give me your mouth. I want to suck my spending from your hot little tongue, you bitch.'

Both obeyed, instantly. With Blanche's face before hers, Charlotte couldn't see what the Mistress and the couple were doing, but the sounds of the paddle sent thrill after thrill trembling through her body. She sucked on Blanche's tongue, not kissing it, but draining it of its spending-spiked saliva. Blanche mewed and panted into Charlotte's mouth. She hung by one hand, which left the other free to twist and torture a golden-ringed nipple. Maria dropped down without instruction, to join Song-li at the fountain between Charlotte's thighs.

Filled with a newfound energy, and charged with erotic

175

power, Charlotte rewarded the two slaves' devotion by releasing yet another orgasmic flood. They slurped and gobbled, slack wet mouths working avidly, drinking in essence of Charlotte, lapping her dry before turning to each other, to tongue up the splatters that had spilled on each other's naked bodies.

There was no mouth at Charlotte's sex. That wasn't acceptable. She had the ability to will herself into an orgasm now, and she needed to use that incredible power. Perhaps her will could have achieved it unaided, but Charlotte's lust demanded that some flesh be in place, to receive her anointing. Drunk with her ability to command her own body, she required that her new proficiency be admired.

Charlotte released Blanche's tongue. 'Get your head down to my pussy! Get your sweet cunt up here, to my mouth, where I can taste it.'

It was the first time in her life that she'd used that word: cunt. It was the first time it had seemed appropriate.

Blanche reared back, supported by her toes, to either side of Charlotte's waist; she kept one hand on the bar above her head. Her free hand fumbled at her waist, releasing the thong that slotted through her sex's lips. Charlotte snapped at the girl's breast, caught a tiny nipple, and pinched it hard.

Blanche gasped, tugged free, and reversed herself. Hooking her toes over the top bar, she let herself hang down, wrapping Charlotte's waist with her arms, and burying her head between Charlotte's thighs.

Charlotte flinched with joy as hard lips clamped on her clit, and a vibrant tongue purred on its tip.

There, spread wide before Charlotte's face, was Blanche's sex. She nudged down with her chin, parting soft folds. She gazed into her slave. Even inside, Blanche was still pale. Her convolutions were as folded and intricate as an elaborate sea shell, translucent pink and glistening. Charlotte lapped.

Now she could see the rest of the chamber. The Mistress was slumped in her black leather chair now. The slick on her splayed thighs told Charlotte that she'd enjoyed at least one wet orgasm. The cat-woman was now arched backward, her hands still strapped behind her, over the chair's padded arm, the back of her head resting on the Mistress's thigh. The Mistress's fingers pinched her cheeks, opening her mouth. A pat directed the eagle-man to kneel up on the opposite arm. The Mistress took his shaft in one hand and drew it to her own mouth. She sucked and pumped, lifting her puckered lips clear off its head and them slapping them back, wetly. The man leant back, pushing his hips forward. His mouth made animal noises and liquid moans. The Mistress's fist blurred on his shaft. He let out a great croak. She tugged hard. He toppled forward, catching himself stiff-armed, flat palms bracketing the cat-woman's hips. He was a bridge, arching over the cat-woman. The Mistress directed his cock down, to within an inch of the open mouth that waited below. He came. Great foaming gouts of his cream squirted, splashing into the woman's mouth and over her face.

As the grinning mouth below the cat-mask licked up the spillings, Charlotte clamped her lips on Blanche's clit and let another of her own orgasms run free, bestowing the blessing of her spending on Blanche's face.

The Mistress pushed her two masked lovers aside, to sprawl on the floor. She writhed to her feet. 'You,' she told the cat-woman, 'get to work on Charlotte's sex. Blanche, take a break. You,' she said to the man, 'may play with Charlotte's nipples.'

Charlotte croaked, 'I want his cock.'

'Of course you do, my dear, and you shall have it. I promise. Not yet though. Not today. That's a pleasure you are going to have to earn.'

Charlotte lost count of her orgasms. The number was greater than a score, she was sure, but had no idea whether it was thirty or forty. They all used their mouths and tongues and fingers on her, except the Mistress. Even she had given Charlotte pleasure, but only with her nimble fingers, milking two shuddering orgasms out of her clit in rapid succession.

When they took Charlotte down she was quite unable to

walk. Her legs refused to obey her. She felt that the only bones left in her limp body were her hip joints, and they'd been disconnected.

They carried her up to her suite and laid her gently in her bed. A few moments later she heard someone hissing at her from the vent, but it didn't matter, did it? All that mattered was to let herself sink into the nice soft darkness that was calling.

Seventeen

Perhaps her multi-orgasmic performance had earned her status, because there was an *eau-de-nil* silk wrap waiting for her after her bath, and Blanche told her she was to go down to breakfast.

The wrap felt comfortable but strange. Her private parts were all covered for the first time since the Mistress had cut her clothes off her body. It wasn't exactly modest though. The silk was thin enough that her golden-ringed globular nipples showed through it quite clearly. It had no fastening but a slippery sash, and was skimpy enough that she couldn't pull it together over her cleavage. She had to leave an open 'v' that stretched down between the vibrant globes of her breasts to where the sash was tied, very tightly, around her narrow waist. When she walked, the front flapped open, flashing brief glimpses of her hairless sex.

The wrap wasn't very long, either. When she sat, to put on the pale blue hold-up stockings and matching high-heeled sandals that Blanche provided, she could feel the nap of the chair's velvet on the bare skin of her bottom and under her sex.

Before the *schloss*, Charlotte would have felt uncomfortably exposed. Now, after all she'd been through, the wrap seemed almost prudish.

When she got down, she and the uniformed nurse were the only two whose bodies were half-way covered. The Mistress wore a tightly cinched Victorian waspie, in lavender and blue vertical stripes, with lavender-gartered blue stockings and a lavender choker. The masked man was bare except for a tiny black satin posing pouch and his heavy leather collar. The cat-woman was in gold lamé high-cut thong panties and quarter-cup bra that offered her breasts like precious gifts. Strings of gold beads circled her neck and waist. Matching bangles adorned her wrists and ankles. Her lips and nipples had been gilded. Her cheeks, the upper slopes of her breasts, her firm round buttocks and the curve of her belly had all been sprinkled with glittery golden dust. She'd been transformed into the erotic centrepiece like one of Rio's notorious carnival floats.

Charlotte felt over-dressed. As she took her seat she contrived to accidentally slide her wrap almost off one soft white shoulder. The slither of silk across the distended tip of her right nipple made something contract nicely inside her vagina.

Breakfast was devilled lambs' kidneys and thick-sliced Wiltshire bacon with a choice of scrambled or fried eggs. The same handsome couple served from silver-domed platters. When all of the plates were full, the two servants took positions just behind and to either side of the Mistress.

'It's my turn today, isn't it, ma'am?' Nurse asked with eagerness in her voice.

The Mistress smiled. 'Impatient, Nurse?'

'It's my favourite part of the training, ma'am.'

'Yes, I know it is. It's a part I particularly enjoy, as well.'

Nurse blushed and looked at her plate. 'Thank you, ma'am.'

The Mistress smiled at Charlotte. 'Today you will have a lesson in breasts. That's a topic that Nurse is particularly expert in.'

She buttered a slice of toast lavishly. As she bit into it, butter dripped on to her fingers. She tutted and said, 'Henry!'

The manservant stepped forward. 'Yes, Mistress?'

'I've butter on my fingers.'

'Should I lick it off, Mistress?' he asked, as calmly as if he'd been offering more coffee.

'No. Take your cock out.'

Charlotte froze with a piece of kidney an inch from her mouth. She should have been accustomed to the Mistress's

180

casual use of those around her, but the man was fully dressed. Somehow that had seemed to exclude him, but she was obviously mistaken.

Without any change in his stone-faced expression, Henry unzipped, reached into his fly, and pulled out a long soft length of bone white cock. The Mistress took it from his hand, massaging the grease from her fingers into its head. It reacted instantly, thickening and lengthening on her palm. She looked at it, her head cocked as if she was trying to decide what to do with it. She shrugged, released his flesh for just long enough to dip all four fingers into the butter dish, and slathered slippery yellow goo over his entire length.

Pumping slowly, she turned back to her plate, picked up her fork, and speared a piece of bacon. She seemed intent on her meal, but as she ate her hand was still steadily slithering up and down Henry's pole, pausing only to rub a thumb's oily ball over his glans.

The man stood erect and impassive, as if this obscene exhibition was part of his everyday duties. Perhaps it was.

Charlotte wriggled on her seat and pretended not to watch, but peeped from the corners of her eyes.

'He's going to come soon, Mistress,' the maidservant observed.

'Would you like it?'

'Thank you, Mistress. As you've got him so nice and slippery, Mistress, may I take him in my arse? He likes that.'

The Mistress shrugged. 'Whatever, just so he doesn't make a mess on the carpet.'

The girl curtsied and circled behind the Mistress to where the man stood. She turned her back to him, bent at her waist, stiff-legged, and tossed her skirts up. She was wearing a frilly black garter belt with suspenders stretched tight across her haunches and down to her ebony hose; she had no panties on. Reaching behind herself, she pulled her own plump buttocks wide apart. The Mistress released the man's cock and wiped her hand on a napkin. The man turned, gripped the maid's naked hips, and lunged. She must have been well-used to that treatment, because his cock slid between her cheeks and on into her rectum without the least pause. He jerked at her hips three times, grunted, and withdrew.

Butter and spunk glistened on his shaft and dripped from his glans. He took a handkerchief from his hip pocket, wiped himself, and tucked his spent member away. The maid stood, letting her skirts fall back into place.

'Will there be anything else, Mistress?' she asked.

'You may clear away. We're all finished here. Charlotte, you may return to your suite. Blanche will bring you down later, when I am ready for you.'

Charlotte almost ran up the stairs. The lewd exhibition that she'd seen had aroused her. The lips of her pussy were tingling. If the ban on her orgasms was lifted now, she intended to use Blanche to sate her urgent need.

She burst into her room to find Blanche seated at the dressing table. She was intent on her lips, which she was coating with Charlotte's lipstick. The vivid crimson of her usually pallid nipples betrayed the way she'd already applied the make-up.

She dropped the lipstick and sprang to her feet. 'I – I'm sorry, ma'am. I had no right. It was just that I wanted to see what my lips and nipples would look like, properly red, like other girls'.'

Charlotte opened her arms. 'That's quite all right, Blanche. No harm done. Come here, dear. Let me see what that lipstick tastes like.'

Blanche cowered away. 'Oh no, ma'am. I've done wrong. You have to punish me.'

'Punish you? No, Blanche. I forgive you, really.'

'No, ma'am. That's not right. I did wrong, so I have to be punished.' She turned and bent to the bottom drawer of Charlotte's dresser. Charlotte was moved to caress the girl's uptilted bottom, but before she could act, Blanche straightened with a length of leather strap in her hand.

'This should do, ma'am. Where do you want me; on the bed or bent over the stool?'

It was tempting, but Charlotte didn't trust herself. When

182

she'd spanked Blanche that first day, the vicious glee of it had overcome her. She was less inhibited now and more in touch with the darker side of her nature. Once she started whipping the girl she might not be able to stop.

She snatched the strap from the girl's hand and tossed it into a corner. 'No! If you want to make up to me, get down on your knees and use your tongue on my clit!'

Blanche looked at the floor. 'Sorry, ma'am, but not till after you've strapped me. It wouldn't be right.'

Knotted with frustration, Charlotte screamed, 'Get out then! If you won't do as you are told, I don't want you here with me.'

Blanche closed the door softly behind her. Charlotte paced up and down, furious with herself. A few token stripes across the girl's buttocks would have sufficed. If she'd had the sense to give Blanche what she'd wanted she could be enjoying the slut's tongue, right now.

She paused in front of the mirror. There was someone behind it, wasn't there? Spying on her? Well, she'd give whoever it was something to look at. She lifted one foot up on to the stool and turned her thigh out, displaying herself. Her fingers eased the hood of her clit back.

The door behind her opened. Charlotte put her foot down.

'Mistress says you are to come down now, ma'am,' Blanche told her.

The Mistress was still in her Victorian madam's outfit, but with a cane in her hand now. The masked pair were unrestrained but bent over a padded trestle. Both of their bottoms were striped with livid welts.

The Mistress turned to Charlotte, fists on hips. 'What is this I hear? You caught Blanche stealing from you, and then refused to punish her? You denied the girl her completion?'

Charlotte stared at the carpet between the Mistress's feet. 'It was nothing. I forgave her.'

'Nothing? Who are you to say it was nothing. The girl feels guilty, and will continue to do so until she is content that she has paid for her crime.'

Charlotte twisted her sandal's toe into the carpet's pile. 'I – I hadn't looked at it like that.'

'Well, you should have. Now I shall have to punish her, for her own piece of mind. This is most inconvenient. Blanche, you know what you deserve. Tell Henry, I said he was to assist you.'

Head bowed and shoulders slumped, Blanche left the chamber.

Charlotte wrung her hands together. 'What is it, Mistress? What is going to be done to her?'

'As you failed to punish her appropriately, her penalty has to be sterner or she'll never get rid of her guilt. She will receive the punishment that she dreads the most.'

'What's that?'

'Do you care? You showed your disrespect for the girl when you refused to punish her. Blanche is proud to serve her betters, and is very good at it. She knows her place. If she does well, there are treats. She is allowed to participate in training the likes of you, for instance. If she errs, she is punished. Rewards and punishments define her life. You tried to spoil that for her. Now I will have to do without her services for a while. I am most put out, Charlotte. Just when I felt that you were responding nicely to my training, you fail me.'

Charlotte fell to her knees and looked up into the Mistress's stern eyes. 'Please, Mistress, forgive me. Punish me – anything you like, but don't tell me I've failed you.'

'Punish you? How?'

'You could use me for your pleasure,' Charlotte suggested, hopefully. 'My body is yours. Or you could beat me? I'll take the cane, or the crop, or you may whip me if you like.'

'Of course I may. I am the Mistress. No – none of those petty punishments would suffice. Think again.'

'Mistress? Whatever it is that Blanche is suffering, I will suffer it too.'

'You'd join her? Go where she has gone? Endure her punishment with her? Side by side, as equals?'

'If that will redeem me in your eyes, Mistress, gladly.'

184

The Mistress tapped the masked man on his bare buttock, and then the masked woman. 'You heard her. Take her.'

They led her away in silence, to the cold and threatening room with the three pillories. There they removed her robe and fitted a yoke to her neck and wrists. It was similar to the one she had worn before, but this one was only half as wide, and the two sections didn't match. One hinged arm was broad and the other very narrow. With the broad section on her nape the more slender part projected no further forward than the point of Charlotte's chin.

When she was secured they led her on, down a long stone passageway. She recognised the path and tried to slow down, but they took the sides of her yoke and hurried her. She had no choice but to keep up or they would have been dragging her. She had too much pride to allow that.

Her dread was justified. The room they took her into was the shadowy one with the big black wooden box.

'Is Blanche in there?'

They ignored her. The cat-woman opened the door. Charlotte peered into the darkness and thought she glimpsed a pair of pale feet, but she couldn't be sure. They propelled her inside, sliding the edges of her yoke into the shelf's slot.

The door clunked shut.

Someone breathed into her face.

'Blanche?'

'Ma'am? Is that you?'

Charlotte's fingers groped, found Blanche's, and entwined with them. Barely three inches separated the two women. A slight movement of Charlotte's foot put them toe to toe. Charlotte could feel the warmth of Blanche's thighs on her own. When Blanche took a breath, her breasts brushed Charlotte's nipples. They stood belly to belly, breathing each other's breath, locked in near contact.

As one, they swayed towards each other. Knees touched. Blanche parted hers. Charlotte's right leg slipped between Blanche's, slithering thigh on thigh, hooking around the girl's calf and drawing her closer. Their mounds brushed together, softness on softness. Belly rubbed belly. Charlotte's proud breasts dragged across Blanche's gentle swellings. Tiny pale nipples flipped swollen globular ones.

Neither could move their necks, but their mouths met. Two pairs of soft lips pressed gently together, and let that slightest pressure part them, so that each inhaled the air of the other's mouth. Each had questions to ask, but this was not the time. Their mouths had more urgent duties to perform. Two slow wet tongues explored, tentative and blind in the utter darkness. They touched. Blanche's slid higher, Charlotte's lower. Charlotte felt the wet glandular softness beneath Blanche's tongue. She probed. Blanche's tongue wagged, slithering from side to side across the upper surface of Charlotte's. It curled up, explored behind Charlotte's teeth, tightened its curl and squirmed between Charlotte's teeth and upper lip.

They drank from each other's mouths. The darkness was no longer their enemy. Being sightless enabled them to concentrate on other senses. A tongue, dabbling, made little wet splashy noises. The soft slide of skin on skin hissed erotically. The hair of Blanche's sex was light and wispy, but Charlotte felt its tickle on the sensitive skin of her own bald mound.

They were aware of each other's warmth, a dramatic contrast to the slight chill of empty air on their naked backs.

Charlotte bent her legs an inch. That tiny movement dragged the skin of her body over Blanche's. Blanche squirmed, caressing Charlotte with her entire body.

Charlotte writhed, letting a ripple run from her toes to her rigidly locked neck. Blanche returned the long slow undulation.

'Ma'am?'

'Not "ma'am". We are equals now, in here. Call me Charlotte.'

'Thank you, Charlotte. Charlotte, my body is so hot for you. I know I'm just a skinny little thing with a body like a boy's, but this body is only for you.'

'You aren't skinny, Blanche. You are slender, and very

186

attractive. If you could feel my pussy you'd know that I want you just as much as you want me.'

'If I could get to your pussy, Charlotte, I'd eat it like a pomegranate. Push against me. Tilt your hips and squish on my thigh. I want to feel your wetness. Yes! Slide on me. Fuck my leg, Charlotte!'

Charlotte slithered the open lips of her sex up and down Blanche's flexing thigh, leaving a warm wet slippery trail. Blanche stiffened the long muscle and pressed up, spreading Charlotte's blossoming petals against the firm resistance of her pubic bone. Charlotte squirmed higher, until her clit was rubbing into the crease of Blanche's groin.

'Twist your hips, Blanche! Get your pussy on mine. Let's see if we can make our clits touch.'

'It's called frottage, ma'am. The rubbing together of two pussies.'

Charlotte jerked her sex from side to side, pressing hard. 'I – told – you – "Charlotte". Say it!'

Blanche thrust back. 'Char–lotte.'

'Twist.'

They rotated their sexes, spreading their lips, squishing the wet inner surfaces together. They pressed so hard that their sexes squeaked. Clit touched clit. Both women juddered. Their mouths were together, but not kissing, just open and brushing lip on lip. A kiss demands attention, and their entire concentration was between their legs.

'Push forward, Charlotte. Feet back – legs wide – belly pressed at me.'

Charlotte untangled her legs from Blanche's and obeyed. Blanche braced her arms and lifted herself. Her calves hooked up over Charlotte's hips. Her legs bent, lowering her core on to Charlotte's. Charlotte's clit felt the warm wet sponginess inside Blanche's sex.

Blanche hissed, 'Fuck me with your clit. Do it hard, until you come. Then we change places and it'll be my turn.'

Charlotte bucked. Her clit's head slithered over and into intricate folds. It felt like an avid tongue's caress, but hotter and wetter. She jerked and jerked and jerked, until she felt the knot loosen; then the flow began, and she gushed.

Her scalding spending cascaded into Blanche's sex.

Blanche unwrapped her legs from around Charlotte and lowered her feet to the wooden floor. 'The box isn't so bad, is it –' she giggled, '– when you've got the right company.'

Eighteen

Blanche's bent-up knee slurped out of the shallow socket of Charlotte's splayed still-spasming, still-flowing pussy. Charlotte straightened from her semi-squat. The air inside the box was thick with the musk of liquefied lust.

'Is there any way we could, and we haven't tried?' Charlotte asked. There was a giggle in her voice, partly from her elation at their having turned their punishment into an erotic game, and part from being exhaustion-drunk.

'Toes?' Blanche suggested. 'If we pushed back, as far apart as we can, I could probably get my foot up between your legs. But my knees are all wobbly. Can you wait till I get my strength back? I'm not like you, ma'am. I have to rest sometimes.'

'Not like me?'

'Insatiable.'

'Am I?'

'Oh yes, ma'am. That's why . . . .'

'Why what?'

'Nothing, ma'am.'

'You were going to say, that's why I was chosen, weren't you?'

Blanche was silent.

'Tell me about Steinreich.'

'What would you like to know?'

'Well, how it's governed, for instance.'

'It's a duchy. The dukes or duchesses rule, usually both at once. The whole family, really. They share the power. Everyone in the family who's of age is an equal ruler.'

'How about elections?'

189

'Elections? There's no need of elections. Your Queen Elizabeth wasn't elected, was she?'

'But she doesn't really rule. Who sets taxes, for example?'

'There are no taxes, ma'am. The House of Steinreich is rich. The family doesn't have to take the citizens' money away from them.'

'But – but the expenses? The police? Old age pensions? Or don't the old and infirm get pensions here?'

'No ma'am, no pensions.'

'You let your poor starve?'

'Oh no. No one starves in Steinreich. Anyone who is poor and can't work applies for a seat, or to emigrate.'

'Explain. What do you mean by a seat?'

'Lots of foreign companies want to be registered in Steinreich, for tax reasons. Our law says that they have to have a citizen on their board of directors. If you are poor, the family selects you to be on some foreign company's board, and that's your income. The minimum pay is about fifty thousand English pounds a year. That's more than most old age pensioners get, in England, isn't it?'

'You said, emigrate. If this is such a paradise, why would anyone leave?'

'For the money. You sell your citizenship. Any foreigner who wants to live here has to buy a citizenship from someone. There's a waiting list. I could sell my right to live here for about a quarter of a million pounds, but then I'd have to leave.'

'Then why don't you?'

Blanche stiffened. 'Leave Steinreich? Leave my home? Leave the service of the family? I couldn't.'

'How about Maria and Song-li? They weren't born here, were they? Are they as loyal to Steinreich as you are?'

Charlotte felt Blanche's shrug by the movement of her nipples against her breasts.

'They don't have citizenships to sell, ma'am. They're just slaves, but we don't call them slaves any more. Tourists get upset.'

'Slaves? They really are slaves?' The thought was disturbing, and thrilling. She'd been thinking of them as slaves all the time, but to have it confirmed as being their official legal status was still something of a shock.

'They're "non-citizen licensed resident workers", ma'am. They are free to leave, if they so choose, but why would they? Like me, they're the sort who were born to serve. Outside Steinreich they'd just have to search for masters or mistresses, to feel complete. They have all they need, right here. Discipline, order, sexual fulfilment, security. What more could they possibly want?'

Charlotte almost suggested freedom, but realised that if freedom was a burden to you, it had negative value. There can be more important things than freedom, like being secure in your place in the hierarchy. People need different things. For some, freedom is vital. For others, mastery over others comes first. For yet others, being enslaved is comforting, provided it isn't accompanied by unbearable pain or back-breaking labour.

And how about her? Was she a natural born slave? Or was she one of the other sorts?

The door opened behind her. Light flooded the box. Nurse unfastened Charlotte's yoke. 'Three hours for rest and food, you two, and you are to report back to the training room. You know how to prepare her, Blanche. Please don't be late, my little darlings. This time it's going to be very special. I'm going to be the star turn.'

Nineteen

Blanche threaded the two loose ends of a looped leather thong through a triangular gold toggle, that was embossed with the Steinreich coat of arms. The leather strips went in through two separate holes but came out of the third together and parallel. 'When you pull either of the ends, the loop gets smaller. The toggle holds it firm one way, so it can get tighter but not looser. To undo it, just pinch down in the middle. Then it releases. Like this,' she explained. She plucked an end free.

Blanche's nimble fingers ran the thong around Charlotte's slender left thigh where it was thickest, rethreaded it, and tugged it tight enough to crease into her skin. Pulling at one end did nothing but fit it more snugly, until she squeezed the golden triangle, which then let her pull the thong out easily.

'Make it tight again, please Blanche,' Charlotte asked. 'I like it very, very tight.'

'Of course, ma'am.'

There was a second thong, a little longer, to cinch Charlotte's waist. As it was tightened inch by inch, her navel was pinched into a vertical slot. A third length encircled her right bicep.

'I look quite barbaric,' Charlotte remarked, twisting at her waist to look back and admire her reflection in the mirror.

'You'll look even more nice and primitive once you've got this on, ma'am.' Blanche held up a number of thongs that were joined together by golden toggles. 'You put it on just like a bra, ma'am, which is what it is, in a manner of speaking.'

Charlotte bent at her waist to dangle her breasts through two thong triangles. Blanche looped a doubled length over Charlotte's head and fastened the strange garment behind her back. A triangle of thin leather now framed each breast. Two thongs joined above each prominent mound, where the shoulder strap of a regular bra would have been attached to its cup.

United by one of the golden triangles, twinned thongs ran behind Charlotte's nape and down to the other thong triangle. A similar arrangement connected the two triangles between her breasts, and also ran around behind her back.

Had the triangles been filled in by some fabric, it would have resembled a normal brassière, except for one important difference, which Blanche took malicious pleasure in demonstrating.

'It's just like the other thongs, ma'am. When I do this –' she tugged on the two leather strips that ran from the bottom of the left triangle, and behind Charlotte '– it tightens, and won't loosen. The same with this one, and this, and ...' One by one, she tightened the three points of each triangle, slowly strangling both of Charlotte's breasts. Blanche didn't pull tight enough to cause actual pain, just enough to groove delicate skin and squeezingly extrude each breast, lifting and separating them. Each compact firm globe was turned into a solidly packed, quivering, tight-skinned balloon of flesh.

It was as if each triangle lifted a breast up and off Charlotte's ribcage, giving it a vibrant life all of its own.

Charlotte gasped. The prickling in her nipples had been constant since the moment Nurse had clamped the golden rings around their bases. Their tingling served as a permanent reminder that she was a woman, and that she was very much a sexual being.

The new restraints intensified that feeling. Her breasts felt swollen and heavy, with nipples that were incredibly dense and engorged to bursting point. The precious rings that pinched her nipples' circumferences seemed to tighten. Each pulse of blood inflated her nipples even further. They were desperate to be touched, and yet so sensitive that the thought of even a cool breeze tickling them made Charlotte cringe inside.

Looking down at herself, she watched the whiteness of her skin blush to a deep pink. A steady throb started just beneath her left nipple, and was strong enough to be felt by a gentle fingertip. It was as if there was a special vein there, that connected directly to her heart.

If there were vampires in Steinreich, and one came to her in the night, would that intimate vein be his sharp fangs' prime target? It was a terrible thought, even as a wild fantasy, but it was a deeply thrilling one, if she was honest with herself.

Her fingers hovered an inch from her nipples' tingling tips. She desperately wanted to touch herself, yet dared not. A dab at one nipple's peak might well crumple her with the divine shock. Each breast, feeling as if it had suddenly grown to massive size, pulsated with thick seething lust.

'Is this,' Charlotte croaked, 'what the Mistress meant when she promised me a lesson in breasts?'

'This is the start, ma'am. The idea is for you to be able to fully appreciate the demonstration.'

'Appreciate? Demonstration?'

Blanche fumbled at her own belly, untying the black silk cord that cinched her waist and ran so cruelly between her slim thighs. 'Yes, ma'am. Now I've got rid of this –' she tugged the restraint from beneath her sex's lips and dropped it on to the dresser. '– I can take you down.'

Going down the stairs was an erotic experience. Each jolt of a six-inch spiked heel on a step sent a shockwave up through Charlotte's body. When the wave reached her chest, the tremor shook the delicate arch of her ribcage. Her breasts had acquired their own massive inertia. They moved, but out of time with her body, bouncing heavily and independently. Every sway and quiver tugged at their glossy tight skin. Each tug sent unbearably ecstatic shooting sensations through a brittle nipple. By the time Charlotte reached the lower floor her essence was running from her sex, coating her inner thighs to her knees.

194

The first thing that she checked when she was led into the training room was the masked man's cock. It was unfettered, for once, and semi-erect. How she would have loved to have coaxed it into its full magnificence! She'd have used her mouth, or her fingers, and tended to it. It would have responded to her loving touch, growing tall and strong. Then she'd have impaled herself. Fast and hard! She'd have slammed herself on to it.

That was what she wanted the most, that handsome man's beautiful cock, bulky and invasive, inside her.

Her nipples needed attention, were hungry for it, but she'd have forgone that particular pleasure if she could just have had that wonderful length of burning maleness throbbing deep and hard in her pussy. Her craving for it was so urgent that she was sure she'd climax as soon as it entered her, and then again, and again, a shuddering orgasm for each and every thrust. She'd soak its hot white skin in her juicy essences, flood after flood. She'd become a torrent, pouring her female emissions over that rod of infinite delight, drenching it time and time again, until it finally melted in the heat of her supernatural passion.

She put her hand on one of two black leather-covered benches, to steady herself. Her knees were trembling.

'She's here,' Nurse prompted the Mistress.

The Mistress was wearing a long black skirt. Criss-crossed leather straps divided her proud naked breasts. There was a long ruby dewdrop pendant fastened to her left nipple by a golden clip that pinched her flesh cruelly, giving her cone an unnatural waist. It had to hurt, but she gave no sign of discomfort.

Breasts and nipples were very much the focus of this training session, Charlotte noted. The woman in the cat mask was wearing nothing but a glossy rubber garment which looked like a skin-tight bolero jacket. It had circular cut-outs for her breasts, which extruded from them. They stuck straight out, unnaturally spiky from her chest. They looked like the sort of nipples you could impale the palms of your hands on.

The Mistress said, 'Yes Nurse. Charlotte is here. I am aware of that.'

'Shall I . . .?' Nurse put her fingers to the front of her uniform, half popping one button.

'Sit up on the bench, please, Nurse. Let the man undress you. You are to be the subject of our little demonstration. Be passive, Nurse. Be "done to" rather than "doing".'

'Of course.' Nurse tugged her uniform's short skirt higher up, to bunch at her hips, and perched on the flat leather surface. Her stockings were white and held by frilly white straps that were stretched up long freckled ivory thighs.

The man stood behind her. His arms circled her waist. He unbuckled her elasticated belt and plucked the buttons of her uniform open with teasing deliberation, one at a time. Inch by inch, the garment parted revealing the incredibly deep cleavage between her two enormous swelling mounds. A bosom of those gigantic proportions should have sagged, but Nurse's breasts were firmly packed and vibrant despite their size. Great swollen nipples, dark brown crinkled plums, stared at Charlotte. Their settings, their haloes, were fawn and the size and shape of upturned saucers.

Charlotte swallowed. She remembered having thought that each of Nurse's nipples was as large as the head of a big man's cock, and almost as mouth-wateringly tempting.

What if she was given the chance to use one like a cock? To ride a pillowy breast, squeezing it between her thighs, that hard nub trapped between her pussy-lips? She could jerk to and fro, working it into herself. She could climax that way; she knew she could.

The man drew Nurse's uniform back over her soft white shoulders and down her arms, to be tossed aside. Nurse leant back on stiff arms, shoulders turned in. The hollowing of her chest emphasised the glorious mounds that the movement squeezed together.

She was naked now, except for her stockings and suspenders. Her body wasn't as plump as Charlotte had thought. She had quite a slim waist, but her breasts and hips were so gloriously voluptuous that she gave the impression of being chubbier when dressed. Her belly was gently rounded, not fat, but with a navel that could have

196

held an egg. The prominent swollen lips of her sex protruded though a thick curly blonde thatch.

Nurse shook her shoulders, shimmying her breasts like a stripper, slapping them together. The man reached around her once more. His palms cupped her. They lifted, feeling the divine weight of her, and then jiggled and wobbled the great mobile mounds.

Nurse leant her head back against his naked shoulder, her face blank and her lips slack, delighting in the wonderful sensations she was enjoying.

'Nurse is fetishistic about her breasts,' the Mistress said. 'She loves to show them off. She enjoys having them caressed in every possible way, from the most gentle to the most severe. Almost all women receive pleasure from having their breasts and nipples manipulated, but dear Nurse is blessed with special sensitivity. We are very fortunate to have Nurse. There could be no finer subject on which to demonstrate some of the less common methods of giving and receiving mammary pleasure.'

Nurse blushed and whispered, 'Thank you, ma'am.'

The Mistress continued with her lecture. 'Charlotte, you have discovered the special delights of having the circulation to your nipples restricted, and are today beginning to find out how nice it can be to have your breasts firmly constrained. With Nurse's expert medical help, we have determined exactly how much bondage can be safely applied, and for how long. The thongs that are compressing your own breasts so prettily, for example, may be left on for several hours without doing the least harm. What we are about to do to Nurse's lovely breasts, though, must stop after no longer than one hour.'

Nurse made a sulky mouth.

'Sorry, Nurse,' the Mistress went on, 'but I must insist on limiting this demonstration to sixty minutes, for your own good. Are you ready?'

Nurse bit her lower lip and closed her eyes. The man had deserted his jiggling and was gripping her nipples softly from beneath, between fingertips and thumbs, rolling them gently.

The Mistress took a swift stride and gave him a cut across his hard tight buttocks with her cane. 'Let her answer me. You know she can't speak when you are doing that to her.'

Nurse found her voice. 'I'm ready, Mistress. Please start. I've been waiting for this all week.'

'Very well. Lie flat. Charlotte, you will have found that engorgement imparts a special sensitivity. To engorge any area, we have to bind it. That can present difficulties when it is breasts that we wish to bind. Medium-sized ones, like yours, cannot be just tied up. They are soft cones, wider at their bases, and tapering. As the cord was tightened, it would just slide up and off. That's why Nurse designed the harness you are wearing.' She turned. 'Blanche!'

The girl sat herself up on the second bench. The Mistress trailed her fingertips across Blanche's delicate swellings, to the girl's obvious delight.

'Breasts like these present an even greater problem. How can you bind that which is almost flat? Still, "where there is a will", as they say. You –' she pointed her cane at the cat-woman '– demonstrate.'

The feline woman brought a coil of white silk cord. Blanche lifted her arms high and wide. With two deft movements, the cat-woman threw loops over her shoulders. The cord crossed between Blanche's tiny breasts and was pulled tight. The end was passed around her narrow chest, immediately below her modest swellings, and was again tightened. The cat adjusted this cord, working it up and squeezing a roll of flesh above. When she was done, Blanche had a trace of uplift. What breast-flesh she had was emphasised by the cutting support. A fourth loop was passed around her, perhaps two inches above her nipples, and tightened. Her diminutive breasts were pinched out, less bulky than compressed halves of lemons, but now as prominent as they could ever be.

Blanche looked down at herself and grinned her approval. Even her translucent white skin was darkened by the throttling cords. The flesh that protruded began to swell slowly. The nipples turned a deeper pink. Tiny though they were, they stiffened. Blanche, her eyes still riveted to her subtle transformation, licked parted lips. She arched her back, pushing her narrow chest forward, presenting her tightly bound flesh for proud display.

The Mistress nodded. The cat-woman stretched out a hand and flicked her fingertips across the very tips of the thorny pink jewels. Blanche jerked. She gasped. A shudder ran through her entire body.

'You see,' the Mistress said to Charlotte, 'even such small breasts as these can be rendered very sensitive when properly compressed. Bondage is a multi-faceted pleasure, don't you agree? It confines and renders the victim helpless, and at the same time it can increase the victim's pleasure many times over.' She leant over Blanche and planted a tiny sucking kiss on her left nipple. 'Thank you, Blanche. Would you like us to remove your cords now?'

'If you don't mind, Mistress, I'd rather keep them on for a while.'

The Mistress looked at Charlotte but her fingers were pinching Blanche's nipple, sending spasms of delight through her delicate young body. 'Such a sweet girl. She really loves her restraints, don't you, Blanche?'

Through gritted teeth, Blanche strained, 'Yes Mistress, thank you Mistress.'

'Now for the main course,' the Mistress said. 'We are going to demonstrate exactly how powerful a stimulant breast-bondage can be. Nurse here can climax from it. Isn't that right, Nurse?'

'Yes ma'am.'

'Charlotte, we are going to prove our point. I want you to come closer to Nurse and observe carefully. Would you cup your right hand over her pubes, please? Heel on her mound? Good. Now, curl your two middle fingers. Nurse will open up for you. That's it. Two fingers inside her? Excellent. Now, don't stimulate Nurse, please. Keep your fingers absolutely limp and perfectly still. They are there as part of our experiment. Nurse isn't blessed with the ability to orgasm quite as wetly as you do, but her internal spasms can be remarkably strong. You should have no difficulty in detecting her orgasms. I want you to inform us, Charlotte, each time you are absolutely sure that Nurse enjoys a climax. Do you understand?'

Charlotte, bemused at having two fingers soaking in Nurse's warm wet internal secretions, nodded.

The man in the mask drew Nurse's arms behind her and bound them in place.

'This isn't necessary for the experiment,' the Mistress said. 'But it increases Nurse's pleasure, and I like to indulge her when I can.'

With Nurse's arms restrained, the man made a running noose, put his left hand through it, tented the fingers of that hand over Nurse's nipple, and slid the loop down. His hand closed, getting a firm fistful of rubbery flesh. His other hand rolled the cord down, working her breast from side to side and up though the noose. When it was snug around the base of her breast, he pulled it tight. The cord bit deep, disappearing into fleshy folds. He tugged, testing. The cord was secure, binding her massive mound.

Nurse squirmed where she sat, wriggling with pleasure. He ran the cord behind her nape, made a second running noose, and repeated the process. When both breasts were secure, he tugged up behind Nurse's neck, lifting her breasts in their constrictive slings, and tied off the slack.

Charlotte stared in rapt fascination. Nurse's breasts were naturally very pale, with a delicate tracery of blue veins showing through their skin. Those veins gradually thickened and darkened. The skin became suffused deep pink before darkening further, to an intense puce. The veins seemed to rise up through her flesh, to lie immediately under her skin, then thickened even further.

Her areolae were puffed up, rising until they stood a full inch from her breasts.

The man's fingertips traced the ridge of one of her pulsing veins. His touch was so gentle that Nurse could feel the individual whorls of his fingerprints.

Nurse's vagina squeezed on Charlotte's fingers. 'That wasn't one,' she assured. 'I didn't come yet. That was just the pleasure building. I don't get off that easy, dearie. Not

200

quite.' She lay back on her bound arms, her incredibly bloated breasts bobbing and swaying high on her arched ribcage. 'I'm ready, Mistress.'

The Mistress wound a small plastic timer and set it aside. 'We start lightly,' she announced. Her fingers snapped. Maria tossed something long, white and floating to her. A second snap brought a feathery snake that Charlotte recognised as the sort of boa that flappers had worn around their shoulders back in the 1920s.

Nurse moved her shoulders, impatient for her delicious torment to begin. Two globes, the size of bowling balls, wobbled and quivered. So engorged were those great spheres that their soft flesh had become dynamically vibrant.

The Mistress laid the fluffy boa delicately across Nurse's left breast. She let the long strip of chiffon float softly down, to settle across Nurse's right breast. A tug moved the tickling ostrich feathers of the boa three gliding inches. With each fraction of an inch that it moved, another curly frond stroked at Nurse's nipple.

Nurse arched. Her thighs spread. Her heels dug into the padded leather and lifted her hips. She gurgled liquid lust from deep in her throat.

The chiffon performed the same tantalising drag. Nurse grunted, deep and feral. Her sex clamped on Charlotte's fingers, palpitating them in an urgent rhythm. Both fabrics moved, slithering across her peaks.

Nurse's clit writhed and grew under Charlotte's palm. A wet rubber vice closed, squeezing Charlotte's fingers almost painfully. As it relaxed, scalding juices flooded.

Charlotte said, 'One.'

The Mistress told the masked man, 'Gentle stroking now. Not her nipples. Not yet.'

His fingers were long and delicate, drawing their tips so softly that their touch could barely be felt. He stroked from one globe's widest circumference towards its vibrant crown, then diverted, making a spiral around it.

Nurse twitched her shoulders, trying to swing her nipple into contact with his fingers, but he drew them back too quickly.

'Look more closely, Charlotte,' the Mistress said. 'Look at the rim's of her haloes. See the raised circles of goose-flesh? All the tiny bumps between the white skin and the brown? There's a nerve ending in every one. Those prickly rings are almost as sensitive as her peaks are, now. Watch what our eagle here does next.'

The man wet his finger in his mouth. Its moist pad ran around the circumference of Nurse's areola. She strained up at him. Ripples convulsed her belly. She threw her head back. Strange strangled noises bubbled up out of her throat.

'Is that pleasant?' the Mistress asked.

Nurse, delirious with her need, made sounds of inarticulate assent.

'Try this,' the Mistress said as she passed the man a strip of deep-piled plum velvet.

Nurse's eyes opened wide. 'No – I won't be able to stand it. Do it, damn you. Do it now!'

The velvet sensation of the nap pulled across Nurse's left nipple, and then her right did the trick. Charlotte was soaked to her wrist.

'No more bloody teasing,' Nurse begged, her accent thickening in her throat. 'Hard fingers, or bite me. Make me feel it good. Do my nipples – do them!'

The Mistress leant over Nurse and stroked her cheek. 'Now, now, Nurse. If you can't control yourself, perhaps we should take a break.'

'No, no, no. No break. I'll be good. Do me more, for God's sake.'

The Mistress beckoned to Maria and Song-li. The man took a breast in each hand and squeezed, extruding flesh between his fingers. The two slaves leant over Nurse, and touched her nipples with the tips of their tongues.

Nurse screamed, and came once more.

The girls pursed. Their heads bobbed. A nipple fucked each pair of young lips.

'Suck me! Bite me, damn you!'

The Mistress nodded. The girls drew back their lips into tooth-baring snarls. Teeth-edges grazed, with infinite

202

gentleness, up and down the sides of those quivering nubs. Nurse bucked up, trying to force more of her breasts into each mouth, but the man's strong hands restrained her.

The lips closed, softly sucking. Cheeks hollowed. Nipple-flesh was drawn in and elongated. The slaves lifted their heads, dragging on their sweetmeats and stretching them high.

Nurse's sex convulsed on Charlotte's fingers again.

'Four,' Charlotte said, and then jerked. A fingernail's sharp point had indented the pad of firm flesh at the base of her spine. The woman in the cat mask! Charlotte tilted her bottom, spread her thighs and arched her back, encouraging further caresses. The nail scratched delicately. The woman moved closer. Charlotte felt the touch of two stiff nipples, one beneath each shoulder-blade. The prickly hairs of the cat-woman's pubes nudged between Charlotte's buttocks.

Nurse moaned deliriously, her head whipping from side to side. Mouths sucked and released, nibbled and nipped. Charlotte's two fingers felt as if they'd been thrust into a throat that was gargling and swallowing. Nurse's sex milked at them and quivered around them. Her hot juices were a constant flow, dribbling on to the black leather surface of the bench. Charlotte wriggled her fingers, just to prevent them cramping. Nurse convulsed into her fifth climax.

The finger on Charlotte's back trailed down, circled the curve of one bottom-cheek, and tickled across the sensitive wrinkled pucker of her sphincter. It continued down to the inside of her thigh, and slid on the oiliness that coated it. Tiny sharp teeth nipped Charlotte's nape, then the lobe of her ear. Charlotte squirmed and then stiffened. The finger that was slippery with her spending was hovering just in front of her left nipple. It dabbed twice, and then smoothed in tight little circles.

Charlotte's sex buzzed. Her clit stiffened. Its head felt as if it had started to glow. She was on the very brink – and then the tantalising finger deserted her nipple, leaving Charlotte suspended over a great aching void.

The slave girls wiped Nurse's nipples dry with small

squares of cambric. The Mistress strode forward, took each nipple in a finger and thumb grip and pulled, pinched and twisted.

Nurse screamed. Her sex convulsed so strongly that Charlotte had to push on her fingers to stop them being expelled. To her amazement, the churning flesh relaxed for half a breath, and then sucked on her fingers, drawing them back inside.

What a wonderful ability! She'd heard tales about sex-performers who could pick up coins with the lips of their pussies or expel ping-pong balls, shooting them for a dozen feet, but she'd always thought of such abilities as rare and freakish, if not fictitious.

Neither of those tricks were ones she felt any great desire to perform, anyway. This though, the ability to work on flesh that was inside you, would be a delightful talent to possess. She could get the man's beautiful cock into her, have him hold perfectly still and, without so much as a twitch of her hips, masturbate him into an orgasm with the clenching and twitching of her internal muscles.

He'd like that. He'd like that a lot. He'd be besotted with her. A woman who had that ability could use it to enslave a man.

Charlotte tried a tentative internal squeeze. Something moved inside her, but weakly. The muscles were there. They just needed strengthening.

Nurse was squealing now, gibbering her lust. The Mistress shook her great mounds by her grip on their nipples, as if she was trying to pluck them off. Nurse came for the sixth time.

The Mistress checked the timer. 'We can fit in one more experiment. Blanche!'

Blanche swung off her bench and scurried away, to return with a bucket of ice and a steaming bowl. Nurse half sat up, saw what Blanche had brought, and sank back with a grin.

It was the man's turn once more. At a sign from the Mistress, he produced an ordinary plastic dildo and turned its base to start it humming. Were they going to fuck Nurse

204

with it? That'd be nice, but it seemed such a commonplace way to complete Nurse's torments that Charlotte felt quite disappointed.

But it wasn't exactly an ordinary dildo. It had an over-sized head and it had been adapted. Its dome wasn't smooth and featureless. A deep dimple had been melted into the plastic; a dimple that was exactly the size and shape of Nurse's engorged nipples.

The cat-woman took her place next to the masked man, with an identical instrument. They lowered their dildos, very slowly, and fitted Nurse's nipples into the buzzing holes. Her belly gyrated. She sucked in a great gulp of air. Her vagina tensed on Charlotte's fingers, and her tormentors lifted the dildos.

As she relaxed, retreating from her erotic peak, the dimples were fitted back into place, then removed and returned. They were keeping her hovering on the brink of climax, intensifying the sensitivity of her nipples, and driving her into a delirium of lust.

They laid their instruments of torment aside, took a cube of ice each, and applied them to Nurse's burning cones.

The cold bit. Nurse screamed. The ice was held in place and then removed. The two slave girls lifted ladles of warm oil from the bowl and poured, anointing Nurse's nipples.

No matter who or what held her, Nurse sat up and rolled into a moaning gibbering ball, folding at her waist, pulling her sex off Charlotte's fingers. She twisted and writhed. The heat, after the cold, had split her very being, cleaving her senses and shattering her.

Charlotte didn't need her fingers to tell her that Nurse was being devastated by a cataclysmic orgasm, her seventh, and all of them were inspired by the things they had done to her breasts. The seventh had to have been the most powerful. The woman's sex was bubbling with it.

The timer pinged.

'There are one or two more techniques that we didn't get to today,' the Mistress said. 'Next time, perhaps.

'Charlotte, you will have noticed that Nurse's internal muscles are very well developed. That will be your lesson for tomorrow. We will start on your vaginal exercises. Do well with them. Work hard, and you will be one step closer to achieving your desire. Very well, Charlotte, you may go.'

Twenty

Charlotte loosened one more screw in the shutter. She tried
to concentrate, but her head was whirling. There was so
much to think about. Nurse's final sobs of joy, for one.
Charlotte and Blanche had been half-way up the stairs
when they'd started.

'That's them untying her breasts,' Blanche had explained. 'Then the vigorous massage. The returning
circulation always does it. It's agony, and she loves it.'

Charlotte had hoped that the release of her own bound
breasts might have done the same for her, and although the
sensation of pins and needles had been intense, it hadn't
been enough to give her the climactic pleasure she ached
for so desperately. Next time, she vowed, she would see
that the thongs were pulled much tighter.

Then there were the other mysterious techniques. What
could they be? Nurse's breasts had been bound, stroked,
tickled, bitten, sucked, frozen and thawed. What was left?
What could they possibly do to her that they hadn't
already done?

And then there was the promise of exercises to
strengthen her internal muscles. What form would they
take? How did you exercise internally?

And, of course, the other promise, of her getting closer
to what she desired most. What did the Mistress mean?
Closer to her freedom? Charlotte wasn't so sure that she
wanted that, not anymore. This was her life now. This was
where she felt she belonged. She was home in a way she'd
never been before, even as a child.

So why was she working so diligently to get the stupid

shutter open? And to what point? She wouldn't be able to escape that way; the window was much too high. All she'd be able to do was determine whether it was day or night.

Was it just a pointless gesture of defiance? One last shred of independence? Why? Could it be that she actually enjoyed the process of becoming enslaved, and feared that once she surrendered absolutely that process would be at an end?

If the Mistress didn't mean she'd be closer to her freedom, then what? Closer to being reunited with her stepsister, Veronica? Yes, she wanted that, but that wasn't her deepest, strongest desire; not now. Did the Mistress somehow know exactly what it was that Charlotte craved the most?

His – the masked man's – cock?

She couldn't know that, could she?

The screw fell out. Charlotte retrieved it and screwed it back loosely into place. Her bed tugged at her. She was tired to the marrow in her bones, but at the same time she owed Veronica whatever comfort she could offer. The *schloss* was probably harder for her stepsister to bear. Charlotte was sexually submissive by nature, so being enslaved and trained was – pleasant? Veronica, though, was sexually dominant. Learning to be obedient had to be a sore trial for her.

In a way, that made Charlotte Veronica's superior, didn't it? Superior in her ability to submit. That was a happy thought.

Charlotte had to be honest with herself. It wasn't kindness towards Veronica that made her deny herself her bed, for a while. It was the itch of lust that, despite her intense weariness, persuaded her to climb under her bed instead of into it. It was her turn, right? She'd masturbated Veronica the last time. Now Veronica could repay the debt.

She removed the grille, put her face to the hole, and hissed through it. As soon as she heard an answering hiss and the sound of something fumbling through the vent, she turned on to her back and spread her legs. Charlotte was too tired for conversation, or for much else. All she wanted was one quick orgasm, and Veronica certainly owed her that.

A fingertip touched the point of her hip. She squirmed up and closer. It traced the crease of her groin. Its pad smoothed the puffy bald bulge of her sex, lingered for a moment where her lips puckered together, and slid higher, to the ridge of her clit.

'Yes,' Charlotte said softly. 'Do it hard and fast. I'm beat. Just give me a quick orgasm and then I just have to get some sleep.'

The finger obeyed. It pressed down on the base of her clit, popping its head from its sheath. That would usually have taken longer, but her clit had been ready. It'd been swollen stiff all day, and even though its rigorous work-out when she'd been confined in the box with Blanche should have sated it, what she'd watched being done to Nurse had revived it fully.

How strange and wonderful! She'd enjoyed more orgasms that day than on any other day in her entire life, and she was still hungry for one last one before she slept. Blanche had called her insatiable. Perhaps Blanche was right. All her life she'd thought of herself as undersexed, but now she just couldn't seem to get enough.

She'd been less than a woman. Now she was more.

The fingertip wobbled on her clit's head. Charlotte lay back, eyes closed, thighs spread limply, only the clenching of her fists betraying the depth of the pleasure she felt. There was just one tiny point of contact between her and her lover. She could fantasise that it wasn't Veronica, but him, the masked man, who was rotating a finger hard and demandingly on her throbbing little nub.

Charlotte's fantasies were always very visual. This time she had lots of material to fuel her fervid imagination. She pictured the two slaves, Maria and Song-li. They had their faces buried between each other's thighs; they were curled together and writhing. They were making love, but doing it more for her entertainment than for their own pleasure.

The Mistress was there as well. She'd been fastened to the wall bars by block at her wrists and ankles, spread-

209

eagled and naked except for one boot. The cat-woman had the other boot, and was working all six inches of its spiked heel into the Mistress's sex. Her panther mask glanced back over her shoulder, seeking Charlotte's approval.

Blanche? She had to be present. Sweet obedient little Blanche. She'd be rolling those tiny nipples of hers, and perhaps using her tongue on Charlotte.

Charlotte pursed her lips, mentally sucking on Blanche's tongue, as the finger on her clit strummed harder and faster; and the boot-heel pumped into the Mistress; and Songli and Maria slurped and chewed at each other while their burning eyes were fixed on Charlotte, who was enjoying being masturbated by . . .

Her body folded around her orgasm, containing it. It was too good to let it escape. The lips of her sex spasmed. It was absolutely delicious, and all she needed to make it perfect was something hard thrusting inside her.

She grabbed the wrist of the hand that was still at her clit, spread her thighs wider – and paused.

The hand – the wrist! They were too big, too thick. They weren't Veronica's. They were a man's.

Her shocked lips gasped, 'Who?'

The hand snatched back through the vent and disappeared. Charlotte heard the grille on the other side being replaced. Stunned, her head awhirl with yet more unanswered, unanswerable questions, Charlotte finally crept into her lovely big soft bed.

210

Twenty-one

The cat-woman was standing naked, facing the wall bars. Her arms and legs were spread. Her wrists and ankles were each lashed to the wood by scores of turns of thin flesh-creasing cord. Her bottom was livid, criss-crossed by a dozen or more crimson weals. The lips of her sex hung pendulous and bloated, clearly visible between her thighs.

The Mistress gave her one last slash, high across her thighs in the creases where they joined her buttocks, and tossed her cane aside. The masked man pulled on a pair of gloves. They were black and furry, perhaps a panther's pelt to match the woman's mask. He knelt behind her, laid his hands gently on her ankles, and began stroking upward. She quivered as fur tickled her calves, and then her bottom tensed. Muscles rippled beneath the multicoloured blotching of her skin. The fur reached the first welt, an inch above the back of her knee.

She gasped. It was as if the tantalising touch of stiff hairs on the lowest of her sensitive stripes was a trigger that released a tightly wound erotic spring. Her hips pounded her sex at the bars. Her back arched. Her shoulders shook. Her head whipped from side to side. A high-pitched lustful keening strained out of her throat. If she hadn't been gagged by the hard rubber ball that had been strapped into place between her teeth, she'd have bitten the wooden bar.

'Keep still!' the Mistress commanded.

Fur stroked the insides of the cat's thighs, their backs, and then across her buttocks; first the left, then the right. She whimpered. The muscles in her thighs, her back, her arms, all knotted. Her bottom's cheeks flinched. Their skin

211

shivered. She was containing her ecstasy, holding it inside, under perfect control.

'Give her another five minutes of that,' the Mistress said, 'and then give her a massage with warm eucalyptus oil – the one that heats the skin and makes it tingle.'

She turned to Charlotte and raised an eyebrow, as if noticing her for the first time. 'What? Oh yes. The vaginal exercises. I'll have Song-li demonstrate for you.'

The tiny Eurasian brought her Mistress a clinking cloth bag. The Mistress took out a single chromed steel ball, a touch bigger than a golf ball. She sat and extended her arm with the gleaming sphere balanced on her flattened palm. 'Show her.'

Song-li bestrode the Mistress's hand. She squatted. The ball nestled into her sex, passed between the cord-spread outer labia, and pressed into the parted pink flesh of her inner lips; less than a hemisphere of the bright metal globe was left still visible.

Charlotte watched in rapt fascination. Song-li dipped no lower, and the Mistress didn't force it upward, but the ball rose. Ripples ran up the girl's flat belly. Her mons twitched, gripped like a clenching fist, and the ball suddenly disappeared.

'Feel,' the Mistress ordered.

Bemused, Charlotte cupped her hand beneath the open funnel of Song-li's sex.

'Inside, you silly bitch!'

Charlotte fumbled. Her fingertips felt their way up the slick warm pulsating walls. No ball. She crouched and pushed her fingers higher. Still nothing metallic. Just how deeply inside Song-li's body was it lodged?

The Mistress said, 'Drop it, Song-li. Give it to her.'

Vaginal walls writhed. The heavy ball plopped into Charlotte's hand.

'That's what you must learn to do,' the Mistress said. 'That's what I consider qualifies a girl to take a cock inside her body. Blanche will be giving you further instructions. Return to your suite. I don't want to see your face again until you can do what Song-li just did.'

212

Charlotte trudged up the stairs. The Mistress didn't want to see her again until she'd mastered that impossible feat? How long would it take her to learn? Weeks? Months? Forever?

On the other hand, the Mistress had said that mastery of that technique was what qualified a girl to have real, natural, man-inside-her-pussy sex. Was that a promise? Learn, and be rewarded? With his cock?

And she was a dancer, wasn't she? Dancers controlled their muscles. She had a head-start.

Charlotte's pace accelerated. She ran up the last few stairs and along the corridor to her suite.

She almost didn't recognise Blanche. The girl was all in glossy black leather. Her scintillating hair had been pushed up under a peaked leather cap. Her jacket fitted tightly but was unzipped down half its front, exposing a deep cleft of startling white. Although her chest was boyishly flat, there was no doubting the sex of the bared skin. It was very soft, very smooth, and very touchable.

Black leather pants clung to her firm flat belly, clutched each of her pertly rounded buttocks separately, and hugged her slender girlish thighs. Her boots were mid-calf in length, with narrow five-inch heels; not quite stilettos, but close.

'What happened to you?' Charlotte asked with a grin.

Blanche stretched out a hand. 'The ball. Give it to me. As for me, I am now your Instructress. You will obey me as you would obey the Mistress. Lie on the bed, face down.'

Charlotte surrendered the steel ball and spread herself. More confusion. Blanche had been her slave, her servant, her friend, her giggle-sharing playmate, her lover, and now this? It all had to mean something, some lesson. But whatever she was supposed to learn, it was beyond her comprehension.

Blanche had blocks ready. She fastened Charlotte's wrists to the headboard, wide apart. Her hand knotted in Charlotte's blonde locks and pulled, straining her neck up and her head back. 'See this?' She showed Charlotte a

213

short leather strap that had been slit for half its length into a dozen thin strips. 'This is for you. You will work hard at your lessons. You will please your Instructress. If you do not ...' She released Charlotte's hair and whipped the strap down across her bottom.

'Yes – yes Instructress,' Charlotte whimpered. She wasn't sure whether this new Blanche was thrilling, or terrifying.

Was there a difference?

'Spread your legs,' Blanche ordered.

Charlotte obeyed. Cold hard smoothness pressed against the lips of her pussy. They parted. The steel ball was forced deeper, until her outer lips closed over it.

'Now pull it in,' Blanche ordered.

Charlotte sobbed, 'How?'

'I've left your legs free to make it easy for you, this time. Squeeze your thighs together until it's forced in a few inches, and then work your vaginal muscles on it.'

Charlotte crossed her ankles and strained. The heavy ball moved deeper by perhaps two inches. It rested, very heavy and totally inert, on the inner surface of Charlotte's pubic bone, about where her G-spot was. She tried to flex on it, with absolutely no effect.

'Try harder!'

'I can't!'

The strap slapped down. Charlotte jerked. The ball slipped out.

Blanche's fingers gripped Charlotte's right buttock, pinching her bruises. She leant down and hissed into Charlotte's ear. 'You want a man inside you, someday? How do you expect to please him? You think he'll be so overcome by your incredible kindness in letting him fuck you that he'll come from that alone?' Her fingers dug deeper into the firm flesh of Charlotte's bottom. 'You need skills, you stupid bitch. Any woman can spread her legs and just lie there. Do you want to be just any woman? Don't you want to be the best damned lover you can be? Excellence has to be worked for; so work for it, damn you, work.'

She snatched up her strap and gave Charlotte two more

stinging blows before reinserting the ball. 'Now do it! Remember what the Mistress told you about the importance of self-control.'

Charlotte concentrated her will. Blanche was correct. In love-making, passion wasn't enough. She'd never thought about it before, but now she did it was obvious. Sex was an art. Like any art, it started with an intense emotional need, but that basic fire had to be worked on, controlled and refined. Wanting to become a concert pianist didn't make it so. It took countless hours of practice. An unschooled passion for the piano just produced noise, not music. A painter had to learn perspective, proportion, technique, or just waste canvas. Sex was no different. The world was full of enthusiastic amateurs. Very few people achieved erotic virtuosity.

She was going to become one of those gifted few. She was determined.

Charlotte compressed the lips of her pussy, narrowing her opening, and gripped the ball. She took a deep breath, closed her eyes, and squeezed with all of her might.

The ball moved.

'Yes!' she cried with elation.

'Higher!' Blanche urged, as excited as Charlotte was. 'You can do it.'

Charlotte strained. Her belly knotted. Her anus clenched. One day, perhaps, she'd expel a baby through her vagina. This had to be easier than that, even though it was in reverse. She bore down, hard. The unyielding lump edged another inch or two into her.

Blanche plopped down on the bed beside her. 'Keep going, Charlotte. Think of it as the head of a cock. He wants to pull back out of you, and if he does you'll lose him forever. Grip him. Hold him in, and drag him in deeper. Take possession of him, Charlotte. Do it, Charlotte, do it!'

Charlotte's muscles contracted.

Blanche hugged her naked back. 'Well done! Now work on it. Push it back down an inch or two, and then suck it back in.'

Pushing down was easier, a more natural movement.

Retracting it, even though she'd managed it once already, took a tremendous effort.

'You're getting the hang of it,' Blanche told her. 'What you need now is lots of practice. You have muscles that haven't been used much. You have to strengthen them. I'm going to trust you, Charlotte. Just keep working that ball up and down until I get back. I owe Song-li's clit a good tongue-lashing and she'll be waiting for me. Keep on exercising.'

The door closed. Charlotte squeezed. The metal ball rolled; it was an alien lump, impossibly heavy, but it moved.

After an hour Charlotte was exhausted. As a dancer, she'd spent countless hours practising at the bar, and pressed on regardless of cramping muscles and complete exhaustion. This was different. This was worse. This time the effort was so incredibly concentrated. The ball never moved more than a few inches. One tiny group of muscles was being worked, over and over.

She could rest, of course. No one would know. Even that hidden watcher behind the mirror wouldn't know whether her internal muscles were flexing or not.

No. She wouldn't succumb to the temptation. She'd develop her control until she was as skilled and strong as Song-li, or stronger. Yes – stronger.

She clamped down hard. The ball moved, gliding beautifully, but then – damn it! She'd squeezed too hard. The ball plopped out, dropping to the bed between her thighs.

She'd lost it, and with her wrists securely fastened to the headboard, there was no way she was going to be able to retrieve it. Was there?

She lifted herself up on to her knees and elbows. Peering down and back between her pendant breasts, she could see the ball, lying there on the coverlet, seeming to taunt her. She spread her knees further apart, folded at her waist, and pressed her sex down. Her mound touched metal. She hunched. Her pussy's lips felt hard smoothness. Charlotte twitched her hips, sliding her sex over the sphere, and applied gentle pressure. She pressed harder, willing her sex to open.

216

The ball slid away from under her, and rolled to balance on the edge of the bed. Charlotte stretched her leg out to it. Her instep touched it. It dropped, to thump on the floor.

She tried wriggling the lower half of her body off the bed and reaching for it with her toes. But she was three inches too short.

She swung back on to the bed and just lay there, sobbing with frustration, until she finally fell asleep.

Blanche woke her with her strap, raining blows on the backs of her thighs until they blossomed with crimson fire.

'You no-good lazy slut! You idle bitch! What's the meaning of this? I leave you alone for a couple of hours, and you sleep. You cow! You no-good whore – no – a whore works at her trade.'

Charlotte hunched up, trying to pull away from Blanche's blows, and her fury. 'It was an accident. Honestly Blanche. I squeezed; the ball fell out and rolled. I tried, but I couldn't reach it. Give me another chance, please Blanche. Just one more. I know I can do it.'

'You really think you can?'

'I know I can. Please Blanche?'

'You think that if you had a cock inside your body you could work on it with your vaginal muscles?'

'Yes, Blanche.'

'You could draw it in, without his help, and push it out again? You could massage its head with your internal muscles. Get him off without his moving?'

'I know I could.'

'And you think you're ready to take the test?'

'Test?'

'Don't get excited. I don't have a man handy, but there is a way to test you, if you are sure you're ready.'

'I'm ready, Blanche. Remember, I was trained as a dancer. I have strong muscles. I just had to get the knack of it.'

'The knack of getting the ball on the floor.'

'I can do it, Blanche. I promise.'

'Very well. I'll test you. Here.' Blanche leant over Charlotte and released her wrists. 'The test comes in two parts.

217

The first part is: you must seduce me. Make love to me, Charlotte. Make me want you. Make me go wild with desire. I don't intend to respond. It'll be a battle of wills. If you win, we'll proceed to the second part: the real test.'

With that, Blanche lay down on her back with her arms straight by her sides, and her legs together. She closed her eyes, and went totally limp. Charlotte sat up, leaning over her, she looked down at her leather-clad ex-slave.

This was a new experience. All of the loving she'd ever had, both before the *schloss* and while a captive, had been initiated by someone else. She'd been seduced by men, and ordered what to do by Veronica. At the *schloss* she'd been tied, strapped, blocked and then been kissed, caned, fondled, tormented and debauched in a dozen different ways; but never before had she had to take the initiative. And Blanche was going to resist.

Where to start?

She pulled Blanche's cap from her head and tossed it aside. What next? A kiss? Perhaps she should plan ahead. Is that what men did when they seduced a woman? Did they work out what caress would lead to what, and how each item of clothing would have to be removed without breaking the mood?

Blanche was sheathed in tightly clinging leather. Her skin was covered, particularly below her waist. Perhaps she should start by getting some of the obstacles out of the way.

Charlotte slid off the bed and went to its foot. Boots first. She took hold of a heel and a toe and tugged. Blanche slithered down the bed. The boot stayed on.

Very well; so it wasn't going to be easy, with absolutely no cooperation.

Charlotte rolled Blanche on to her face, sat herself on the back of one slender leather thigh, bent Blanche's leg at the knee, and tugged a heel upward. The boot came off. Then the second one. That wasn't so hard, was it?

Next the trousers. She rolled Blanche on to her back again and searched at her waistband for a fastening. There was a hook and a zipper to the left. Once undone, the leather worked down over Blanche's narrow hips without too much trouble, until it was bunched at her knees. Charlotte hopped off the bed again, found the zip that ran from the legs' cuffs up the insides of Blanche's calves, and minutes later had the garment discarded on the floor.

That left just a leather thong-bikini below Blanche's waist. That could be removed later. Taking it off her wouldn't spoil the mood.

Good. Now she had Blanche bare except for her leather jacket and her bikini. There was lots of naked flesh to work on, and nothing that would delay the smooth progression of a seduction. Charlotte felt quite proud of herself. Her next task, as she saw it, was to kiss and caress Blanche until the girl could no longer resist responding. That's what men did, when they got a girl under their power.

That's what she had, hadn't she? A girl under her power. Of course, there were straps and thongs and cords in the dresser's bottom drawer. The easiest way to seduce her would be to swiftly tie the girl up, and have her way with her.

Was that what Blanche expected of her? Was that the lesson? If you want someone, you must overcome them, bind them, and do with them as you will. No. It couldn't be that simple. This was a test and somehow or other, sooner or later, it was going to involve those aching internal muscles of hers. Blanche had something else in mind. Having to seduce Blanche was just the first stage of her trial.

She'd best get on with it. Perhaps there was a time limit; a hidden clock ticking away somewhere.

With all the dragging, getting Blanche's boots and trousers off, the girl was pretty close to the foot of the bed. In fact, her legs were dangling from her knees down. That opened up possibilities. She was well positioned for cunnilingus, but a seduction didn't start with a tongue in a pussy, did it? That came later.

Charlotte climbed on to the top end of the bed, took Blanche by the shoulders of her jacket, and dragged her back up. The little bitch just flopped and lolled like a disjointed doll.

219

Charlotte would change that. She'd get a reaction from Blanche whatever it took.

She straddled her subject's waist, unzipped her jacket, and spread it wide. Now she had a naked body to work on, naked except for the scrap of glossy black leather that cupped her pubes. She had to admit that it was a remarkably beautiful naked body.

Beauty comes in many forms. Both the Mistress and Nurse were gorgeous in their own special voluptuous ways, though the Mistress's body looked much firmer than Nurse's. One day, Charlotte resolved, she would explore that firm lush body, in detail.

Blanche's beauty was totally different. She was stretched smooth and taut over her bones. Nowhere was her flesh layered deeply, except perhaps for the cheeks of her bum. Hers was a fragile beauty. It was finely sculptured, not softly moulded. Your fingers could feel the delicate arches of her ribs, and the prominent sharp bones of her hips. The pad of her mound was shallow. Press down on it and you'd feel her pubic bone. If you caressed Nurse, you only touched flesh. Stroke Blanche's skin, and you were close to her bones. It was so incredibly easy to reach down into her. She had no protective layers. When you gripped her, you reached her; all of her.

Charlotte felt her desire for this strange girl rise up as a lump in her throat. It wasn't just physical. There was emotion in it as well. There was compassion and caring. She wanted Blanche, not just as a body to play with, but as a real thinking, feeling person. Just as she, Charlotte, was more than a collection of body parts so, she suddenly realised, was Blanche. There was a person inside Blanche, looking out. It was that deep inner being that Charlotte lusted to reach.

She lowered her head slowly, and brushed Blanche's cheek with her lips. She snuggled down, naked skin on naked skin, her breasts squishing flat on Blanche's narrow chest. The spread zip of Blanche's jacket scratched the softly swelling sides of Charlotte's breasts, but she didn't care. If anything, the pain was pleasurable.

Her lips, close to Blanche's translucent ear, whispered, 'I want you, Blanche. I want to know your body. I want to pleasure you.'

Her tongue flicked an earlobe, then curled behind the ear and tickled its folds. She took the point of Blanche's ear into her mouth and sucked on it with infinite tenderness. The tip of an ear is not usually considered an erogenous zone. That was exactly what made the caress so incredibly erotic. Nipples are usually the focus of desire whereas ears are not.

'Lie still, my love,' Charlotte crooned. 'I am going to taste you. I am going to touch you. I am going to know you, in all your wonderful intricacy. I am going to learn to know your sweet young body as well as I know my own.'

Did Blanche's cheek press gently against hers? Were her words, her affectionate words, reaching something inside Blanche? Was tenderness as seductive as kisses and caresses?

She kissed the corner of Blanche's mouth. That soft touch parted the girl's lips, just a fraction. The tip of Charlotte's tongue pressed, not into Blanche's mouth, but just into the tiny soft crevice. It felt the texture of her lips. It tasted her lipstick.

The gloss-on-skin feeling was so good, Charlotte slid her tongue along, testing the difference between the corner of Blanche's lips, where they were thin, to the full plump ripeness of her lower lip, at its centre. A slight pressure, and that lip yielded. There was wetness waiting inside. Warm sweet wetness, and the hard surface of teeth. When Charlotte's tongue wagged from side to side, she felt its tip ripple as it passed from tooth to tooth.

It curled. The inside of Blanche's upper lip was soft and flaccid. It wasn't limp because it was weak or lifeless. It was totally relaxed because it was receiving a caress, not giving one. It was a receptor, sucking in sensation.

Satisfied that Blanche's lip had felt her tongue probing, Charlotte nibbled at it, intensifying the tactile communication. Blanche's mouth softened, melting. Charlotte took it as an invitation. She extended her tongue, wriggling it into

221

humid depths. It touched Blanche's, lying there in her mouth, totally quiescent. Tip slithered on tip. Charlotte's tongue moved Blanche's to the left and then to the right. She trilled on it.

It lay still, as if sleeping, perfectly relaxed. Charlotte wondered whether, had their roles been reversed, she could have maintained that iron self-control.

She lifted her head and gazed down. Blanche's mouth was soft, not with the slackness of desire, but simply at rest. Charlotte's two fingers drew Blanche's lower lip down, hooked into her mouth, and pulled her jaw open. Blanche's mouth sagged, unresisting.

Charlotte lowered her mouth on to Blanche's, and worked her lips between the girl's. Charlotte found Blanche's tongue, and drew it out gripped between them. Blanche's tongue flowed into Charlotte's mouth, almost liquid. Charlotte sucked, smoothed, caressed and nibbled. The tongue she was making love to, allowed her. No resistance. No response. It was just there; warm, wet and sweet; alive but perfectly relaxed, limp in Charlotte's mouth.

Charlotte released it and it simply fell back to where it belonged.

Very well. Charlotte reared up and swooped down, stabbing her tongue into Blanche's mouth three urgent times before retracting it and slithering it across the girl's cheek. She kissed Blanch's soft eyelids, then pecked tiny dabs across her face, and down to the throbbing vein at the side of her neck. She nipped, little vampiric bites, all the time trailing lower. Her tongue squirmed in the hollow of Blanche's shoulder.

There was no reaction. None at all. The fragile body she was pressed to was under the control of an indomitable will. Or else Blanche was simply indifferent to Charlotte's loving. No. That couldn't be. That mustn't be.

Charlotte kissed Blanche's collar bone. Her tongue laved the hollow of her neck. It wandered lower, across the delicate skin of her almost-flat chest, to a nipple.

Her tongue's tip circled, feeling the subtle difference between the texture of breast skin and aureole skin. That sensitive circumference wasn't marked by a ring of goose-flesh like Nurse's, but there was a difference. The breast skin was warm satin. The aureole skin was warmer silk.

Her tongue spiralled in, found the stiffness at the centre, and flickered on it.

Something twitched under Charlotte's palm, where it rested gently on Blanche's belly. A reaction?

She sucked Blanche's nipple between her lips, mumbled on it, and let a growl rise up from deep inside herself to vibrate it.

The tiny muscle twitched again.

Charlotte clamped on Blanche's nipple. Her teeth teased it. Her tongue flicked, hard and fast. She drew forcefully, and released, then drew again. Her suction pumped the pea-sized polyp between her lips.

Blanche might have sighed, but Charlotte couldn't be sure. It might have been just a fractionally deeper breath.

Charlotte pressed her cheek to Blanche's skin, over her heart. She could hear its steady throb, and even feel it. Her fingers toyed with Blanche's other nipple, pinching it between finger and thumb while dabbing gently at its tip. She rolled it, squeezed it, and drew it out to its full diminutive length.

Blanche's chest rose and fell. Her breathing was deeper, definitely deeper.

Still teasing the nipple with her fingers, Charlotte extended her tongue, flattened it on Blanche's skin, and dragged it down, slithering it over the corrugation of her ribcage, to her lowest rib. Then she went lower still. The skin of Blanche's midriff was stretched tight. Charlotte's tongue flirted on it, staccato, playing it like a drum.

She worked her mouth, squeezing saliva from under her tongue, and wetting it thoroughly. Dripping, it flattened once more, hard on the resilience of Blanche's body. When it moved again, it left a wet trail. It slathered in circles, each one extending lower until it felt the complex dimple of her navel.

Charlotte wriggled down until her breasts were between the sprawl of Blanche's thighs. Her arms bracketed the girl's ribs. Her palms pressed in on the sides of her love object's diminutive breasts, while fingers and thumbs tweaked and tugged her nipples.

Her lips pressed Blanche's navel as if it were a mouth. The tip of her tongue ringed the minute hard dome deep inside that soft declivity.

Blanche's ribcage inflated. Charlotte gave the slight swelling of the girl's belly a quick nip, pressed her wet mouth on it, splaying her lips, and dragged lower still. Blanche's pubic mound was under Charlotte's chin. She pressed gently, working her jaw from side to side. She exhaled, stirring the thistle-soft down that was so fine and translucent, she had trouble focusing on it.

Blanche gave a delicate moan. One thigh moved aside, perhaps an inch.

Charlotte was sure that those two subtle signs indicated rising lust. Blanche wanted Charlotte's mouth to be lower, breathing out on to her sex, breathing in its delicate musk.

She was going to have to wait.

Charlotte knelt up and back, edging to the foot of the bed. When her face descended again, it was to plant a tiny kiss on the inside of Blanche's left knee. As she tickled there with her tongue's tip, her hands closed on Blanche's hips, where the tight thongs of her bikini cut grooves into her flesh. There were bows there. Her fingers found trailing ends and tugged, just an inch.

Blanche was sensitive. Her sense of touch had been elevated to the point where a breath on her skin would thrill it. She'd feel the slow loosening of her bows. She'd know what that promised.

Charlotte inspected the skin of Blanche's inner thigh. It was translucent white, almost a milky blue. There were veins beneath it. Those just above her knee were deeper and paler. Further up, beside and below the long muscle, where the shallow vale that led up into her groin started, the veins were closer to the surface and more visible.

Charlotte pulled again on the bows fastening the bikini thongs; they loosened a little more.

Her tongue touched skin, where a vein pulsed. It traced

that fine blue line higher. The left bow fell apart. Then the right. Blanche's leather bikini lay loose on her mound. The slightest movement would brush it aside, exposing her sex to the air and to Charlotte's eager eyes.

The wandering tongue reached mid-thigh and stopped. It deserted that leg and started again just above Blanche's right knee.

Blanche's body seemed to subside into the bed, as if disappointed that the tongue's progress had been delayed.

'You want my tongue, don't you?' Charlotte purred.

Blanche didn't answer, but her head flopped to one side. It was the most she'd moved since she'd first fallen back limply.

Charlotte rolled on to her back, with her face in close to Blanche's leg. Two hands lifted Blanche's knee over Charlotte's face. Charlotte extended her tongue and gave the back of Blanche's knee three long strong licks.

Blanche gasped.

Charlotte licked again, thoughtfully. Should she wriggle even lower, off the bed, and use her mouth on the girl's toes? That retreat would tease, wouldn't it? Even as Blanche enjoyed the oral attention, she'd be wanting Charlotte's tongue to be squirming into her sex rather than between her toes. Charlotte was tempted, but her own desire forbade it. She was as eager to taste the girl's pussy as it was to be tasted.

She rolled again, spread Blanche's thighs wide with one firm decisive shove, and returned her tongue to its vein-tracing.

Her hands pinned her victim's legs flat to the bed. Her tongue worked harder and faster now, climbing higher, sometimes pausing for kisses and nips, but always moving nearer and nearer to her delightful soft wet destination.

There were tiny hairs in the hollows of Blanche's groin. Charlotte tickled them with her tongue's tip. She rested her cheek on the rounded heat that radiated through the scrap of leather. A twist of her head dislodged the bikini. Charlotte nestled her cheek on bare damp spongy flesh, and continued with her tongue's teasing of Blanche's groin.

225

There was a crease there, as fine as a hair. Her tongue traced it. The movement lifted her cheek from Blanche's sex. The girl groaned a protest.

Charlotte licked and lapped, following the crease until it disappeared and only an intricate tracery of blue veins showed the divide between Blanche's haunch and her torso.

'I might lick your pussy, if you were to ask me.'

Blanche made a sound, but it wasn't a request, just the suppression of one.

Charlotte's mouth browsed across Blanche's mound, above her clit's ridge. Blanche's hips twitched. Charlotte let her breath heat Blanche's ridge. Blanche swallowed a sob.

Charlotte crouched lower. Her hands forced Blanche's legs still wider. Charlotte laid her cheek on the bedclothes between Blanche's thighs, turned sideways, and inspected her pussy.

There was a vertical puckering between swollen fleshy lips. Charlotte blew on it. The lips thickened. Their engorgement slowly uncrinkled them. They became more defined. They parted at their centres. Charlotte pursed her lips, put them close, and let out a sigh of air. The edges of Blanche's pussy fluttered. The soft dark slit widened.

Charlotte planted a kiss, as delicate as the brush of a butterfly's wing. She exhaled into Blanche.

Beside her cheek, a sinew twitched.

Two strong thumbs spread Blanche's sex. Charlotte stared into her. 'You are so beautiful inside. Your skin is the palest pink, delicately mottled with deeper shades, and all underlaid with fine veins. Deeper, my love, you are shadows and folded intricacies. Your flesh forms a soft labyrinth. I'm looking inside you, Blanche. I can see into the intimate depths, where you are so incredibly internal. My breath –' she puffed '– is wafting up inside you. You don't have to speak, my dear. There is a pulse that speaks for you.'

Charlotte wet a fingertip, then probed it beneath Blanche into the crease of her buttocks, and found the wrinkled puckering of her anus. She traced its rim, feeling

226

the delicate radiating creases. There was a responsive twitch.

'Your pulse spoke to me,' she said. 'When I do this –' she rimmed again. '– it tells me, "Yes. Do that again".'

With Blanche's sex spread, where its lips joined, a little cup of flesh was formed. Charlotte flicked that soft cup's edge with the tip of her tongue.

Blanche groaned.

Charlotte asked, 'Am I being too gentle? Would you like to really feel my touch?'

The sound that Blanche made could have been one of deep pleasure.

Charlotte hooked her left thumb down into Blanche's sex from above, and her right thumb up, from below. She gently pulled her thumbs apart. Blanche's sex became a tight vertical slot. Charlotte closed her teeth on it, not hard enough to hurt, but threatening pain. Her tongue squirmed into the compressed slit and slithered up and down, whilst moving in and out. Perhaps it was psychological, inspired by Blanche's snow-white skin and blushing pink interior, but Charlotte thought she detected the flavour of fresh vanilla, with a hint of ripe strawberries. She sucked hard.

Blanche gurgled her approval.

Charlotte's firm thumbs then stretched Blanche's sex out to either side. She pressed her mouth into the gaping oval. She hummed, vibrating the lips that were pressed against her cheeks. She puffed air in, and followed it with her tongue, burrowing as deeply as she could press.

When her tongue lapped to the sides, it tasted Blanche's essence. Her sex was beginning to ooze lust. Blanche's hips humped up at her. Charlotte was winning.

She withdrew her face and spread Blanche's sex once more. The cup where its lips met was full now, filled with a clear aromatic fluid. Charlotte pursed her lips on it and sucked it up.

'You are delicious, my love. Your juices are so sweet. I'm drinking you, Blanche.'

Blanche half sat up and then lay back, remembering the rules of the game.

227

'Would you like my finger inside you?' Charlotte teased. 'Like this?' The index finger of her right hand slid in, pressing up behind Blanche's pubic bone. 'I'm feeling for a rougher spot,' Charlotte said. 'Your G-spot. If I rub on it, you'll flow, my sweet. I'll be able to drink at your fountain. Ah, here it is. Is that nice, when I rub hard in little circles? Does it make you melt inside? I see it does. Your pussy is weeping, Blanche. It's crying for something. What does it want, dear? I don't have a cock for it. Tell me, Blanche. Tell me what your sweet little pussy wants, and I'll do my best to please it.'

Blanche croaked, 'Clit. For God's sake do my clit!'

Charlotte slid a second finger in alongside the probing first, and maintained a steady massage as she lifted herself higher. Blanche's clitoral ridge was bulging thicker than Charlotte had ever seen it. A tiny pink arrowhead was peeping out of its hood. Charlotte dipped lower and planted a gentle kiss on the shy little nub.

Her lips were so close that their movement brushed it and the breath of her words tantalised it. Charlotte whispered, 'Do you want me to suck you, or lick you? Tell me, little one. What is it you want, this –' she pursed on it and drew in whistling air '– or this?' Her tongue pressed it back into its sheath and polished over it.

Blanche's entire body stiffened, and spread like a starfish. Her belly rippled. The sinews that ran up the insides of her thighs stood out in corded ridges. 'Just do it to me, bitch!'

'Then I shall.' Charlotte took a two-fingered grip behind the head of Blanche's clit and skinned its sheath back as if it had been a man's cock. It was bare beneath her face, naked, exposed, tender, swollen and needy. She pecked at it with hard lips, then clamped down on it, and sucked with all her might. Her tongue wagged on it.

Blanche cried, 'Yes, yes, yes!'

The girl's passion was contagious. Charlotte half-rolled to her side. She folded at her waist. Her legs scissored out, wrapped around Blanche's left shin, and drew it to herself. As her fingertips polished Blanche's G-spot and her tongue flickered on her clit, she humped her sopping wet core at the side of Blanche's calf. Her writhing body lifted up, to get her sex splayed on Blanche's shin, and edged higher, almost curling her into a ball. Blanche's hard knee fitted into the warm wet socket of Charlotte's sex. Blanche pressed up as Charlotte hunched down. Charlotte used Blanche's leg to pleasure herself, but neither her tongue nor her fingers forgot their first duty; to pleasure Blanche.

Blanche stiffened. Her hips rose off the bed, lifting Charlotte. Charlotte, realising that Blanche was on the brink of an orgasm, paused. She counted to six, and then started over, laving the head of Blanche's clit in a different rhythm, her tongue wagging from side to side instead of flipping up and down.

Blanche gurgled. She squeezed out, 'Bitch, bitch, bitch. I was close.'

Charlotte hissed around Blanche's clit, 'Yes. Beg for it. You don't come till you beg me for it.'

'I beg! I beg! Give it to me, fuck you.'

Charlotte made a dagger of four bunched fingers. Her tongue resumed its up and down motion, harder and faster. She stabbed into hot spongy wetness, driving the spike of her fingers in far enough to stretch the lips of Blanche's pussy. She withdrew and stabbed, with an accelerating tempo. The room was filled with squelching noises and the heady aroma of woman-musk.

Charlotte nibbled at Blanche's clit. She growled on it. Her hand jammed into Blanche, harder and deeper until she was almost punching.

Suddenly Blanche cried out and grabbed Charlotte's hair, crushing her face down on her pubes. Her hips jerked. She ground her sex on Charlotte's teeth. 'Uh, uh, uh, uh – enough!'

She rolled, tossing Charlotte aside.

Despite the violent trembling of unsated lust that seized her, Charlotte crawled close and managed to ask, 'Did I pass the first test?'

Blanche pulled her close. 'Yes, my dear, you passed the first test. Now, if you will check under the pillows, you'll find what we need for the second part of your trial.'

Twenty-two

Charlotte's fingers closed on pliant, firm plastic. She pulled it out from under the pillow. It was a simple dark blue cylinder, about an inch and a half thick, perhaps twenty inches long, and rounded at both of its smooth ends. Its shaft was covered with tiny bobbles like the surface of a table tennis bat. It was flexible for its entire length.

In Charlotte's erotically charged condition, it looked absolutely gorgeous.

'Am I to use it on me or on you?' she asked.

Blanche's eyes twinkled. 'Both. It's big enough for us to share, don't you think? If we don't get greedy.'

Charlotte's eyes widened. 'Certainly. I'd like that a lot. But what's the test?'

'I'll explain when we get to that stage. First, I'd like to watch you use it on yourself. Are you shy to do that?'

'Shy? I would have been, before coming here. Now? No. Now I'm proud of my sexuality. If it gives you pleasure to watch me masturbate, and you'd like to see how turned on I can get before I climax, I'll find that very satisfying. Is there anything special you'd like me to do with this?' She stroked the full rubbery length across the tip of her left nipple, delighting in its dragging texture.

Blanche rolled on to her hands and knees and crawled over. She stared down into Charlotte's eyes. 'You're ready for it, aren't you Charlotte?'

'Ready? Of course I am. What have I been doing for the last hour? I've been making love to a gorgeous girl. I've had to work on her lovely body while she lay like a beautiful warm statue, defying me to make her react.'

'And you did make me respond, didn't you? I tried to resist you, Charlotte, but you were too much for me. I was ready to ignore being bound, spanked, nipped with your teeth, or any of the other things I was expecting. You fooled me, Charlotte. You were kind and gentle, and you gave me tenderness. I couldn't resist that.'

'Does that mean that you wouldn't like it if I was to tie you up tomorrow and paddle your pretty little bum till it glowed bright pink?'

Blanche giggled. 'Of course not. I love it when you dominate me, Charlotte. But that's tomorrow.' She put on a mock stern expression. 'For today I am your Instructress. Today, you have to obey me.'

Charlotte found she had to pretend to be meek, even though a submissive attitude was supposed to come naturally to her. She cast her eyes down, looked up at Blanche through her lashes and asked, in a very soft sweet voice, 'And what does my so-very-demanding Instructress require of her obedient pupil? Speak, and I will obey.'

'I want you to get yourself so hot that your insides curdle from it. I want you deaf and blind with lust. I want you to crave an orgasm so badly that your muscles knot and you drool. I want you to melt. I want to see your pussy boil with passion.'

Charlotte let the craving that bubbled inside her show in her eyes. 'I'm not far from being that hot, Blanche. Making love to you got to me, even though you did absolutely nothing in return for my caresses. I was just moments away from coming all over your knee when you tossed me aside. I might look calm now, but I'm still simmering inside.'

'And that's exactly how I want you to be. I want to feel passion radiating from your skin.'

'Touch me,' Charlotte whispered. 'My skin is hot. I'm in a fever from wanting you.' Her hand took Blanche's and drew it to her breast, then dragged its fingers down her body, towards her sex.

Blanche snatched back. 'No! I mustn't touch you yet. For now, I want you to do it to yourself. Love yourself, Charlotte.'

231

'Then watch me closely, and I will. You want to see me as a sex-crazed slut? Well, here I am.'

She pulled a pillow down from the head of the bed and sat herself on it. Her hands gripped her ankles and pulled them up; her right ankle went over her left thigh, her left ankle over her right thigh; she sat in lotus style. The simple yoga position tugged her sex wide open, which was exactly the way she wanted it. She wanted Blanche to see the indisputable proof of her lust glistening on the swollen and gaping lips of her sex.

The way her pussy drooled liquid honey when she was aroused and flooded with her warm wet climax had always been a source of shame for her. Now she was fiercely proud of it.

She was going to soak the bed before she was done.

Charlotte mentally recited a mantra for physical self-control. Two deep breaths expanded her diaphragm, and she was ready. She arched. With her arms stretched sideways, she doubled her torso backward. She bent at her midriff. Her ribcage expanded. Her waist shrank. The skin on her belly stretched taut.

Charlotte's long blonde hair, dangling behind her, flopped against her buttocks. She strained. The top of her head crept lower and lower, until she felt her crown touch the bed behind her bottom.

She laid her fingers on her hip bones and stroked up, across her tightly stretched midriff, over the twin fans of her ribs, up the quivering undersides of her breasts that were now pointed at the ceiling, to her golden-ringed hard-bead nipples. She tugged them straight up and bounced on her haunches, giving the illusion that she was lifting herself by the grip on her own sensitive flesh.

Charlotte twirled those sensitive peaks, let herself give a soft responsive moan, and flipped upright again. She grinned slyly at Blanche, still fondling her own engorged nubs, bowed her head as her left hand lifted, and took the precious dark pink bud into her mouth.

Her lips curled back into a snarl, exposing her teeth and showing Blanche that they were gripping the metal band that strangled her nipple. Her head tugged back. She shook, sending voluptuous tremors through the mobile flesh of her breast.

Her lips closed. Her cheeks hollowed. Her suction drew her nipple into the humid depths of her mouth, dragging as much of her breast after it as her mouth could contain. She bit. She chewed.

When Charlotte opened her mouth and let her breast fall from her teeth's vicious grip, there was a ring of tooth marks, purple dents, half-way down its soft sides from its throbbing peak.

Two hands circled that tooth-defiled self-abused tender cone, and squeezed it, offering it to Blanche's mouth. Blanche shook her head, reluctantly.

Charlotte massaged both of her own breasts, milking at them, coaxing even more blood into their constricted tips. Already dark from the blood that pounded in them, they darkened further. Charlotte kept massaging them, working at their engorgement until the pulsating pressure was just short of unbearable.

'They ache,' she told Blanche. 'They ache and throb. If you were to touch them, I'd scream.'

Blanche swayed towards her pupil, drawn by the temptation, but restrained herself.

Charlotte stroked the soft curves of her breasts' undersides, then drifted spider-fingers down her ribcage, caressed her own waist, let her palms smooth the curves of her hips, and fondled her own belly. Unaided, her feet lifted from her thighs. Her legs straightened and spread wide, until her toes were pointing to either side of Blanche's kneeling body.

Charlotte's fingers teased the insides of her own thighs. Still stroking, she lowered herself back. The pillow beneath her elevated her hips. Her mound was arched high.

She let herself whimper as the fingers of one hand parted the lips of her sex and teased the flushed inner surfaces of her outer labia. Her other hand took a two-fingered grip on the skin of her clitoral sheath, directly behind its head, and drew back. A tiny pink pearl popped out, glistening and ready.

233

The pointed nails of one hand indented the softness of her sex's petals while her other hand slid her clit's hood slowly and deliberately up and down its shaft.

Charlotte concentrated. She willed the channel of her vagina to widen and deepen. From where Blanche crouched, she'd be able to see inside Charlotte. Charlotte wanted to expose herself to as great a depth as possible. She wanted Blanche to see into the most intimate, internal places.

'Look at me, Blanche,' she said huskily. 'Look into my pussy. See how sweet and wet it is? It's running with my juices. Wouldn't you like to taste them? I need that, Blanche. I need your tongue. I need your fingers. Play with me, Blanche. Feel me, inside. Bite my lips. Chew on me. Push your tongue deep inside me. Suck my clit; please Blanche? Give me pleasure. Make me come, I beg you.'

'The dildo,' Blanche reminded.

'Oh yes. The lovely long thick dildo. Use it on me, Blanche. Use it hard.'

'You have to do it yourself.'

'Do it myself? Oh, of course. It's part of the test. I'd forgotten.'

Still masturbating her clit, Charlotte groped blindly sideways. She lifted the dark blue plastic length to her mouth and sucked on its head. She slavered over it, coating it with her saliva. She fumbled it between her thighs, two-handed now, and felt the hard smooth bulb at one end press into her yielding looseness; she urged it inside.

Her sex was ready for it. The slick head sank in. She pushed harder. Her lips felt the dragging caress of the knobbed surface of the shaft.

'No hands now,' Blanche ordered. 'This is when you show me just how skilled those internal muscles of yours have become. Pull it in, Charlotte.'

Charlotte's hands released it. She spread her arms to either side, and concentrated. Grip, compress, convulse inside. Grip, compress, convulse inside. Her labia sucked on it.

Inch by inch, with unbearably slow rhythmic precision,

her sex swallowed the dildo. At first three inches, then four, then five, were engulfed. The shaft's nobbles dragged her outer lips in, inverting her, but her vaginal muscles were inexorable.

'Now stop,' Blanche commanded.

'What?'

'My turn.'

Blanche crawled across the bed to Charlotte. She straddled her thighs, and humped up to half-sit in Charlotte's lap. She reached down and bent the protruding length of blue plastic upward, almost at a right angle. Reaching under the pillow, she found a bottle of oil. Her teeth twisted the cap off its nozzle. She squirted, coating the dildo's free end, and then inserted the nozzle into her own sex to lubricate herself. Her palm massaged the oil that oozed out, rubbing it all over her pubes and pussy. Dropping the bottle, she raised and then lowered herself.

Charlotte lifted herself on her elbows to watch. 'I have a cock now,' she exclaimed, 'and I'm going to fuck you, Blanche!'

'Exactly.' Blanche's hips writhed, forcing her down and impaling her. She wriggled lower and lower until her pubic bone was pressed hard on Charlotte's; the full twenty inches of firm plastic were embedded deeply, and shared equally between them.

Charlotte humped up.

'No! You mustn't move your body. Now is when you use those internal muscles, Charlotte. Fuck me. Fuck me with them.'

Charlotte squeezed, bearing down on the plastic invader with all of her might. Her pressure expelled it, despite the drag of the little bumps on its sides.

'Yes,' Blanche hissed. 'Now suck it back, and do that again. Faster and faster, Charlotte. Fuck me with it.'

Charlotte's vagina sucked and pushed at the dildo. After the first dozen strokes she found it came almost automatically. Her internal convulsions just kept pumping the dildo into Blanche, but the abdominal strain was enormous.

'I have to come from it,' Blanche gasped. 'But our

Mistress's instructions said nothing about our not using our fingers. Like this, Charlotte.'

She fumbled and found Charlotte's clit. Her thumb pressed it down against Charlotte's pubic bone, and wobbled on it. Charlotte reached to their squishy plastic-distended juncture, discovered Blanche's clit, and rubbed its oiled little head.

Despite herself, Blanche humped and ground, assisting her lover's desperate efforts. Her eyes glared down into Charlotte's, love and lust and hate seemingly intermingled into a ferocious devouring intensity.

Then her pupils lost focus. She threw back her head and cried, 'I'm coming, Charlotte!'

'Wait for me.'

'I can't!'

Charlotte gave an extra-hard push, driving the dildo further into Blanche. Blanche shuddered, stiffened, and collapsed to one side, twitching. Her share of the dildo, glistening with a mixture of oil and her essences, sprang free. Charlotte, desperate in her need, sat up and gripped it in both fists. She pummelled it into herself, stabbing and stabbing until she felt the floodgates open and she poured her lust out to saturate the bedclothes.

The two girls grinned at each other, wearily.

'Did I pass the test?' Charlotte asked.

'Oh yes. You passed.'

'Is there a prize?'

'The Mistress told you there would be. A real live cock for you to play with, and more.'

'More?'

'Much more. More than you could dream. You'll see. Tomorrow, in the morning, you'll see.'

236

Twenty-three

The naked girls kissed and hugged a reluctant farewell in the doorway.

'I can taste myself on your tongue,' Blanche said.

'Same here,' said Charlotte, smiling.

Blanche stroked Charlotte's cheek. 'You know what I'd like?'

'No, what?'

'I'd like a nice man to come in my mouth, and then have you suck his spunk off my tongue.'

'Mmmm. Someday, perhaps.' She tugged at her lover's arm. 'Blanche, come back to my bed. Talk dirty to me. I'm getting horny again, already. Spend the night with me. Wouldn't it be nice to wake up in each other's arms?'

'Or with our faces between each other's legs? I'd love to, but I have my orders, Charlotte. Another time?'

'Of course.'

Charlotte closed the door softly. Almost in a daze, she sat herself at her dressing table to brush out her sweat-soaked hair. After a dozen strokes she decided that the morning would be time enough. Even though the last traces of lust were still tingling the lips of her sex, she was too weary to even think straight. As she laid her brush aside her glance fell on the shutters over her window. There were new screws. Every slotted head had been replaced by one with a little square dimple.

Her hours of work had been for nothing. Somehow it didn't seem to matter. She'd passed her test. Things were going to change. She had no idea exactly how they would change, but she was sure they would, somehow.

237

She turned back rumpled bedclothes that still smelled of Blanche's musk.

'Charlotte!'

It was Veronica, through the vent. Almost disinterested, Charlotte crawled under the bed and removed the vent's grille.

'Your hand,' Veronica whispered.

Charlotte stretched through. A strong hand gripped her wrist.

'Who's that with you, Veronica?'

There was no reply. The hand dragged, pulling Charlotte's shoulder to the vent. It twisted, turning Charlotte's hand palm up. Something cool poured into her palm and over her fingers. Oil. Despite herself, Charlotte was curious. What did they intend, Veronica and her mysterious male companion?

Her hand was pushed down, on to warm flesh, firm but resilient. She groped, exploring. The undercurve of a smooth belly? The compact resistance of a pubic mound?

The hand bore down on her wrist. Her palm rotated. Her fingers brushed the insides of spread thighs and touched the sponginess between.

She was supposed to fondle Veronica's sex? Very well. She applied her own pressure, massaging oil into sensitive skin.

The hand lifted her wrist. More oil soaked her. A second hand cupped her fingers, folding them around – yes – a man's burning hard shaft.

Trapped by two strong hands, her palm and fingers were smoothed up and down, slowly masturbating. Their grip was quite unnecessary. She'd have stroked of her own volition, willingly and eagerly. It seemed like an age since she'd felt the pulse of a man's cock throb against her palm.

His fingers opened hers. When she felt his cock again, it was its naked head that was under her palm. She was supposed to polish his glans, coating it with oil.

More oil poured; overflowing her palm, it ran to drip down her forearm. It would be spilling on to Veronica, saturating her sex.

He moved her fingers once more, to grip his shaft just beneath its head. He bore down, bending the head of his cock lower. Her thumb touched hot flaccid flesh. Veronica's pussy!

He released her.

Charlotte pictured the scene in the next chamber. Veronica was on the floor by the vent, lying on her back with her legs spread. The man had to be tented above her, his cock the only point of contact. Her hand, Charlotte's, gripped his shaft. What was required of her was obvious. She bent his cock down to Veronica's sex and rubbed his oily globe in tight little circles, pressing it on Veronica's clit. When her stepsister responded with a grunt and a lifting of her hips, Charlotte directed his dome to the yielding entrance. He pressed. His fiery column slithered though her fingers, into Veronica.

He was making love to – no – fucking Veronica, but she was the instrument. Their joining was under her control. Her hand directed the angle, and regulated the depth. She was the mistress of their pleasure.

She pulled him out, feeling the eversion of Veronica's clinging lips. She rotated him once more, pressing harder and moving faster, masturbating Veronica's clit with his glans.

Her stepsister began to grunt with a guttural rhythm. She was getting close to her climax. Charlotte frotted as fast and hard as her wrist would move. She tightened her grip, throttling his stem. The plan that had occurred to her required that Veronica reach the pinnacle of her pleasure before the man did.

He arched back and tried to thrust between Charlotte's fingers, but she was adamant. This was for Veronica. He would have to wait.

Veronica screamed, and slumped. Charlotte shoved, pushing the man aside. She snatched through, over Veronica's twitching body, grabbed her far hip, and tugged. Veronica rolled closer to the vent, on to her belly. Charlotte groped. Her fingers found his wagging cock and closed around it, taking control once more. She bent it down, found the soft cushions of her stepsister's rear, and guided him into their deep dividing crease.

Yes! The joint of her thumb felt Veronica's tight anal ring. A twist of her wrist presented the man's cock-head to it. Without prompting, he sank. Charlotte's fingers felt Veronica spreading over his dome, letting him in. As he moved deeper, Charlotte squeezed.

Just the head of his cock was inside. His shaft was in Charlotte's grip. He pulled. His glans popped out from the muscular constriction. He leant forward. It forced its entry anew. He pumped, fucking Charlotte's tight oily fist, just the head of his cock popping into and out of Veronica's sphincter.

That was the sensitive part. Charlotte, inexperienced in anal sex as she was, knew that much. Veronica was being denied the deep distending that her rectum craved, but her anus was getting the full benefit. Each thrust penetrated with maddening shallowness, tantalising Veronica beyond endurance.

A sound came from the man's chest, deep and vibrant. His thighs began to tremble. Every muscle in his body strained. Charlotte felt pressure against her hand; not the pressure of his thrusts, but an internal swelling. He barked, short and hard. Charlotte released him. Her hand, spread on Veronica's buttocks, felt the hot wet splashing as he poured out his liquid lust.

When he flopped down on to Veronica's body, squeezing Charlotte's hand flat between her stepsister's bottom and his belly, she tugged it out and back through the vent, to lick the musky sweet-sourness from her fingers.

Charlotte didn't know if they heard her whispered, 'Goodnight.' It didn't matter.

Twenty-four

After Charlotte's morning shower, Blanche wrapped her in an enormous, warm, fluffy robe.

'What's this?' Charlotte asked when she saw her breakfast waiting on the dressing table.

'Black bread and goat's cheese, with a mug of wine and water. It's traditional, ma'am.'

'Traditional?'

'For Saint Clothilde's Martyrdom Day, ma'am. That's what today is.'

'Oh? Is it an annual celebration?'

'Oh no, ma'am. The annual one is just Saint Clothilde's Day. This one is much more special than that.'

Charlotte nibbled and sipped, not wanting to dishonour her father's land's customs.

'You're to wear this, ma'am.'

'Is that traditional as well?'

'Oh yes. It certainly is.'

Blanche helped her into a long white gauzy dress; it sat off the shoulder, and had embroidery at a gathered waist. 'I have to do your hair now, ma'am.'

She dressed Charlotte's long blonde curls with a wreath of tiny white roses.

Charlotte asked, 'Do all the girls in Steinreich dress up as Saint Clothilde on her day?'

'Not all, ma'am. Just those who want to give themselves do.'

'Give themselves?'

'You'll see, ma'am. Stand up and turn around.'

'Those are the blocks I arrived in, aren't they? Are they

really necessary? I'm obedient now, aren't I? I'm not likely to run away.'

'Just be good, please ma'am?'

'Oh, very well.' Charlotte allowed Blanche to block her wrists behind her back. As they left Charlotte's suite, she went to turn towards the staircase.

'Not that way, ma'am. Not today.' Blanche led Charlotte along a long carpeted corridor, to a large pair of double doors. Henry stood to one side and another handsome footman, who Charlotte hadn't seen before, stood on the other. They opened the doors with deep bows. Blanche curtsied to Charlotte and waived her in.

There was open air. That was the first thing Charlotte noticed; in front of her big french windows stood wide open and led on to a broad balcony, with a crystaline blue sky beyond. Then she saw the people in the room. The Mistress was dressed like a proper *châtelaine*, in a grey ankle-length button-through jersey dress; it was figure-hugging but modest. And the masked woman was now in a clinging black silk dress with a dramatic plunging neckline. The man was still in his eagle's mask but otherwise dressed in medieval costume. He wore a plum velvet doublet and breeches, with a snowy white shirt, open at the collar. White silk hose sheathed his muscular calves and he had gleaming buckled shoes on his feet.

The Mistress bowed her head. 'Welcome, Clothilde. You must call me Matilda, now. I am your most humble servant.'

Charlotte felt her mouth fall open.

The man and the woman both removed their masks. The woman's hair cascaded down her back, a gleaming torrent of liquid midnight. It was Veronica! As for the man, Charlotte had seen him before. 'You – you're the flight attendant!'

He bowed. 'I couldn't resist, Clothilde. I had to see if you were truly as beautiful as Veronica and my father had told me.'

'I . . .' Charlotte dried up.

Veronica crossed to her and took her in her arms. 'You

242

are entitled to some explanations,' she said. 'Our mutual stepfather was the rightful duke. Steinreich is traditionally ruled by a triumvirate – the duke, the duchess, and our spiritual leader, The Clothilde. When the Iron Curtain fell, father left his beloved duchy. He wasn't running away. His parents sent him, to prepare and to find suitable mates for his son. Now Steinreich is free once more. We can return to the old ways. Carlos here, our father's natural son, sought us out. He made my acquaintance, by a ruse, and seduced me. He soon decided that I was qualified to rule by his side. I could rule, being as harsh as was needed. I could submit to the larger good. I was someone he could bond with, for harmony between the members of the triumvirate is a necessity. We are equals, you see. We three must rule as one.'

'But me?' Charlotte asked.

'I satisfied Carlos that you could submit, but was unsure that you could be stern. I had my doubts that you should stand by our side. I feared that you would be too submissive, dear stepsister. We decided to test you – to put you through a modern equivalent of the trials of Saint Clothilde. That seemed only fitting, as it is under the title of that saint that you must reign.

'You passed all the tests, Charlotte. You can withstand tribulation, unflinchingly. You care for the pleasure of others, but are not unmindful of your own physical needs. We three are compatible. In the council chamber we might well disagree, but Carlos and I are sure that there will be no major rift, for the strongest bonds are forged in the heat of the bedchamber. If we are angered, we can vent our spleen on each other instead of declaring war or some other such nonsense. If we make mistakes, we can be punished and so shed the burden of guilt. By allowing ourselves private catharsis, we can maintain our public sanity. Come, Charlotte, Clothilde of Steinreich. Your people are waiting.'

She led Charlotte out on to the balcony, Carlos and Matilda following. Below, in a great flagged courtyard, a crowd awaited. The front row consisted entirely of girls, all dressed as Charlotte was, loose breasted under semi-transparent gauze. Every one had her wrists blocked behind her, and was accompanied in the second row by a sturdy young man.

The crowd roared. Carlos, behind Charlotte, turned her by her shoulders, showing the assembly her blocks. The crowd cheered again. He turned her to face them once more and made a great show of smacking her lightly-clad bottom, to further tumultuous cheers.

'We must go back in,' Veronica whispered. 'There are many lusty young men and bawdy girls down there, who are anxious to get on with their own celebrations of our ascent to the three thrones.'

Carlos leant close. 'I, too, am anxious to celebrate,' he said. 'You were promised a cock, a real one, were you not? Mine is ready for you, Charlotte. It's been aching for you since first I saw you, aboard the plane.'

They retired to the chamber. Matilda released Charlotte's wrists.

'Let me get this straight,' Charlotte said. 'We are all rulers here? Each of us commands, and each has to obey, when the orders are appropriate? We rule well, and sanely, because we release our emotions in private?'

'As you say, ma'am,' Matilda confirmed.

'Then get out of your clothes, all three of you. Show me the way to the room with the three pillories. You kept a tally of my days, Mistress Matilda? I had to pay for my every slightest error and was allowed some small reward when I performed well. I too have been keeping a tally. I have some spleen to vent, before I reach emotional equilibrium. My account book needs to be balanced. Blanche, attend me. I hope your wrist is strong. These three are about to discover that Clothilde can inflict some trials of her own. And then, my dear, perhaps we shall realise that special fantasy of yours; the one that you told me about last night.'

Licking her lips in anticipation, Blanche followed Charlotte from the chamber.

NEW BOOKS

Coming up from Nexus and Black Lace

Lydia in the Bordello by Philippa Masters
July 1996   Price £4.99   ISBN: 0 352 33092 9
Lydia, now back in England from her African adventure, is concerned by the double standards inherent in Victorian society. She is also fascinated by Brighton's brazen working-girls. When the mysterious Lady Amberson asks her to help provide some very special entertainment at her private parties, Lydia is initially shocked, but realises that to refuse would be to be guilty of the hypocrisy she so despises.

Rue Marquis de Sade by Morgana Baron
July 1996   Price £4.99   ISBN: 0 352 33093 7
Charlotte's inborn lust and submissive, masochistic tendencies temper her fear and hatred of Veronica, her sadistic stepsister, with whom she will soon be reunited. The sisters' destination is Steinreich, a tiny principality with some very bizarre laws and customs. Veronica seems quite at home there, but Charlotte dreads to contemplate what she will have to endure, in order to claim her share of her father's legacy.

Annie's Further Education by Evelyn Culber
August 1996   Price £4.99   ISBN: 0 352 33096 1
Helped by some obliging and enthusiastic friends, servants and fellow members of the Flagellation Society, Annie establishes Redhand House Academy – an institution for women desiring disciplined education. Yet it is soon evident that success has gone to Annie's head, and that she, too, has some harsh lessons to learn before her own education is complete.

The Chaste Legacy by Susanna Hughes
August 1996   Price £4.99   ISBN: 0 352 33097 X
Shipwrecked in a storm, the beautiful Corinda Chaste finds herself the prisoner of Constantine Stephanikis, a Greek pirate. As he teaches her to satisfy even the most bizarre sexual tastes, she proves to be an eager and totally uninhibited pupil. She is, however, unaware that Stphanikis has other – more sinister – plans for her.

Forbidden Crusade by Juliet Hastings
July 1996   Price £4.99   ISBN: 0 352 33079 1
1186, the Holy Land. Forbidden to marry beneath her rank,
Melisende, a virginal young nobelwoman, determines to use her
cunning – and her sensual body – to seduce the chivalrous young
man she loves. But will her resourcefulness and appetite for sexual pleasure allow her to survive imprisonment in the harem of a
Saracen Emir?

Lord Wraxall's Fancy by Anna Lieff Saxby
July 1996   Price £4.99   ISBN: 0 352 33080 5
1702, Lady Celine Fortescue agrees to marry the debauched Lord
Wraxall, on condition that he spares Liam, her lover, who has
been wrongfully condemned. Wraxall reneges on his promise, and
Celine resigns herself to a life of subjugation. Liam, however,
escapes and, allies himself with the lustiest pirates in the
Caribbean . . .

The Houseshare by Pat O'Brien
August 1996   Price £4.99   ISBN: 0 352 33094 5
When Rupe bares his most intimate desires over the Internet, he
does not know that his electronic confidante is Tine, his landlady.
With anonymity guaranteed, cybersexual encounters are limited
only by the bounds of the imagination, but what will happen
when Tine attempts to make the virtual real?

The King's Girl by Sylvie Ouellette
August 1996   Price £4.99   ISBN: 0 352 33095 3
The early 1600s. Under the care of the decadent Monsieur and
Madame Lampron, Laure, a lusty, spirited young Frenchwoman,
has learned much about darker pleasures. Sent to the newly es-
tablished colony in North America, she tries – and fails – to
behave as a good Catholic girl should, and is soon embarking on
a series of wild sexual adventures.

NEXUS BACKLIST

All books are priced £4.99 unless another price is given. If a date is supplied, the book in question will not be available until that month in 1996.

CONTEMPORARY EROTICA

THE ACADEMY	Arabella Knight	
BOUND TO OBEY	Amanada Ware	Feb
BOUND TO SERVE	Amanda Ware	Sep
CANDY IN CAPTIVITY	Arabella Knight	Jun
CHALICE OF DELIGHTS	Katrina Young	Mar
THE CHASTE LEGACY	Susanna Hughes	Aug
CHRISTINA WISHED	Gene Craven	Apr
CONDUCT UNBECOMING	Arabella Knight	
CONTOURS OF DARKNESS	Marco Vassi	
DARK DESIRES	Maria del Rey	May
DIFFERENT STROKES	Sarah Veitch	
THE DOMINO TATTOO	Cyrian Amberlake	
THE DOMINO ENIGMA	Cyrian Amberlake	
THE DOMINO QUEEN	Cyrian Amberlake	
ELIANE	Stephen Ferris	
EMMA'S SECRET WORLD	Hilary James	
EMMA ENSLAVED	Hilary James	
EMMA'S SECRET DIARIES	Hilary James	
EMMA'S SUBMISSION	Hilary James	Oct
FALLEN ANGELS	Kendal Grahame	
THE FANTASIES OF JOSEPHINE SCOTT	Josephine Scott	
THE FINISHING SCHOOL	Stephen Ferris	May
THE GENTLE DEGENERATES	Marco Vassi	
HEART OF DESIRE	Maria del Rey	

Please send me the books I have ticked above.

Name . . . .

Address . . . .

. . . .

. . . .

. . . . Post code . . . .

Send to: **Cash Sales, Nexus Books, 332 Ladbroke Grove, London W10 5AH.**

Please enclose a cheque or postal order, made payable to **Nexus Books**, to the value of the books you have ordered plus postage and packing costs as follows:

UK and BFPO – £1.00 for the first book, 50p for each subsequent book.

Overseas (including Republic of Ireland) – £2.00 for the first book, £1.00 for the second book, and 50p for each subsequent book.

If you would prefer to pay by VISA or ACCESS/MASTER-CARD, please write your card number and expiry date here:

. . . .

Please allow up to 28 days for delivery.

Signature . . . .

Please send me the bound introductory issue.

_____

Name _____

Address _____

_____

_____

Send to: Club 3-four Century Books, 331 Ladbroke Grove,
London W10 5AE.

Please enclose a cheque or postal order made payable to
Century Books, to the value of the books to cover postage
and packing costs as follows:

UK and BFPO — £1.00 for the first book, 50p for each subsequent book.

Overseas (including Eire) — be of £1.50 — £2.00 for the first
book, £1.00 for the second book, and 50p for each subsequent
book.

If you would prefer to pay by VISA or ACCESS/MASTER-
CARD, please write your card number and expiry date here:

_____

_____

Please allow up to 28 days for delivery.

Signature _____